THE RISING

THE PATRICIAN PROPHECY | BOOK ONE

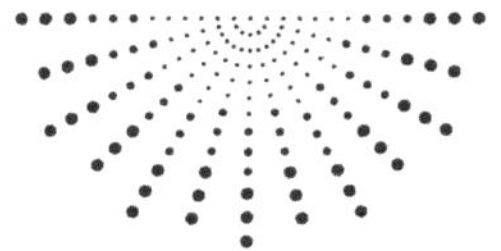

MICHAEL PENOSKY

THE PATRICIAN PROPHECY BOOK ONE: THE RISING BY MICHAEL PENOSKY

Published by Brimstone Fiction

1440 W. Taylor St. Ste #449

Chicago, IL 60607

ISBN: 978-1-946758-61-3

Cover design by Elaina Lee, www.forthemusedesigns.com

Interior Design by Meaghan Burnett, www.MeaghanBurnett.com

Available in print from your local bookstore, online, or from the publisher at: www.brimstonefiction.com

This is a work of fiction. Names, characters, and incidents are all products of the author's imagination or are used for fictional purposes. Any mentioned brand names, places, and trademarks remain the property of their respective owners, bear no association with the author or the publisher, and are used for fictional purposes only. Scripture taken from the NEW AMERICAN STANDARD BIBLE(R), Copyright (C) 1960, 1962, 1963, 1968, 1971, 1972, 1973, 1975, 1977, 1995 by The Lockman Foundation. Used by permission. Brimstone Fiction may include ghosts, werewolves, witches, the undead, soothsayers, mythological creatures, theoretical science, fictional technology, and material which, though mentioned in Scripture, may be of a controversial nature within some religious circles.

Brought to you by the creative team at Brimstone Fiction:Rowena Kuo and Meaghan Burnett.

Library of Congress Cataloging-in-Publication Data
Penosky, Michael.
The Patrician Prophecy Book One: The Rising / Michael Penosky 1st ed.
Printed in the United States of America

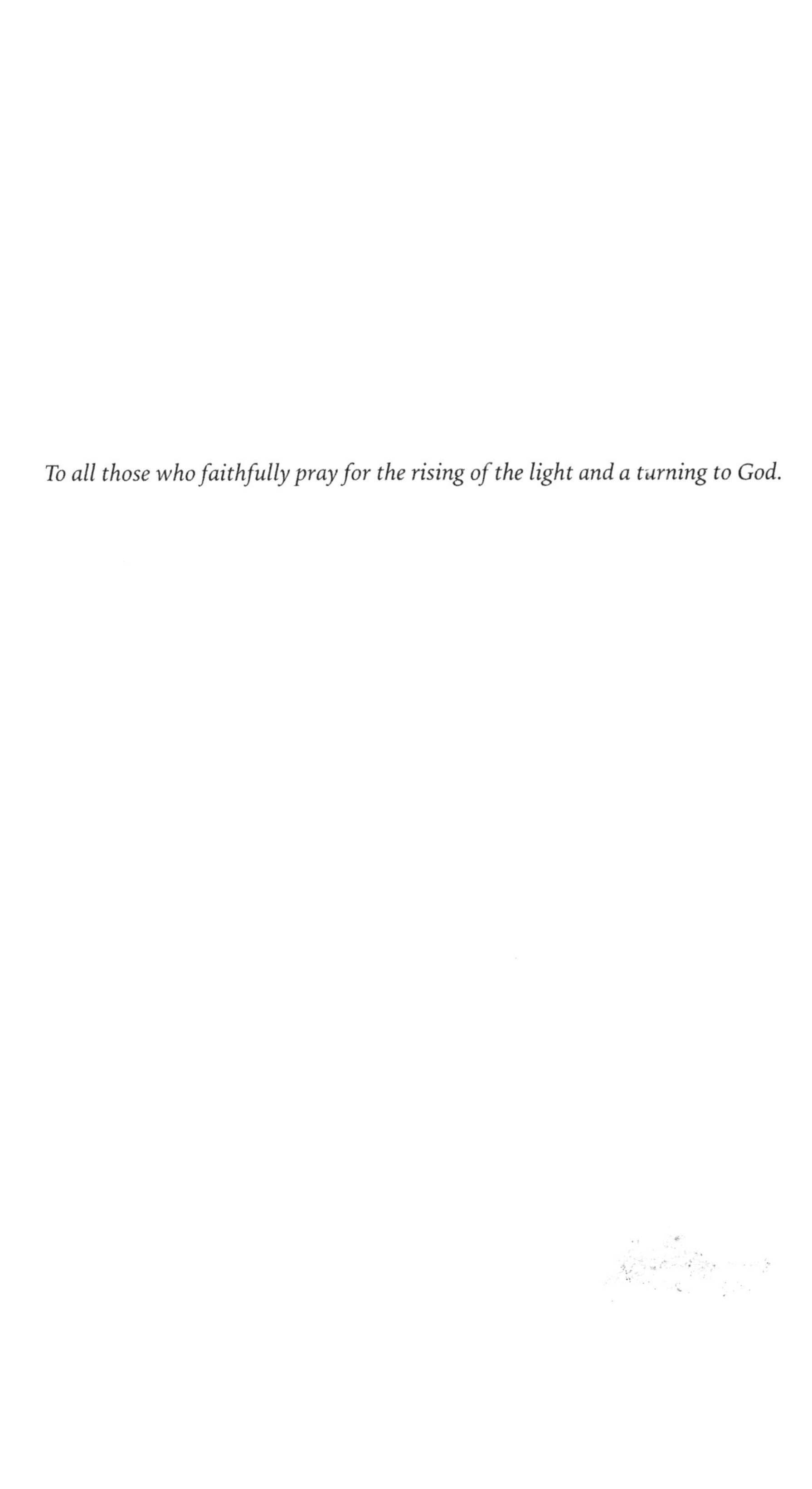

To all those who faithfully pray for the rising of the light and a turning to God.

"For I would ride with you upon the wind,
Run on the top of the disheveled tide,
And dance upon the mountains like a flame."
— W. B. Yeats, *The Land of Heart's Desire*

"And it shall come to pass … that your old men shall dream dreams."
Joel 2:28

CHAPTER ONE

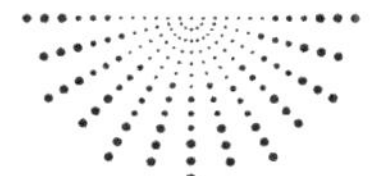

Old man Shaw's irregular heartbeat didn't stop him from putting on his best pair of pants and his favorite grey flat cap. His wife, Aryana, had gotten it for him last month for his eightieth birthday. He hadn't been venturing out much the last few weeks on account of his new heart problem. As he peered out the window at the grey-stone walls that lined the twisting farm road that led up through the hills of Antrim, a strong palpitation rocked his chest. He fought it off even as the thought occurred to him that stone walls last forever, but the organs of men do not.

An old chalice would get him out the door today. Answers to his most pressing questions about it awaited him.

He'd discovered the chalice only because of the wild visions he started having weeks ago. Night after night, as his mind gave way to sleep, he found himself in his dreams moving dirt, shovel in hand, in a foggy mist near the giant oak on the back end of his farm and bringing up all kinds of treasure. Then one morning, he woke from one of those dreams and, despite his bad ticker, went out and started digging.

And the dream came true—he'd actually unearthed something.

A valuable artifact, that much he could tell, but just how valuable? And what about that strange, indecipherable writing on the bottom of it? From what time period? How long had it been in the ground? And who put it there?

He fetched it from the china cabinet and examined it once again, for what had to be the hundredth time. It had an ancient yet timeless mystique about it. Silver, with a ring of diamonds studded around the circumference, it sparkled in spite of the bits of peat moss that still clung to it. The bogland of his farm had acted as a powerful preservative, it seemed, even against normal tarnish.

There had to be some greater mystery to it all, though, he just knew it. Today he would get some answers. Maybe that would reduce his stress level, and his heart would improve. With that in mind, he looked into Aryana'a teary eyes and kissed her on the cheek. "I'll be right as rain in no time, don't fret over me."

She pulled him close for one last hug. "You sure you don't want me to go with you, George?"

He flashed her a wry grin. "I'd just as well be at the pearly gates already if I can't go anywhere alone from now on."

"I just don't understand why you won't get yourself a cell phone like the rest of the world." She looked back up at him into his eyes. "Will you at least give me a call from the store phone when you get there?"

He nodded, kissed her on the forehead, and stepped out the door.

Two hours later, he ambled toward a clerk, a pudgy forty-something chap who stood at the counter of Abby's, one of the premiere antique shops in Northern Ireland. Devoid of any other customers, the store had just opened for the day on a crystal-clear mid-week morning. He loosened his grip on the prized relic and placed it on the counter.

A slight pucker formed on the lips of the clerk's otherwise poker face. "What have we here?"

"You tell me."

The clerk pushed his glasses onto the bridge of his nose. Taking the chalice in both hands, he studied its contours, then tipped it over to examine the bottom. "Did you see the inscription?"

"I presumed it to be Latin. I was hoping you could translate it."

"Were ya now?" The clerk raised an eyebrow but never took his eyes off the writing on the bottom of the chalice. He squinted hard. "There's the Latin word *propheteia*. Means 'prophecy.' I can say that much."

George smiled at hearing the word *prophecy*. Some of the tension released from his shoulders.

The clerk continued his study of the inscription. "But the rest of it ... I'm going to need to take it back to the office, examine it further."

Before George could protest, the clerk whirled with curio in hand and hustled off through the door behind him.

As George stood there sans chalice, staring at the closed door, the regrets lashed down on him hard, like a cold rain out of the north. He should have found another way to learn more about the chalice, one that didn't involve leaving the serenity of Antrim to make the long trip to the city centre of Belfast.

A pain flared through his chest, settled a moment, and then left. The same vexing ache he'd felt for the first time a few days ago when he'd dug the chalice from the ground. He told himself to relax. The stress was going to kill him.

WITH THE OFFICE DOOR CLOSED TIGHT AND LOCKED, THE clerk set the chalice on the desk, picked up the phone, and dialed a number. On a secure line, he rang his boss.

The strange symbol on the bottom—just after the prophecy—required the call. A cross, sword, shield, and breastplate. You needed a magnifying glass to see it. But the boss had once admonished him that if it ever showed up on anything, to call.

No answer. No surprise. The guy mentioned he would be vacationing in the south of France this week.

The clerk took some photos of the chalice with his phone and uploaded it to an antiques forum and then began to search online for anything that looked similar to the chalice in front of him.

Maybe somebody would contact him who knew something about the chalice and the strange inscription with the symbol on the bottom.

He withheld one thing from the old man—aside from the Latin word for *prophecy*, he'd recognized another word—*Patricius*, the Latin version for the name *Patrick*.

When fifteen minutes passed without any sign of his artifact, George raised a hand and flagged down a store employee from the front of the shop. "Can you bring out the gentleman inside the office."

The employee knocked on the office door, seemed to have heard a response, and then turned to George. "It should be just another minute or two."

A razor's edge pain once again arced through George's trunk. He drew slow, deep breaths as he limped around the counter toward the office. Before he reached it, the door swung open and out sidled the clerk, his face flushed, clutching the chalice.

"Please excuse the delay. I'm afraid my exam was ... inconclusive. The owner would like you to leave it until someone more experienced can have a look."

Rubbing the closed-cropped beard on his chin, George gave a slight nod. "But what do you feel in your gut about it?"

The clerk shrugged, looked away, wouldn't make eye contact. "Not sure, but, of course, the owner will want see it."

George was done here. Some other source would have to deliver the information he sought. Maybe another place in Belfast would be able to examine it today. He mustered the strength of years long past and wrested the chalice from the hands of the clerk who'd probably never suffered a hard day's work in his life. "I'll be on me way. Thank you for your time."

"Wait a minute," the clerk said. "I placed a photo of the chalice with an online forum. Maybe somebody will respond with some information. The store closes early today, one o'clock on Wednesdays, you know. Six p.m. the other days of the week. You could go to lunch, return later. Come through the rear entrance. I'll be in the office down the hall, doing some work for about a half hour after closing. The front door will be locked. Maybe I'll have something for you then. Or you could just leave me your number, and I could call you?"

George simply turned away without a word and angled out the front entrance. He crossed the street, passed his beat-up, former-British-army-issued Land Rover parked at the curb, and headed into a pub called *O'Devany's House*. Once inside, he sat at the bar and ordered a pint and a stew. A rugby match already streamed on the piped telly above him.

The pain left his chest with his first sip of Guinness. And the time passed easily. He asked around the bar if there were any other antique shops nearby. Everyone said the place across the street was the best. It did have a solid reputation, the reason why he had chosen it in the first place. And he really didn't know where else he could get his answers. Perhaps he would check with the clerk one more time after lunch as suggested and maybe he'd even bring the chalice back again sometime with the owner present. When he finished eating, he called Arayana and told her not to worry, but he'd be a wee bit later than anticipated.

"Just be careful," she said. "You'd put the heart in me crossways if you were to have an accident on the way home."

When he hung up, he left a wad of Irish pounds on the bar next to his check and headed out into the sunlight. A few minutes shy of one-thirty. No doubt the clerk was still there.

The shiny black SUV parked behind George's old land rover barely registered as a concern on his radar as he came to the front door of the antique shop. The store was locked with a *closed* sign in the window, just as the clerk had said. George slow-walked around the building to the back-alley entrance and went inside.

Voices from the office way down the hall echoed off the walls.

Gingerly, George crept forward down the long corridor.

Something about, "unlocking the hidden prophecy." Those words came out clearly.

Were they talking about his chalice?

George stopped, listening at the partially closed door.

An angry voice asked, “Who else did you talk to about it?”

The sound of a hand smacking flesh.

George peered around the corner of the doorway. Two large men in suites stood over the clerk whose eyes were swollen and bloodied. One of the large men had a jagged scar on his forehead and a neck as thick as a wooly sheep.

“No one, I swear!”

Another slap. “Where’s the old man now?”

“I don’t know. Please.”

I gotta get help. Now.

The old man moved down the hall as quietly and quickly as he could, the pain in his chest returned with malice. Almost at the exit, he stumbled into a garbage can.

Had they heard it?

They had to have. No time to look back.

A muffled gunshot sounded as the door close behind him. A gunshot from a silencer?

This was bad.

George bee-lined for his rover, the pain stabbing his chest. Where was a police station? Or a policeman for that matter?

The next thing he knew he was at his vehicle, opening the door, plopping down in the seat, firing the ignition.

He pulled out into the street and saw them coming. They headed for their black SUV.

Down the street, he accelerated.

Have to lose them. Quick.

He turned wildly to the right down one street, then left down another, then right down an alley and out onto another street. A check of his rearview mirror showed no black SUVs.

What should he do now? That crucial question vexed him. He had no phone, and his hands were shaking so wildly he could barely keep them on the steering wheel. If he saw a hospital, he’d turn in and get his heart checked. But what if the SUV showed up on his tail? What then?

Panicked and confused, he found himself heading out of Belfast, away from the city, toward home, toward Aryana. She'd help him, tell him what to do, if he could just make it to the farm, to the hills of Antrim. To home.

HE DIDN'T NOTICE IT FOLLOWING HIM UNTIL HE WAS WELL over an hour outside of Belfast meandering his way through the hills of Antrim.

When George slowed, the SUV slowed, keeping itself almost out of sight. The game continued until his rover crested a deserted, sinuous stretch of rippling country road. The SUV blurred in the old man's rear-view mirror as it sped even with him in the lane for opposing traffic.

A jolt of high-octane fear slammed him hard. Foot to pedal, pedal to floor, he bolted to a lead. But only for a few feet before the SUV matched him again. With the realization that he wasn't going to shake it, two thoughts swarmed his head in rapid succession. First, he wished he were as well-armed as his friend Finn, who was now a commercial fishing boat captain but in a past life had smuggled guns for the IRA. Second, his mind leapt to the dream that had caused him to dig for the chalice. He could have sworn that it foretold of his grandson, Ian, making a trip across the ocean from the States to help him with the mystery the artifact posed.

Had God led him this far only to have it end like this?

He looked to his right and saw the man with the scar.

A spasm of pain seared George's chest, and everything went black as his rover careened over a hill and toward a ravine.

"DO YOU WANT ME TO PUT A BULLET IN HIS HEAD?"

"Is he dead?"

"Not breathing, no pulse, yeah, I'd say he's dead. But he doesn't seem injured much. He's an old man, I think he had a heart attack."

"Perfect."

"Uh huh, nice and clean this way."

"The main thing is we got the chalice. Lorcan will be flying high when we give him the news."

The man with the scar laughed as he reeled off a string of profanities. "Let's get out of here."

CHAPTER TWO

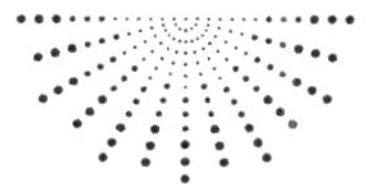

Professor Saorla O'Rourke attempted to focus on the normally mellifluous voice of Dean Grady, but his words seemed blaring, cacophonous now. Her eyes drifted to the Greek letters etched in gold calligraphy on the wall behind him. She translated them in her mind: *Prove all things, hold fast to that which is good.* It was the school motto, which reflected the college's Christian tradition of searching out the truth wherever it led. She was trying desperately to hold fast to the things of the past that were good and true and right, but they seemed to have slipped away like a lone ray of sunlight, fast disappearing under the onslaught of a raging Irish rainstorm.

She scrambled the Greek letters in her mind, forming fewer hopeful sayings in a dozen different languages, both ancient and modern. Then, she took the gold wedding ring from her pocket, rubbing it between her fingers, as she often did, not daring to put it on, but keeping it near as a constant reminder of all that she'd lost.

Saorla fought back tears in the middle of a meeting called by the dean of Arts, Humanities, and Social Sciences at Trinity College, Dublin. Ostensibly, the meeting was to be about improving community engagement and general public relations, but impending staff cuts had been the main topic of discussion on campus the past few weeks.

Rumors had been flying wildly that there were going to be some serious layoffs. More than fifty professors, associate professors, lecturers, and assistants gathered in a large lecture room as Dean Grady did his best to avoid the elephant that had to be on most everyone's mind, except Saorla's, that is.

The cuts were simply not at the forefront of her mind at the moment. No, it was something much more primal.

These days her eyes welled with tears at even the most insignificant signal—a glimpse of broad male shoulders to her periphery, a flash of a profile with a thick black beard, a few syllables spoken with a certain tone and Scottish-Gaelic accent to it, a sincere smile, a particular fragrance. Or a late evening walk down Grafton Street, seeing a couple holding hands and then each turning to meet the other's lips.

In these odd moments, her whole body ached for Stuart with an inconsolable yearning. Sometimes she'd wake in the night and reach for him.

The ache faded only in those dreams.

She returned her gaze to the dean, as a hand shot up in the first row and a professor proceeded to ask a question about the across-the-board cuts that were rumored to be coming soon to many of the departments. It was said that all the jobs of all the tenured professors were, of course, safe. But many of the non-tenured contract employees would be forced out.

As the youngest member on the faculty, Saorla had consequently earned the least seniority. She had served as a professor for three years. The first year was bliss, with Stuart. But she'd been hired on a non-permanent contract basis, which would end in two months.

The crisis registered in her logical brain, but the only part of her that really mattered could barely muster the energy to match her socks in the morning, and she hadn't done anything special with her hair in months.

"Will you be addressing the rumors of staff cuts at some point today?" the professor in the front row asked. "And if not, will you at least tell us whether there is any truth to the rumors."

This should be good. A professor named Meegan had just told

Saorla recently how she could always tell when Grady was lying—*he pushes his glasses up hard onto the bridge of his nose and then looks down at his shoes before he delivers his best falsehoods.*

Saorla eyed Grady carefully. He jabbed at his glasses sending them upward and stared toward the floor for a long moment before saying, "There is no truth at all to the rumors, not even a smidgeon."

Finally, the dean concluded his remarks. A flicker of late sun shone through the window. Some of the faculty escaped in a trot to continue their busy lives. Others inched up zombie-like, seeming almost too stunned to move from their seats. Did they, too, know that Grady was lying?

Last of the stragglers, Saorla rose to her feet, unsteady and shaking. She avoided the dean in the hallway and darted the way back to her office where she flipped the light switch, illuminating the centuries old studio bursting with books. Settling into the chair at her well-worn wood desk, she kicked off her knee-high boots from over her leggings and slipped on her walking shoes. She leaned her head back in her chair, closed her eyes, and sighed.

How could she save her job? And what would happen to her dear friends among the faculty? Two articles were brewing in her head as possibly publishable, she supposed, along with another book about the Old Irish language and its development. If she had time to finish these projects to a successful conclusion, her chances of surviving the cuts improved. But what about some of the other faculty? Something needed to be done that was more immediate and inclusive.

A sudden knock at her partially opened door shifted Saorla's attention. Claire Curran, a fellow Irish Studies professor who'd joined the faculty a year before Saorla, peeked in from behind the door. Claire was a petite redhead in her mid-thirties.

"Hey, love," Claire said. "Is it a good time?"

"Would it make a difference if I said no?"

"Funny, love. I'll tell Dean Grady you have a new closed-door policy. That should move you up the chopping block for layoffs."

"Layoffs? Is that what you came to talk about?"

"Not really. I'd rather talk about income inequality and gender discrimination and the capitalist pigs running amok. But don't get me started."

"Sounds like you already are. But hey, we all think the same on those issues. Tell me what you think about the across-the-board cuts that are coming like an army of British dragoons to quell the Irish moon from rising?"

Claire smiled, probably at the metaphor, then shook her head. "I think there's a real danger one of us gets the noose."

"Yeah? What's your theory?" Saorla asked, with only a modicum of curiosity.

"Grady is bucking to become the next provost in charge of the college. It's all political with him. He has more ambition than you think. His big idea is to push more diversity."

"But we're *women* professors. I thought we're the *sine qua non* of diversity."

Claire shook her head. "Grady has other ideas. *Push forward* has become his mantra. Making a name for himself as one who increased transgender and third-world professors is his goal. Word among the faculty has it that he resents your hiring because you're native Irish. Not diverse enough in his book."

"But we're *Irish* history professors."

"I think I can survive, but I'm pretty sure Grady has you in his crosshairs." A teasing glitter shone in Claire's eyes. "Actually, I'm making that last part up. I think we're probably shipmates of the same boat wreck. We started about the same time in the same department. You're Irish. I'm American with Irish ancestry."

"There has to be a way to get past these cuts," Saorla said. "Somehow we have to boost enrollment and/or the financials. Then we can all keep our positions."

"You are an optimist, love."

"Optimist? You have no idea how wrong you are about that."

"Well then, time to join the club and get working on plan B. Are you dusting off your resume?"

There was another knock at the door. It was Myrna Cahdan, Saorla's twenty-two-year-old grad assistant. Her hair was cut above her ears and dyed a space-age silver. Two nose rings hung from the side of each nostril. Nearly every week she threatened to show up sporting a tongue piercing.

"Sorry to interrupt. I thought you two would be needing help in getting your articles published ASAP. So here I am, ready to research whatever you need."

"Is she always this cheery on Friday afternoon?" Claire asked.

Saorla nodded. "Just be thankful you're never around first thing in the morning when she moves in on the coffee."

Myrna began dancing about like she was performing in the show *Riverdance* in an obvious effort to help illustrate Saorla's point. When Myrna finally tired of the display, she turned to Claire. "So, Professor Curran, rumor has it you're flunking Kevin Tierney?"

Kevin was a second-year undergrad who was as well known for his perfect academic record as he was for his controversial conservative views.

"Can you keep a secret?" Claire whispered.

"Depends," Myrna said.

"I'll take that as a yes. Let's just say there are ways to get around the anonymity of the test-taking system. During class discussions, Tierney made the mistake of badmouthing the Green Party and taking a stand against increasing the minimum wage. I know how his voice sounds—it's the same on paper as it is in class discussions."

Claire pulled out her cell phone and checked the time. "My evening lecture starts in ten minutes so I've gotta leave." She turned to Saorla and placed her hand on her shoulder. "Remember, love, it's time to get a plan B in motion."

Saorla watched Claire close the door tight as she left. The doors of Saorla's world also seemed to be closing tight, her whole life turning into one big plan B.

"I'm glad you stopped by," Saorla said to Myrna. "We've got lots of work ahead, and it starts in a big way Monday. But are you up for it? How's your personal life holding up with your class load and your duties with me?"

Myrna plunked herself down in a chair. "That's sweet of you to ask, especially given all you've … Sorry … anyway, I like to juggle with my life, or else I get bored. The more stuff going the better. My boyfriend is gone—don't ask why. I tend bar at Milton's Pub in Temple Bar twice a week. That takes up a good chunk of time, but the money almost helps to make ends meet. I'm having a hard time paying my rent."

"Why don't you find a cheaper flat?"

"Everything around here is just as high."

Saorla had an idea of a way she could assist. "Listen, the cuts will probably affect grad assistants as well. How much are you paying?"

"Sixteen hundred euros a month for a wee studio barely big enough for my bed."

"Really? Can you get out of it?"

"Just signed on for another six months."

Saorla had worked with Myrna over the past year and had grown comfortable enough around her. She had an extra bedroom and was sure she could establish some rules to prevent Myrna from infringing on her privacy. "Why don't you sublet it and move in with me in Ballsbridge? It's a little farther out, but you could save your euros for whatever comes down the road. We could put it in writing right now. That way, if something happens to me, you would be entitled to stay there until the estate is settled, which could take years."

"What do you mean, *if something happens to you*? That's a bit macabre, don't you think? Even for all you've been through."

Tears again banked the corner of Saorla's eyes. *Of course Myrna wouldn't want to live with the depressed basket case that she'd become*. "Forget it. It was just a silly idea I had."

"Are you kidding? It's the opportunity of a lifetime—unless you start in on a curfew. I have a social life to maintain, you know."

"Yeah, I remember what it was like to be in school."

Myrna's pale blue eyes trained on Saorla, studying her curiously for a long moment. "What about *you* and a social life?" she finally asked. "You don't go anywhere. You're young for a professor, you could meet someone and—"

"It's not in the cards for me," Saorla said, feeling her voice quiver. The tears stung her eyes, and she was already having second thoughts about helping Myrna out with an offer of a room. She turned away from her and grabbed a tissue.

"Sorry, I shouldn't have upset you. I'll leave now."

"It's okay, I—"

"I gotta go anyway. The Milton's bar patrons will send out a search party if I don't show. Nobody can mix a whiskey sour like yours truly."

CHAPTER THREE

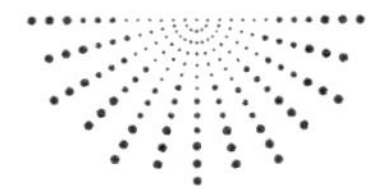

Ian Shaw paddled on his surfboard and searched over the thundering waves back toward the Northern California shoreline some two miles away. Clouds obscured the low-lying October sun that hunted for the patch to poke through, as it barely buoyed its way over the hills to the east. It had been more than ten months since he'd last tested himself at Mavericks. The unique underwater rock formations triggered Mav's waves to break far from shore and had been a recipe for surfer death a number of times in the past.

As he watched and waited for the agitated giants to roll in, his pulse rocketed and sweat gathered under the cap of his wetsuit, despite the fifty-seven-degree temps in and out of the water. A surfer about forty yards off was duck diving, trying hard to get out back behind the breakers to Ian.

"Dawn patrol, dude!" the surfer bellowed when he paddled close enough to be recognized as "Shark," a quintessential surfer dude that Ian had befriended the past year.

The sea springing up from near where Ian lay on his board was a billowing monster. The surf was at thirty feet and going higher. Unusual inasmuch as the big-wave season didn't usually kick off until around the first of the year. But the weather had conspired to bring an early start to the madness.

Shark maneuvered his board next to Ian's. His face had the pasty look of a well-earned hangover.

"You okay?" Ian asked.

"Late night. Draggin' my butt a little."

"Dude, you gotta get right. Those bad boys will eat you alive!" Ian pointed at a surfer rising on a behemoth. The wave sliced on, and the squatting figure abruptly vanished. Silence fell between them for a moment. The effort to communicate over the roar of the sea was draining, and Ian was wholly engrossed in selecting the perfect wave.

"Sure glad I don't have to go to some stuffy law office like you, bro," Shark finally said. "Ocean's my office."

Now it was Ian's turn to lose focus. He'd have to leave for his work at Horowitz, Dunlap & Connor, in an hour or so. The agenda for the day suddenly flashed through his mind, and he remembered the meeting scheduled with the partners for later in the morning. But tomorrow was Saturday, which meant he'd be free to surf all day after he finished his early-morning, mixed-martial-arts training.

A glimmer of sun poked through the clouds, and Shark pointed toward it. "It's a sign of good karma."

"More like God's blessing."

"Ah, man ... my religion's the waves."

"That can't be true."

Shark smirked. "I'd swear it on a stack of seaweed, bro. The waves are my deity—"

Ian peered past Shark to the west, his brain registering a sign of a different sort—the brewing of an epic wave.

"Go for it, bro," Shark shouted.

Ian paddled hard, sucking in the cold ocean air. He sensed the presence of someone paddling behind him but dismissed it as impossible. He rose to his feet, struggled to gain his balance, but then stuck it firm.

Standing on his board like the mythical god Thor, he rode through the sky, while the wave grew and undulated. He became one with a summit of water, billowing up, presiding over the rolling, crescendo of thunder.

His lips tasted the pungency of the ocean salt. His eyes remained unblinking at the wonder and terror as he alternately surveyed the crest of the hills at the coastline so far off in the distance and then the level of the sea falling away below his board while he rose in unison with the climbing swell. The effort to keep equilibrium and the impossible height caused his heart to pound hard against his chest. The powerful wave was the strongest he'd ever seen, much less ridden. He lived for this combination of fear and pleasure—the half-ecstasy, the half freaking-out.

Traveling at the speed of lightning, all his problems faded in the intensity of the moment. The tunnel crept closer. He began ascending again. Rising, gravity waned, and he soared to an impossible height.

Despite the roar of wave and wind, Ian heard a shout as a surfer sliced in under him. "Bro! Party wave!" Sharks laughter somehow carried over the rumble of the sea.

Ian flinched hard, and he ended up in a crouch so low he was almost seated on his haunches. He darted reflexively for a lower position in the wave. But Shark was already there below him.

Ian let out a groan. To be in the clear up here alone as he was fighting to keep his balance and possibly his life four or five stories above the level of the sea was one matter, but Shark had added exponentially to the danger level. Two surfers, two boards, and a wall of water. The odds had shifted toward a bad ending.

Ian glided onward, tucking into the tube. The wave jerked and twisted him forward, sending him hurtling and summersaulting. The wall of water behind and above converged rapidly. A scream pierced the air. "Wipe-ooout!"

Concrete slabs of water pounded him, hurrying his descent. Ian took a last gasp and plunged down and down under the water. The Velcro strap that connected his leash to his board tore apart with the force. The board flew toward the surface, and he would probably never see it again.

Through the water, he plummeted, baptized to a depth of thirty to forty feet under the sea.

Ian found himself spinning violently and uncontrollably, the water churning about, holding him under. His lungs shrank to half their size, and he was sure an elephant was stomping on his chest. The urge to breathe was unbearable now.

Up was survival, but the more he sought it the more out of reach it seemed. The water and the churning wouldn't free him for a second. So he tried to relax by going limp. Dead man's float.

He opened his eyes and looked down. The salty water stung his retinas, but he fought to peer through the inky murk of the ocean. Billy "the Shark" Williams' leash was wrapped around a rock, with his board on one side and his body counterbalanced on the other. The churning water had him imprisoned, unable to reach the Velcro strap near his ankle.

By some miracle, Ian was able to bob a moment above the surface, allowing him to take a gulp of air. Then the churning plunged him down again. He lunged toward Shark, lungs still crying to breathe. The washing machine spun Ian around again. A pair of blue jeans in the final stages of a spin cycle.

The awful churning released Ian momentarily. He made another surge toward Shark. Groping about, blinded by a seething swirl, he felt for Shark's leg, found it, and with one sweep, he released the Velcro strap at Shark's ankle. Board and former rider rocketed free.

Now it was Ian's turn. He broke the surface, gulped a huge influx of air and then another, before letting out a desperate gasp.

And then the next tumult hit.

The wave was a blue giant with a plunger, and Ian was a Lilliputian going down the bowl. Whirling and shaking, no air remained in his lungs. Without warning, the plunging Gulliver stopped the torment and catapulted Ian to the surface. He gulped another chunk of air and reflexively began treading water.

Relative calm settled.

Floating face down in the water, a body drifted.

"No!" Ian moaned. Shark floated only a few yards away. A couple of hard strokes and he was on him.

He yanked Shark backwards.

Not breathing.

Placing an arm under his armpit, he secured Shark and began flailing toward shore. The going dragged as Ian steadied Shark's head with his hand. A mile and a half to land. Ian stroked with all he had left.

Nausea overcame him, and he almost vomited, both because he'd nearly drowned and because his buddy probably had. The lack of oxygen had cut his peripheral vision to where he could only see through a tunnel. And his arms and legs were "noodled."

Never give up, he told himself. *Even if you die trying to do this.*

He strained a few yards further before he heard the sound of watercraft. In seconds, a couple of emergency jet skis appeared.

A man with dark hair and a red orange vest lifted Shark onto his craft and sped away. The other jet pulled near Ian. Glasses and a black Giants baseball cap was all Ian could make out. "Get on," the man yelled.

Ian mustered the strength to hoist himself, but his effort fell flat, and he fell back in the water. The guy finally pulled him aboard. The craft powered toward shore.

"When I saw you on that wall of water, I couldn't believe it," the man yelled over the whoosh of the wind. "I'm a big wave photographer. Got it all on film. That was epic, man! You had to be up there at least five stories. They'll still be talking about this ten years from now —mark my words."

"Thanks for coming," Ian gasped.

"When I saw you rag dolled, I knew you'd need help—and quick."

Words exhausted Ian so he just nodded. The Giant's cap persisted nonetheless. "That's when I threw my camera down and headed out. This baby does fifty-five per hour, max. Technically, I'm not licensed to operate at Pillar Point. But I always bring my ski when I'm shooting with my cam. Just in case. Right, man?"

Ian nodded again. They were already at shore. The rescue had only taken a minute or two, tops.

Was there hope for Shark?

Paramedics swarmed the beach. Mars lights flashed from vehicles farther up where a significant crowd had gathered. Ian stumbled off the ski and ran toward the flashing lights. On his third stride, his legs noodled and his face landed in the sand, his head narrowly missing a large boulder.

"Let me check you out, sir."

Ian jerked his face up and saw it was an EMT.

"Naw. I'm okay. I ... just wanna know how's Shark?"

"You had a shark out there with you too?"

"No, the other guy ... His name's Shark." Ian put his chin down on the sand.

The EMT eyed him closely. Ian tried to suppress indications he might need serious medical treatment. "Really, I'm fine. How's the other guy?"

"I think he's going to be okay."

Ian exhaled.

By now, his eyesight had fully recovered, and a grin creased his face when he spotted Mike Clark and Jeff Kinzler rushing toward him. The two men had a beach ministry for surfers.

"Coulda sworn you had a death wish when we saw you up there," Jeff said.

Ian popped up and flashed a wry smile. "I was thinking about heading back out to catch another one."

He waited for their faces to register shock. "Just kidding. I'd really have to be crazy to do that, huh?"

The glimmer of a smile formed on Mike's face. "We want to watch over your soul, so you get to heaven, but not that soon." Mike and Jeff both laughed nervously.

"I need to check on Shark," Ian said.

The trio made their way over to the EMT truck but had to wait about fifteen minutes before they could see him. When the paramedics finally opened up the back of the truck, Shark was spread out on a stretcher with a Grinch-who-stole-Christmas grin. Ian flashed Shark a Shaka sign, extending out a thumb and pinkie finger, before heading off to get ready for the meeting at the office with the partners.

CHAPTER FOUR

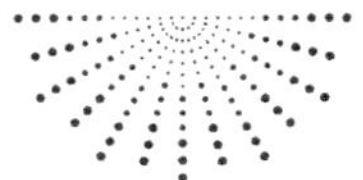

After the meeting with Myrna, Saorla began her normal three and half kilometer trek home. Darkness had descended, and a cool drizzle fell on the city, muting store lights in the foggy air. She walked past the shops on Grafton Street, marveling at the large, thin glass window of a woman's clothing store. A sudden urge seized her to hurl herself through it. Instead, she grasped her hair, moist and dark, flipped it over her shoulder, and kept walking.

Further on, a vision of herself lunging in front of an oncoming bus tempted her mind. She kept walking, though—but, honestly, she didn't know why—until a high-end liquor store came into view just ahead. She stepped inside and hunted for the best bottle of French wine they had.

A 2012 vintage Bordeaux blend produced by the Chateau Lafite Rothschild estate that sold for three-hundred and ninety-eight euros caught her eye. It stood like a toy soldier on the shelf behind the clerk at the checkout line, like a harmless amusement for a child.

"I'll take that one," she said to the man behind the counter.

He raised his eyebrows and then pulled the bottle from the shelf. "Somebody is in for a big night," he said, as he scanned the price.

Saorla didn't reply.

Big night? It was all relative.

She paid out all the euros in her purse, left her change on the counter, and walked out with the Bordeaux.

The desire to wrestle through another night dimmed. Maybe the morning would not be waiting. She was going to get through this evening, or she wasn't—only time would tell.

The large burgundy front door of her two-story Georgian home greeted her with all the allure of a prison gate. The ivy grew thick now, mostly obscuring the salmon-hued brick facade on either side of the door, climbing up as if reaching out for a better existence. Stuart would have cut it back, but she hadn't had the time for it.

Surviving was a full-time occupation.

Inside, the place was empty, of course. She'd reluctantly come to accept that. On most days anyway. But this wasn't most days.

Saorla entered the kitchen and grabbed two wine glasses and a white tablecloth. She took them upstairs to her large master suite bedroom, flicked on the gas fireplace, and pulled open long, beige curtains to expose the view from the veranda of the lighted and heavily tree-lined street below. She spread out the white cloth and set the table near the veranda for two.

Sitting in one chair now, she poured a glass of vintage Bordeaux and placed it on the table in front of the empty chair across from her. Then she slowly poured herself one.

She raised her glass, as if toasting and said to the chair, "Happy third anniversary, Honey. October eighth." Then she took a long, solid sip.

October eighth was supposed to be a fun, joyful day for the rest of her life. A time to celebrate and remember.

The tears were coming full on now, running down her cheek, and one dropped into her wine glass. Tears and wine, mixing together, she would drink them both to the dregs if this was what God or the cosmos had for her.

God? Ha, what a joke that was.

It's definitely the cosmos, darling pretty. Even though you once thought different, you know now, if you know anything at all.

"I will always love you. Bottoms up. Here's to plan B, love."

She chugged it down without bothering to savor it and then poured another glass. Repeating the process until the bottle was gone and then downing the glass across from her, the ache finally subsided, a bit.

A careful search of the house for more wine failed to uncover any. Liquor had been her frequent friend of late, so much so her formerly well-stocked home was now a complete dry zone.

She flipped on an Irish folk music station, advertised as the place where sad songs were never that sad. On this night, however, that boast could not be true.

Back in her bedroom again, she pulled a book from the shelf: *Easter Moon*. Not just any book at random but one that Stuart wrote on the history of the Easter Rising of 1916, which was the main salvo of Irish nationalists against British hegemony that ultimately led to independence several years later. The more she read, the more she knew she was going to need her own personal rising at some point before it was too late.

She suffered through an hour or so of distracted reading. The wine had so clouded her eyesight that she couldn't tell whether her bedroom clock read nine or ten. She decided it was only nine o'clock, too early to go to bed. All she wanted to do now was forget ... sleeping pills would make it happen. She could sleep, and she could forget.

Maybe forever.

IAN HIT THE ELEVATOR BUTTON STILL SHAKEN FROM THE events at Maverick's earlier that morning. The door opened, and he pressed *forty-six*. The three chief partners of the firm operated out of the entire forty-sixth floor of the building. The rest of the crew had the four floors below.

On the way up, Ian racked his brain, trying to imagine why he'd been summoned. Perhaps they wanted to give him a raise. Yeah, right.

God knew he could use a raise. He'd just bought a condo a few blocks from the bay and was now saddled with a mortgage on par with the national debt of a small country.

The elevator stopped at the forty-fourth floor, and Jarvis Reed stepped in. Jarvis was a Yale Law grad who grew up on the East Coast and worked a couple of years in a New York firm, before flipping coasts four years ago to take a job with Horowitz, Dunlap & Connor. Jarvis was Ian's chief competition for partnership.

Ian glanced down at Jarvis's prematurely balding head and asked, "Let me guess, forty-sixth floor?"

"You're uncanny," Jarvis said with mock surprise.

"Any idea what's going on?" Ian asked. "Are you working on something important?"

Jarvis chuckled. "Everything I do is important. You should know that."

"Spoken like a true Ivy-leaguer just upgraded from gofer status at his new firm."

Jarvis laughed. "The truth is, I have a tedious statute-of-limitations issue in a personal injury case that just came across my desk. Nothing else that important on the horizon either. What about you?"

"The criminal cases can be dicey at times, but I don't have a high-profile murder case right now. Yet there are some pretty big stakes in play for one of my current clients."

"Tell me about it."

The elevator stopped, and the two men stepped into the hallway outside the partners' offices. They paused beside a virtual jungle of indoor plants and the fountain they surrounded to continue their conversation.

"I'm representing a twenty-three-year-old math teacher named José Calderon. The State says he committed a drug trafficking crime when he was fourteen that kicks up to a felony murder count because someone died from an overdose of the drugs the gang was peddling. Now, nine years later, the State wants to try José as an adult."

"Can they do that?"

"I'm hoping the judge buys my argument and says no. I'll file a motion to dismiss on Monday. If the judge denies it, he'll want to start trial midweek."

"Is he a good kid?"

"Yeah, he's avoided trouble ever since that bad stretch in his youth. He graduated from college last year, now he's teaching at a school in East Palo Alto. If he'd been arrested before the age of twenty-one, all he'd probably have gotten was a slap on the wrist—perhaps some community service, maybe some sort of probation. But now, at twenty-three, he's too old to be tried in the juvenile justice system, so the state is seeking to punish him in adult criminal court, where he could face thirty years."

"Why wasn't he arrested earlier?"

"He was in a gang way back when, cleaned his life up, moved on. But one of the gang members ratted José out in hopes of leniency for his own offenses."

"Sounds like the kind of case that could make the evening news," Jarvis said. "I suppose it's possible the big wigs would call you in to make sure you have a handle on it. But I still have no idea why they would want to see me."

Ian opened the door of the reception area. "I guess we'll find out soon enough."

As Ian expected, both Mr. Horowitz and one of the other founding partners, Kenneth Dunlap, were there. Nobody, in the last couple of months, had seen much of Terrance Connor, the third founding partner whose name appeared on the office stationery.

Ian had only visited Mr. Horowitz's office a few times since joining the firm. The large suite harbored a vast array of exotic plants. Fine art frescoes adorned the walls. A replica of the Resolute desk at the White House rested near the ceiling-to-floor windows, and a spacious conference table designated itself at the opposite side. The view of San Francisco Bay dazzled the eyes.

"Good afternoon," Ian nodded slightly to each of the partners as he stood in the entrance. "I hear you wanted to see us."

Mr. Horowitz beckoned them in. "Yes, sit over there, Mr. Shaw and

Mr. Reed." Horowitz pointed to chairs on the other end of a conference table across from the two partners, and they all sat.

"Actually, we want to talk about you today, Mr. Shaw. Mr. Reed is here for purposes that will become apparent."

This was odd. They usually called him Ian.

Probably not here to talk about a raise.

Horowitz glanced down at the notes on his legal pad and then back up at Ian. "I want to get right to the point, Mr. Shaw. It has come to our attention that you were involved in an altercation in the Castro District back in July. Is that true?"

So that's what this is about.

"I'm not sure if it was Castro or Haight-Ashbury, but it was somewhere over there. And I wouldn't call it an altercation."

"What would you call it, Mr. Shaw?"

"Self-defense. The police came. There were no charges brought. But some of those folks should have been arrested."

"Tell us what happened." Horowitz's words were innocuous enough, but the sarcasm in his voice set Ian's teeth on edge.

How had the partners learned of the incident? Why were they making so much of it? And were their minds somehow poisoned against him?

He took a deep breath and remembered that night. "It was a Friday evening in July. I'd been over in Santa Clara watching the Earthquakes play the Chicago Zephyrs. I like to watch soccer, used to play a bit myself. It runs in the family you could say. My—"

"Just get to the incident."

"Yes, sir. I was on my way home—it was a warm night, and I had my windows down— and I heard music followed by some loud shouting. I was stopped at a red light, looked over to my right at a park. I could see that something wasn't right."

"What wasn't right?"

"The chatter in the air sounded angry."

"Why did you feel it was *your* job to get involved?"

Ian suddenly felt like a judge ought to be here, at least one person to officiate what seemed like a courtroom drama. None of his prior experience with the partners suggested that they were biased against him. Nor had he heard any rumors suggesting they were unfair. The firm was well respected in the city—tough, but generally honest, was the consensus in the legal community. But he couldn't give them a full explanation for his actions. The truth was he'd been training steady at mixed martial arts for more than a year at that point, and he wasn't diffident about testing his new skills outside the gym. "There were a bunch of men. They looked violent. They surrounded a small group of people, mostly innocent-looking girls, who had guitars out trying to sing some songs in the park. Acoustic guitars, nothing amped up. I then—"

"Who were these people?" Horowitz asked.

"I didn't know at the time, but I learned later they were a group of Christians who'd gone into the park to pray and worship. That's all. Sometimes they'd engage people in low-key conversations about their faith. Nothing pushy. The other group, the violent ones—there were a good number of them. They were calling themselves the Neo-Pagans. Looked like a hard-core motorcycle gang to me. Anyway, they were accusing the Christian group of being Prop 8 advocates and—"

"Prop 8? That is so last decade," Horowitz quipped.

"Yeah," Ian nodded, thankful they had something they could agree on. "So I parked my car off to the side of the street and got out to find out what was happening, and that's when it went from PG to R-rated. The Neo-Pagans screamed every vile name in the book at the Christian group. There were just five of them—three or four girls, early twenties probably and a couple of boys with guitars who weren't much older."

"I have it from reliable sources that you caused some injuries that night," Horowitz said, with a frown.

"I had to do something. By the time I got to them, the gang had them surrounded. They were smacking the men with their fists. They had them on the ground. Pummeling them. Then they start abusing the girls, trying to—"

"Mr. Shaw, we don't need the R-rated version here. Just tell us what your role was."

"I decked the biggest one first. Knocked him down, probably broke his jaw is what I thought at that moment, but he later turned out to be all right. The second biggest came at me with a knife and swung it. I ducked, he missed. And then I kicked him right in the chest. He went down like a bag of sand, probably had a broken rib. The other three wanted no part of it after that. Somebody called the police, and we sorted it out when they arrived. The Neo-Pagans told the police that the Christians were hassling them. The police weren't buying it thanks to a couple of neutral eyewitnesses. They allowed the big fellas, the pagans, to go off with the EMT crew, who worked on them a bit, and then they all left. Even the one with the broken rib slunk off."

Horowitz was still frowning. "This meeting was a chance to give you due process before we took any action in this matter."

"Excuse me, but what action are you talking about?" He also wanted to ask, *Due process for what?* But thought the better of it. He had to maintain his decorum before the partners. But how could they say they'd given him due process when they'd not even given him notice of what this meeting was about?

"Mr. Shaw." Dunlap spoke for the first time. "It is our judgment that your behavior on that July night was unbecoming of an attorney of this firm."

The reprimand smacked of a foregone conclusion. Otherwise the two would have conferred. His opportunity to speak in his defense had apparently been nothing but a sham.

"We deem this to be a violation of the attorney code of conduct in our firm's employee manual," Dunlap said. "As a consequence, we are suspending you for one month without pay, effective immediately."

Ian couldn't breathe. It was as if a gut-punch had knotted his stomach. And he was still lightheaded from his earlier ordeal at Mavs. He tried to speak, "I ... I think—"

"—Moreover," Dunlap continued, "you will in the next month apologize to those men you hurt, or you will be terminated from your position with this firm. Is that clear?"

Indignant rage clouded his vision and clogged his throat. He forced out a "yes."

"Mr. Reed, you will take over Mr. Shaw's workload effective immediately."

A clammy sweat clung to Ian's forehead. Random thoughts whirled in his head like a bevy of bouncing squirrels, incapable of giving form to speech. He'd never had trouble remaining calm in the courtroom, but it was much harder to keep his emotions in check in this setting, especially in his weakened physical condition.

The partners stood and ushered Ian and Jarvis out the door. Ian walked slowly to the elevator with Jarvis.

"Listen, I think I know what's behind this," Jarvis said.

"You do?"

"Yeah." A goofy grin spread across Jarvis's face. "Horowitz has it in for you because he realizes now that I'd make a better partner than you someday."

Ian slowly nodded, unable to register any feigned indignation at Jarvis's ill-timed attempt at humor.

"Okay, I know, bad joke. But I really do think I know what's behind this. It's the appeal you filed on behalf of that Hollywood exec sex molester that's been in the news for weeks now. The partners don't want the publicity. And rather than coming out and ordering you to drop it, they think it cleaner to just cut ties with you now. And the scrap you got into over in the Castro district provided a convenient opportunity. They know you're stubborn and probably won't comply with their ultimatum."

Ian slowly shook his head. That's why he was at the firm—to provide criminal defense for people accused of crimes, people who were entitled to representation and the presumption of innocence. "I don't get. Publicity for a law firm in this sort of situation is usually good, even when the firm represents someone who is infamous for their alleged crime?"

"That's not the way they see it this time. The guy's so toxic, the partners don't want to become victims of a cancel campaign. Best option, they probably feel, is to look like they are fighting the evil by letting you go. The question is what are you going to do about it?"

"Surf," Ian muttered, still not completely clear-headed after getting worked in the washing machine earlier that morning.

"My advice is you apologize and quietly drop your representation on the appeal but let the partners know it's been done."

Ian shook his head. "Listen, I have a motion to dismiss the indictment and a brief in support that needs to be filed Monday on behalf of José Calderon. I'll leave it on my desk for you. There's going to be an expedited hearing before the judge later in the week. Please don't let the kid down."

Jarvis nodded and stepped into the elevator. Ian's cell phone pulsed and began playing Timba. The number and picture of his paternal grandparents in Northern Ireland popped up. Fumbling the phone in his still languid hands, he secured it, and then answered with the swipe of a finger. He hadn't talked to his grandparents in a couple of months, and it would be a treat to hear their voices after the double trauma he'd endured out on the water and now here at the office, so he took the call, and waved on Jarvis, who headed down on the elevator.

"Oh, it's so good to hear your voice, honey," his grandmother said. "We've missed you much."

A tone of sorrow was etched all through her Irish lilt.

"I've missed you too, Nana. And Papa, too."

"I'm afraid I've got bad news," his grandmother said.

Ian's heart started pounding as if he were again riding the epic wave on which he'd crashed and burned.

"Listen, hun. It's your grandfather. He had an accident. He's okay, I mean ... he's alive, albeit barely. And something very valuable was stolen—a silver chalice he'd dug up on the farm was taken from his car. The authorities are saying he simply had a heart attack, blacked out, crashed, and someone took advantage. But George says it was an assault that triggered it because someone intended to steal the treasure. The doctors say his condition is serious." Nana was sniffling now.

"Oh no," Ian said. "Is Papa in the hospital? Can I talk to him?" He pulled at a fistful of his hair. "Where did it happen?"

"Driving in the hills near the farm on his way back from Belfast."

Ian could picture his grandparents' sheep farm in the Hills of Antrim and the rolling country roads nearby. He'd lived with them for two years when he was a teenager after his parents split up.

"Listen, Ian, I'm trying to contact Rory too. Have you spoken with him lately?"

"Nah." The truth was he hadn't spoken to his father in over two years. "And that's not likely to change with the playoffs coming up in less than three weeks."

"I think he's going to want to take some time off coaching and come and see Papa."

"Please tell me he's going to be all right."

"They have him in the intensive care unit, and he's asking for you." She started to cry softly and couldn't talk.

Ian waited for her to regain her composure.

"He wants you to come," she finally said. "The authorities won't believe him. They say their investigation shows no signs of foul play, and he says he needs your help. Look, there are things he's found on our property, strange things. And he says he'll hold on until you get here."

"What things?"

"A silver chalice for one. He found it in the bog the day after he had a dream that led him to dig. The chalice is, we think, very valuable. He says there's more artifacts to be found. He took the chalice to Belfast to have an expert examine it. On the way home, he had the accident. Then, the chalice was stolen before the hullabaloo surrounding the arrival of a good Samaritan who performed CPR and the medical help. He insists he had the heart attack because someone frightened him on the road and planned to steal the chalice."

Ian took a deep breath to settle himself. "How can I help? I'll do anything I can, of course."

"He wants you to come and find out who stole the chalice. He doesn't trust the authorities. But I think he should just forget about the whole thing—his heart hasn't been well, and you know how he never listens to the doctors."

CHAPTER FIVE

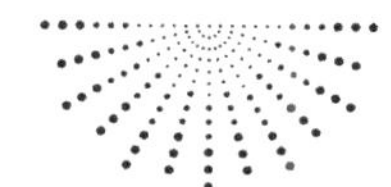

Saorla trudged toward the medicine cabinet in her master bathroom like a death row inmate headed for a hangman's noose. The pills in the yellow prescription bottle seemed to smile up at her cynically, like mocking prison guards. The psychiatrist who prescribed them for her two years ago had told her that they would "take the edge off." She'd never taken any to find out if that were true and hadn't been back to see the gentleman. But she was about to find out now. The chances that she would ever report back to him after today would be zero, she guessed.

She took a few of the pills in hand and placed the bottle on the granite sink countertop. Too many at one time and she might choke to death. But what did it matter anyway?

She shoved a couple of them in her mouth and chased them down with a glass of water that was already waiting for her.

Taking the bottle of pills in hand, she stared at them for a long moment, debating, and already the drowsy fog was pouring over her.

Her cell phone buzzed to life in her pocket, startling her, breaking the sad spell she'd fallen under. The bottle of pills dropped from her hands to the floor, the pills spilling like a hundred shattered pieces of crystal dreams.

She stabbed around at her phone in her pocket and eventually hauled it out.

Papa? It was her father.

There wasn't a single person on earth she could think of that she would answer that phone for. Except him.

"Hello, Papa," she said with a sniffle and trying not to slur her speech.

The words on the other end came in a rush of Gaelic, *"Is ceol mo chroi thú,"* and were pronounced phonetically as Is Cyoal mu khree, perfectly in fact, as only a lifetime of saying them could produce.

"You're the music of *my* heart too," Saorla said, her voice weak and cracking. The shame over taking the pills pounced on her now and wrestled against the sleep she felt spilling over her eyelids. She pushed herself toward her bed and eased herself down.

"I thought you could be needin' a little cheerin' up. Was I wrong, girl?"

"Maybe more than a *little* cheer—" She let out a deep yawn. She hadn't meant to let her guard down as much as those few words conveyed.

"I hope I can be of help with that."

She yawned again. "Very tired tonight ... Papa ... getting sleepy."

"It's rough on anniversaries." He said it like a man who knew from experience.

"And all days that end in Y," she said in a near whisper into the phone propped on her pillow next to where her head lay.

He'd traveled the same hard road of grief when Saorla's mom died a few years back. That loss had been tough on Saorla too, but Stuart's passing so close on the heels of her mom's was a full solar eclipse, the one grief blocking out the other.

"That will be changin' for ya soon. I know it will. You're young and beautiful, you'll meet someone, fall in love again. The grief will fade into the past, and the memories you'll have without the pain someday. Just keep your faith in God."

"You still think he exists, or that if he does, he even cares?"

"I know he does, you'll see. I've been praying for ya at Mass every day this week, and I know ya will come back around to Him even if it doesn't look exactly like *I* think it should."

"I haven't been to Mass since Stuart ..." She couldn't quite get the rest of the words out, not because of grief—the ache that was always there had loosened its grip, detached a wee bit of its bludgeoning force with the wine and the comfort of her father's voice—but it was the sleep that was coming fast, and she couldn't fight it much longer.

"I don't suspect you have."

"So tired, Papa."

A pale grey slumber closed her eyes. She knew her father was about to end the call by telling her he loved her, he'd probably say it in the Irish language. She said it to him first, *"Is breá liom tú."*

If he said it back to her, she would never remember hearing it.

MUFFLER RATTLING, SOPHIE ZAWORSKI JERKED HER twelve-year-old Volkswagen Golf to a halt and parked it on the curb on Baggot Lane. She was running way behind schedule in her list of homes to clean in the Ballsbridge area of Dublin but that didn't stop her from singing the worship song that had been playing before she got out of her car. She usually got to Ms. O'Rourke's Georgian much earlier, and this Saturday morning was already creeping up toward the noon hour.

Sophie punched the five-digit code into the wrought-iron gate, and it slid back. She got back in her vehicle and drove past the stone fence that separated Ms. O'Rourke's property from the public sidewalk out front and parked next to the professor's dark green Land Rover and black BMW. Even after cutting the engine and music, she continued singing.

Sophie admired the condition of the brick facade as she opened the burgundy door with the large silver knocker and went inside, a striking contrast to the run-down area of Dublin north of the River Liffey and east of O'Connell Street where she lived.

Ms. O'Rourke had told her from the beginning to enter without knocking and to call her Saorla, not Ms. O'Rourke. In the kitchen, with tea and American muffins ready to be shared, was where she usually found the professor. In the early days of her employ, Sophie relished the chance to practice her English over morning tea.

The first day Sophie met the professor, the lesson was on how to correctly pronounce Saorla, "See-er-la." The professor had explained that it was the old Irish word for Sarah. Of late, their relationship had turned from pupil-teacher toward friendship, and Sophie had come to recognize the spirit of mourning that hung over Saorla like an old wool coat two sizes too big. She would continue to pray for her. On the drive over, the Lord had provided a scripture verse to share.

On this day, however, all was quiet, as she entered the first floor sitting room off from the kitchen.

No one there. Just the framed photos over the mantle of Ms. O'Rourke with her deceased husband, Stuart MacLean. Sophie had never met the handsome man in the pictures with the bushy dark beard. Ms. O'Rourke had explained that she'd kept her maiden name after marrying him because she'd published a number of academic articles using the name O'Rourke and was developing a reputation of her own and didn't want to coast on the laurels of her husband.

Sophie pulled back her hair and tied it in a ponytail. She grabbed her cleaning supplies and began to make quick work of the downstairs living area. After about twenty minutes on the first level, she ascended the stairs to the bedroom chambers. Sophie called out before going through the open bedroom door.

No answer.

An empty wine bottle stood on the table with two glasses. Had the professor had company?

Over near the entryway to the bathroom, a bottle of pills lay spilled on the hardwood floor.

Tingling electricity spiked down Sophie's neck. By instinct, her legs bounded toward the smaller bedroom opposite the master. She yelled in Polish all the way.

She scanned the floor on the other side of the bed, and then glanced out the large frame window at the back of the house.

A body lay face down on the lawn in the courtyard below.

She reeled herself around. What to do? Call 999?

No, go to her first.

Sophie flung herself down the stairs and out the french doors to the back patio and courtyard. She charged to the body and tugged the woman over onto her back.

Was she breathing?

Yes, she was breathing, but faintly.

Sophie patted her on the cheeks. "*Prosze, obudzsie*! Please, wake up!"

CHAPTER SIX

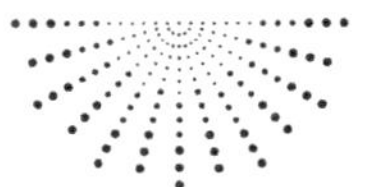

After Ian's flight landed in Dublin, he cleared customs and boarded a train at Connolly Station for the three-hour trip to Antrim. Once seated, he pulled out a piece of paper from his pocket. The flight attendant's full name was Cheryl Miller, she was highly attractive and had flirted with him throughout the connecting flight out of Chicago O'Hare, calling him "James Bond." She included her phone number and a note with a smiley face saying she would love to meet him sometime in Dublin. She had layovers there all month and knew of plenty of sites they could see together. Ian shoved the paper back in his pocket and settled in for the ride that took him up the east coast of the island.

The terrain flitted and danced as he gazed out the window, somehow convincing him all over again that he'd never seen green before. From the stupendous cliff-laced shorelines to the untamed bogs to the peaceful pasturelands bespectacled with heather and gorse to the lonesome mountains and hill country, the green varied in shades and intensity.

Ian soaked it all in, feeling his spirit refreshed. But as the train grew closer to the town of Antrim, where his grandfather was hospitalized, his head started to swim with questions.

Would the old man hold on until he got there? If he were still alive, would he be awake? Able to speak? And what did he want to tell Ian that was of such urgent importance?

He disembarked at the Antrim station and remembered he hadn't turned his cell phone on after leaving the airplane. He did so now, and a text message from his grandmother popped up.

Papa released from the hospital early this morning under hospice care, so go straight to the house.

The change to his plans sent Ian in motion. He hailed a taxi willing to make the fourteen-mile trip to his grandparents' farm. They lived in County Antrim in the North, in the shadow of Mount Slemish, a brilliant, green-domed hill formed by an ancient volcano that rose massively above the bogland and sheep pastures. From the top, the Antrim Coast and the Irish Sea loomed in the distance.

The taxi deposited him at the culmination of a long gravel road and at the front of an old white, one-story farmhouse. Ian rushed his way to the entrance and knocked gently before entering. The acrid smell of rubbing alcohol greeted his nostrils with a sting.

A light flicked on in the foyer, and his grandmother came into view. Ian bridged the distance and hugged her fiercely. He fought off the moistening in his own eyes, as he pulled back to search her face. Tears crawled down her cheeks. The dark hair he remembered had grayed some since the last time he saw her, and she had added a wrinkle or two more, but otherwise she looked the same.

"Nana, I've missed you both. It's been too long."

She smiled through the tears. "You're here now. That's all that matters."

Ian nodded. "How's Papa?"

"The will to live and a strong spirit, he has. He wants to tell you of his find and the things he sees when he sleeps. These dreams he's had for years." She paused, freezing Ian with her eyes. "He thinks you're called to help him get to the bottom of some great mystery."

What was his grandmother talking about? He'd never discussed any kind of dreams or a mystery with his grandfather before. He knew him to be a practical, God-fearing man who studied the Bible, prayed every day, and attended a Presbyterian church in the small town of Buckna, not far from the family farm.

"I'll do what I can, of course," Ian found himself saying. Papa had always been there for him. Especially, when he was a teenager and his parents divorced, sold the house, and all three of them went their separate ways. Ian spent the next two years after the divorce with Papa and Nana, taking refuge on their farm and growing into a man. Since the divorce, Ian hadn't seen his father much but still kept in close touch with his mother, who lived in Seattle.

"What really happened that he wound up in the hospital?" Ian asked.

"I think that would be better coming from him. I don't know what to believe. And I have a feeling he isn't telling me everything about what happened."

Ian scratched his head as he considered Nana's comment. "What about his health?" he finally asked.

"As far as external injuries, he sprained his arm pretty bad and had some minor scratches. The real concern now, though, is the condition of his heart. I don't think he has long."

Ian could see the lines deepening in Nana's forehead. "How's he doing today in terms of staying awake?"

"Slept most of the morning. He was up two or three hours ago, for sure, looking grand for about ten minutes and then went off again. That was when we first got set up here at home."

A nurse came from the back of the house, holding a patient medical chart. She scribbled something on it. "Sorry to interrupt, but he's conscious now and knows you're here. He wants to see you."

Ian bounded off the second he heard Papa was conscious. He found him in a bed set up in the living room. An IV was hooked up to his left arm, his right arm wrapped in a sling. His thick white beard was due for a trim, and his thinning hair desperately needed a comb and cut.

"Looks like they're getting the better of you, Old Guy," Ian said, hoping to cheer him up.

"Don't bet on it!" Papa managed to croak out.

This was a good sign. The old man had his wits about him. His robust baritone, however, was now reduced to a frail whisper.

"Sit down." Papa motioned toward two folding chairs.

Ian sat next to Nana. Reaching over, he placed a hand on Papa's veiny wrist, being careful not to disturb the IV needle and tube running from the upper part of the arm. Overexerting the old man was the thing Ian feared the most. But Nana had impressed upon him the urgency of Papa's message.

Papa motioned for Nana and the nurse to leave the room. When they were gone, he turned to Ian. "I've been having these dreams. Sometimes every night for a week. At least twice a month. Started a few years ago. I thought they were from God. But didn't know what to make of 'em. You follow so far, lad?"

"Yes, absolutely." Ian wanted to tell of his own newfound faith but didn't dare interrupt. A silent prayer that this wouldn't be their last conversation eked out of him.

"Good man," Papa said, unblinking, continuing to fix a stern gaze on Ian. "Then, I started to have a lot more of them recently. In my dream, I am diggin', always diggin'. And then I hit the most amazing thing. You know what I hit?"

Ian remained silent, while Papa, breathing heavy, paused to catch his breath. He gathered himself and then continued. "Artifacts, ancient things. Whatever I find in the earth in these dreams, I bring up and examine. There's always a clue or a riddle to it. When I figure it out, it leads me to the next place to look. I am led from one bloody mystery to the next. Finally, a clue leads me to a huge treasure chest."

A bony arm with an IV needle in it swung out to show just how big a chest, but then abruptly stopped, the old man obviously fatigued. When he finally rallied, he said, "A chest trunk like you would see in a pirate movie. After I dig it out and clean it off, I'm given a key, and I open it. It's filled with gold coins. I'm thinking, wonderful, this is a treasure beyond quantifying. Then it starts to float upward, turning to golden bubbles that rise to the sky. They fill the atmosphere and suddenly begin popping and descending to earth. They land as rain on people all over the island, infecting them with joy. There's dancing and laughing."

"These were just dreams I was having until a few nights before the accident. I heard a voice in the dream as clear as if someone were speaking to me while awake. It says to dig near the large oak tree. You remember that bogland just after the last tree on the east side of my property?"

"Sure," Ian said.

"The voice said to dig there, and the next night in a dream I was shown a picture of the exact spot. So I went there and started cutting the bog and moving dirt. That's when I found the silver chalice with writing on it."

"So then you took the chalice somewhere to have it looked at?"

"Abby's, an antique dealer in Belfast. The lad there thought it was old, I could tell. They wanted to keep the chalice at the shop. I got nervous and left with it. But then I went back and saw the clerk there being interrogated. I tried to get help, then I heard a gunshot, and they were after me. Then it was stolen from me. Someone tried to kill me for it."

"Whoa, slow down, Papa. What happened after you fled the store?"

"Coming back from Belfast a black SUV was about to sideswipe me. I panicked and lost control, probably that's when I had the heart attack. A tree finally brought me to a stop, I'm told, after I plunged off the road at a curve. A farmer who lives across the heather found me. I was in a coma for several days, until the day your nana called you. The PSNI, the police that is, say that the heart attack is why I crashed. But I know I was almost *sideswiped before* I crashed and had the heart attack.

"You told the police this?"

"They say there was no sign of foul play at the store or the accident sight."

Papa pounded his fist into the sheets and then wheezed. He took a sip of water from the cup by his bedside. "Shortly after I found that chalice, I found a small silver cross in the field—a cross with a sword, shield, and breastplate engraved over it. That night I had a dream. You were there in it, Ian. You were taking over, and you were there for the golden bubbles and the rain and the laughter."

"Whoa," Ian said, holding out the palm of his hand in effort to slow things down. "Do you know what it all means? The objects? The dreams? Is there a larger purpose? And who tried to kill you?"

Papa's eyelids drooped. Fighting to keep them open, he continued to face in Ian's direction. "You must promise—"

The voice of the nurse interrupted. "It's time to let him rest."

Papa disregarded the interruption and grasped Ian's hand. "I want you to promise me something," he said again. "Promise me that you'll do everything in your power to get to the bottom of this."

Ian wondered what it was exactly that he was about to get into, and how he could possibly stay and help, with his job in jeopardy at home. He studied his grandfather's eyes. What did the old man expect him to get to the bottom of anyway? Maybe the conspiratorial tone was simply due to old age, and his grandfather growing more child-like, making things a bigger deal than they needed to be.

Papa seemed to sense Ian's hesitation and confusion. "I'm going to tell it to you plainly, lad. I believe the dreams promise a great Christian revival for Ireland. And, Ian, remember, someone tried to kill me. There are dark forces out there that want to stop this. The dreams warned me of that. Will you help me, lad?"

"Yes," Ian finally found himself saying as he nodded his head. What would it hurt to look for some trinkets for a couple of days and investigate a crash site? And in the meantime, he would be able to spend some much-needed time with this old man, who he deeply loved and would surely miss when he was gone. And then he could go back home and save his job. "I'll … figure this out for you. Whatever it takes."

The old man's eyes were watering. "Good man you are."

Ian had so many questions, but Papa was drifting off. He nudged the old man's arm just a bit. "What's the next step?"

Papa moved his hand enough to point a finger at Ian, but his eyes were closed. "You should always remember—"

The nurse appeared again from the kitchen, glaring at Ian. "Visiting time is over," she commanded.

Ian just stared at her, wondering if she was for real.

She pressed her tactical advantage. "I am going to have to ask you to let him get some rest."

Ian glanced over at his grandfather. Eyes shut, his head had fallen to the side on the pillow, chest rising and falling at a comfortable pace.

"Yes, ma'am." His questions would have to wait.

THE BLUE SKY GLISTENED AS SAORLA SLOWLY OPENED HER eyes. Why was she wet all over, and who in the world was slapping her on the face? All that was nothing, though, compared to the pounding in her head. She jerked her hands up to stop the hand on her forehead. A woman was praying in broken English.

"Jesus, bring her to wake. Heal mind."

Slowly, it came back to her now. The bottle of Bordeaux on the veranda and the early exit to bed. But how did she end up out on the lawn?

"Are you able to come up?" Sophie asked.

"Yes, I … what time is it?"

"Almost eleven-thirty," Sophie said. "I take care of you now. Take you in house."

"Just a bad case of Irish flu."

Saorla's eyes cleared enough to see the puzzled look on Sophie's face, framed by blonde hair in strands from a loose ponytail.

Saorla tried again. "I ended up paralytic, I guess."

That didn't work either. A thousand words to describe a hangover were in every Irishwoman's lexicon.

"I drank too much wine," Saorla said at last. "And I had a couple of sleeping pills," she added sheepishly.

Saorla was grateful to have Sophie helping her, but her privacy was also being invaded. Someone on the outside was moving too close to her world inside.

After a hot bath and some well-brewed tea, Saorla found herself chatting at her kitchen table with a caring and kind young woman. Saorla had never before asked Sophie any questions beyond those of a mundane nature, mostly out of fear that Sophie might reciprocate with a few intensely personal questions. And normally, Saorla would have been eager to trek over to Trinity, where she had a couple of meetings scheduled with students, but with the head pounding and the stomach churning, she decided her job at the college would have to wait. Instead she would risk a foray into the personal. She owed Sophie that much after the help she'd provided.

"So, what brought you to Ireland? I don't think I've ever asked you. And what was life like for you in Poland?"

A momentary look of surprise flashed across Sophie's face that was soon replaced by a relaxed smile. "When I was little girl," she paused to put her palm down about a meter off the ground, "communism fell and people dance in street. My father, he was strong man. But then get so sick, he go to hospital, get pneumonia, and never get well. He loved his little girl and tell me I must always follow God and listen close for his voice. I always want to know God. To listen for his voice."

"Do you have other family?"

"Yes, my mother came with me, and we live north. I have also sister here. Two brothers in Poland still. I send money, tell them both to come. One of them sends the money back to me always. The other saves it, he will come soon maybe."

Saorla was thinking of another question, but the ache in her head was growing worse.

"Would you like to not be so sad anymore?" Sophie asked.

The query startled Saorla and sent the tears forming. "Yesterday was my wedding anniversary. My thirtieth birthday is at the end of the week. My anniversary follows so closely on the heels of my birthday for a reason." She paused, risking a complete and utter breakdown. But Sophie's kind eyes encouraged her. "On the mid-August night Stuart proposed, he said he intended to make me a married woman before my next birthday. Too lovesick to protest the short notice, I said, 'yes,' and made plans. But the church was fully booked all the way out to the week before my birthday. The one available date was October eighth, just for us."

Snapping free of these unexpected recollections tested her sorely.

"I can pray for you," Sophie said. "Jesus can heal the broke heart, make you glad, like oil pouring over to take away the pain."

Head down, Saorla felt Sophie's warm hand on her shoulder.

"God take away spirit of sorrow from sister."

As Saorla soaked in the prayer, a little crack appeared in the obsidian wall of depression that had been suffocating her, and a sliver of something she hadn't felt in a long time slid through, tiny as it was —simple hope.

After a few minutes, Sophie finished praying, took Saorla's hand, and locked eyes with her. "The Lord told me a special message for you as I was driving. He say from his word to you, *'It is the glory of God to conceal a matter, but it is the glory of kings to search it out.'*"

Saorla waited for Sophie to say more, but nothing followed except a long silence. "What does that mean?" Saorla finally asked.

Sophie shrugged a shoulder. "I thought you know. If not now, later maybe you know."

Saorla wasn't sure how those words would ever apply to her. But she did notice that her headache was gone.

CHAPTER SEVEN

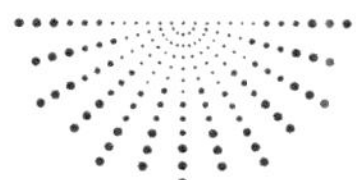

Late Sunday afternoon, Ian grabbed a shovel out of the stone shed near the farmhouse and tossed it onto the bed of Papa's white Nissan pickup truck. The plan was to investigate the sites his grandfather had been digging up. He was determined to keep his vow and make the best effort he could to get to the bottom of all that burdened the old man's heart.

Papa's two border collies, Yeats and Lance, scanned Ian's every move. Yeats, the alpha of the two dogs, took his name from the famous Irish poet Papa often quoted. Ian recalled how his grandfather bellowed lines from Yeats's "The Second Coming" while the old man did his chores around the farmyard. How Papa had settled on the name for the other dog, Lance, was uncertain. Ian prayed for more time, the time to ask Papa about Lance and other more important matters too.

Ian patted his leg. "Let's go, boys." The dogs leapt forward and catapulted themselves onto the truck bed. Panting and tails wagging, they were obviously ecstatic to have some attention again after their master's absence over the past several days.

Before leaving the house, Ian had received the full report from Nana on Papa's prognosis. The old man's heart had been so weakened that the expectation to survive the month was shaky. The doctors had, however, reassured Nana that Papa had stabilized enough for him to be at home under hospice and palliative care. Comfort became the priority, and the family could say their good-byes within the privacy of their home.

Ian drove the truck down the gravel and dirt road past the stone gate that separated the house yard from the rest of the farm. The sun climbed above a thin row of pale grey clouds. As Ian recalled from the time he'd spent on the farm as a teen, the visibility could change in a moment.

All along the road, gorse bloomed intermixed with honeysuckle splashed by shafts of sunlight evading puffs of low-hung clouds. Beyond the road lay rolling verdant mounds of grass stretching to the horizon—a thousand hills sprawling in every direction, with cattle or sheep on each one.

Ian headed to the area of the farm where the large native oak tree grew that his grandfather had mentioned yesterday. Although much of the interior of the island had been covered with them at one time, the stubborn oak stood alone, its siblings largely deforested in the seventeenth century.

It was in the vicinity of this tree Papa had found the silver chalice with the engraving of Latin words. Last night Nana had shown Ian a photograph of the chalice. It certainly looked old. But he knew nothing of its provenance.

He needed to know more, and he would need an expert to dive deeper.

Another idea clicked in his head as he neared the oak. Instead of pulling off by the tree, he continued east until the road curved to the south and let out at the public thoroughfare. Ian took a left turn and headed for the site where Papa had crashed. The road snaked along the lush hillside. It would be easy to have an accident with serious injury or death in this rolling countryside.

In another minute, he arrived at the scene of the crash. Papa's vehicle, a roofless jeep-like contraption, remained where it had come to rest at the bottom of a hill with the front bumper firmly smashed and adhered to a tree. Off to the side of a lonesome stretch of barely paved roadway, Ian parked and exited his vehicle. There were no skid marks. He grabbed a flashlight out of the glove compartment. "Stay," he commanded the dogs, who just looked at him curiously.

After descending the hill about forty feet, he noticed that due to the downward slope of the landscape, the front end of the vehicle was propped up about four feet off the ground where it met the tree. He propelled himself beneath the underbelly. Focusing the flashlight on different spots of the undercarriage, he searched for some indication of brake failure or other malfunction. Everything appeared as it should. Was it simply a case of an old man taking a curve too fast in the hills of Antrim while having a heart attack?

He continued to poke around the scene and was about to quit.

And then he saw it.

A business card from the antique shop where Papa had taken the chalice. On the back was written, *Let it go or you will regret it.*

A warning? It had to be.

Ian returned to the truck and drove away short of breath, both from sprinting back up the hill and from the confirmation that his grandfather's accident had been deliberately planned. He pondered calling the PSNI but reconsidered. Ian wasn't sure Papa would welcome the attention at this point, and he'd been adamant that the authorities didn't believe he'd been run off the road. Ian doubted the business card would change that. Instead, he would journey to the oak tree and examine the area.

Ian retraced his route and pulled off about twenty feet from the oak. Tire tracks were present in the thick grass. He walked to the tree. No signs of digging. He wandered further to a mile-wide stretch of treeless bogland so typical to Ireland, with its slow plant growth other than the foot-high shrubs that blanketed it. As the futility of his search dawned on him, Ian remembered the dogs.

"Yeats, Lance, come, boys!"

The dogs bolted from the pickup bed, becoming two balls shot from a cannon. Front paws slammed his chest with rapid thuds.

"Down, boys," he said sternly. Long, sharp nails untangled themselves from his coat.

Sitting at his command with their two tails wagging like windshield wipers gone haywire, the beasts awaited further orders. He bent over to pet them behind the ears, one with each hand.

"Find," he yelled. "Go find the dig." The duo darted fifty yards to the east and then stopped to bark in a circle.

Ian grabbed his shovel and headed toward the dogs. They pranced around an area carved out of the bog about eight square feet.

"That was rad, boys!" Both dogs had their paws on Ian's torso again, and he wrapped his arms around them. "I have some steak bones coming your way, dudes. Awesome job."

The dogs alternately watched and slept as Ian dug for the next hour. The sun remained visible in the sky, but thicker clouds developed rapidly to the west.

The shovel suddenly struck something solid. Maybe a flat stone? A few more scoops of the shovel, and he heaved it out.

The flat stone was actually a monument of some sort about three feet long, a foot and a half wide, and an inch or two thick. It appeared to be broken. Down the middle? From the looks of it, he probably had roughly half of it. A few cursory stabs of the shovel around the area where he unearthed it did not reveal anything else hard.

Brushing the crustiness of the bog from the stone, he perused the surface. An inscription of some kind was carved into it. When he returned to the farmhouse, he would clean the rest of the grit away.

His goal shifted now to finding the other half. The sky turned increasingly ominous, and a light sprinkle began. He had almost persuaded himself to quit for the day when the shovel thumped something softer than rock but harder than dirt. Abandoning the shovel, he dug out the peat soil around the object with his hand. A few short scoops later, he pulled out a leather satchel from the earth.

He wiped it carefully, bit by bit, and then placed it on top of some clumps of peat next to the monument.

Rain fell harder, issuing a race against the gathering storm. He scattered peat over the area he'd been working.

Turning to the heavy stone object and satchel, he squatted and heaved them up, curling the items under his arm.

"Yeats, Lance, let's go, boys."

The shelter of the truck beckoned as large pellets of rain stung his face. The downpour hit just before the dogs jumped onto the bed, and Ian made it into the cab.

Deep in his heart, he feared Papa wouldn't wake to see the new discoveries.

THE RAIN FELL IN SHEETS WHEN IAN ARRIVED BACK AT THE farmhouse. He snapped up the stone slab and satchel from the truck and sprinted for the front door. The dogs shot inside ahead of him, shaking the water from their coats.

Nana smiled, holding open the front door. "A new nurse is here now. Her name's Maureen."

Ian kissed his grandmother on the cheek as he passed through the door. Water dripped from his wet clothes to the blond-colored hardwood floor. Turning back to her, he held out the satchel and slab. "I found these out in the back forty."

"Amazing! They look ancient. He'll be pleased."

"Yeah, the bog has quite the preservative effect, it seems. There's going to be a lot of work to do though." Ian couldn't bring himself to tell her about the message on the business card. He pushed on into the living room.

Papa was asleep. A nurse in a light green uniform, Maureen presumably, sat in a sofa chair, knitting what appeared to be a small blanket. She glanced up, and Ian waved. The nurse blinked and returned her gaze to the blanket on her lap.

Ian dripped his way to the guest room, divested himself of his wet clothes, and changed into a dry sweatshirt and jeans. Now comfortable and warm, he glanced over at the table where he'd placed the leather satchel and the stone slab. Next to them lay the silver cross and the photograph of the chalice. The excellent condition of the finds astounded him. What time period were they from? What ancient secrets did they possess?

Testing and expert analysis would not be cheap. Money would be in short supply with his salary suspended and his mortgage payment coming due. A return to San Francisco would also be necessary at some point to deal with the mess he'd left there. The clock ticked on the ultimatum the partners at the firm had given him. And Jarvis no doubt waited in the shadows to take over his spot as the leading candidate to become a future partner at the firm.

Ian fired up his laptop and researched the question of who could best analyze the objects. His search led him to a number of authors, professors, and antiquities dealers he considered qualified. The more he looked, though, the more he was profoundly convinced that his best option was a professor of Irish History and Philology at Trinity College, Dublin.

Her curriculum vitae was spelled out on both the university's website and Wikipedia.

Name: Saorla O'Rourke. The first name was pronounced See-er-la, the entry said. Ian thought the name beautiful, but more importantly, smart, like a wise old seer.

Professor O'Rourke had authored numerous articles and one book on the formation of the early Irish and middle Irish language. She was also an expert on the history and lore of the island.

Ian studied her photo on his screen. There was no indication from her looks that she possessed the wisdom of the aged. Just the opposite, she was young, about his own age. But he felt strangely that her name matched her appearance. Sheer black-brown hair fell well past her shoulders, framing the allure of her face. Slightly-flushed skin radiated health, and her teal-blue eyes were serene, strong, steady.

He would call her immediately and arrange a meeting as soon possible.

A sudden, loud knock on the front door pierced the country silence.

Who was calling so late on a Sunday evening? The sun had set an hour ago. What if it was his father unexpectedly arriving from overseas? He wasn't in any mood to deal with that right now with barely any sleep in the last twenty-four hours. Ian dismissed the thought that his father could be at the door. He'd be too busy back in the States for a visit this time of year.

Peeling the curtains back from his window, he peeked out to the front porch in time to see Nana happily greeting a rough, grey-bearded man. It wasn't his father, and Ian slowly exhaled. But it was an imposing figure nonetheless: a gruff fish-boat captain named Finn Hooligan who was a friend of Papa's. Ian remembered the captain from his occasional visits during the time when Ian had lived with his grandparents. Captain Finn fished the Irish Sea for cod and had a cottage on the Strangford Lough on the east coast of the island. He'd probably received word of the old man's troubles and had come to pay his respects.

Relieved that it wasn't his father at the door, Ian dialed Professor O'Rourke's number and left a message.

CHAPTER EIGHT

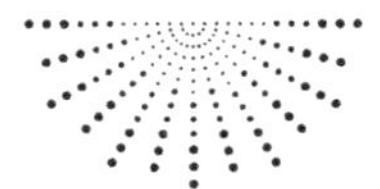

Ian had left one message on Sunday night and two during the day on Monday for Professor O'Rourke but hadn't heard back. On Monday afternoon, he decided to drive to Belfast and poke around at the antique shop where Papa had taken the chalice, a place called Abby's Archives. The clerk who'd waited on Papa was nowhere to be found, but after the store closed for the day, Ian followed a stock boy to his car where he was able to pump him for information.

The conversation started with Ian handing him a crisp €200 banknote. The clerk in question, Ian learned, was off until next week. The boy was relatively certain there was nobody named Abby involved in the ownership of the store, but he had never met the actual owner. Ian asked if any store employees ever talked about who they'd consult in a difficult case. The boy didn't know. Ian asked him to keep his ears open, wrote a number where the boy could reach him, and told him he had more cash if he had any answers.

Ian awoke on Tuesday morning determined to finally make some progress in reaching Professor O'Rourke when he heard his grandmother stirring in the kitchen around 5 a.m. Living on a farm, Nana and Papa were habitually early risers. Ian was pleasantly surprised to find Papa awake now too, lying on his side in bed.

"Hey there," Ian said. "How you feeling?"

Papa looked even weaker today. "I can't complain."

"You were up late?"

"That old Cap Finn kept me awake for over an hour. Trading stories. He got to talking about his gun-running days with the IRA. That part is sad. His conscience bothers him, but his fish stories are a gas. Sometimes he's as mad as a box of frogs."

Nana entered the room and stood next to Ian. "Last night, Rory called." She placed a hand on Ian's shoulder while addressing Papa. "He's on his way and will be here sometime this week."

Butterflies rose and fluttered in Ian's stomach. He hadn't expected his father to make it overseas, even if it were to see his own dying father. As coach of the Chicago Zephyrs in the MLS, Major League Soccer in the United States, Rory was in the final push of the season to make the playoffs. It would be a shock if he were even thinking of leaving his team at such a crucial juncture. And his father's coming would only exacerbate an already tense situation here. He wouldn't understand Ian's quest to help Papa or the prediction of a spiritual sea change.

"Aw, he should wait till his season is over," Papa said.

Silence fell over the room.

"It's for the best," Papa said at last. "We don't get to make all our plans the way we want. I need to see Rory. It's been too long for sure."

It wasn't too long for Ian.

He would travel to Dublin this morning and initiate a meeting with an expert to analyze the objects. How long that would take was anybody's guess. Maybe he would be lucky enough to miss his father's visit entirely. He dismissed that wish, however, and valued the limited time left with his grandfather, even if that meant a collision with Rory. Still, Dublin was calling. He prioritized shedding some light on his grandfather's mystery, and he would do it before all the sand in the hourglass sifted from the old man's life.

CHAPTER NINE

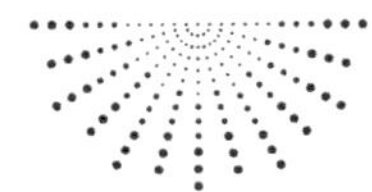

Ian parked his car at a parking deck on Fleet Street about two blocks from Trinity College and walked south on Westmoreland Street. Despite his previous stint in Ireland, he had hardly spent any time in Dublin, except for one visit to the National Museum with his grandmother more than a decade ago. Thus, the city's environs remained unexplored territory. The college, he discovered, stood in the heart of central Dublin, just south of the River Liffey.

Westmoreland Street teemed with life—pedestrians, tour buses, and sidewalk vendors with carts. Even though the intense summer crowds had dissipated, a significant tourism presence endured, and the city had the feel of a world-class, cosmopolitan melting pot.

Soon the college loomed ahead with its castle-like stone walls in classic eighteenth-century architecture. Corinthian columns rose at the gates of the main entrance from the north along a street called College Green. As he entered, he noticed the large bronze statues of the poet Oliver Goldsmith and the philosopher and political thinker Edmund Burke, both alumni.

The buildings inside were arranged to face inward toward a series of quadrangle lawns, with cobblestone squares, walkways, and fences.

The grounds and buildings covered about forty acres, providing a world in itself, aloof from the city streets beyond its confines.

The shallow sun shone in the east, just after nine in the morning. Ian had departed from his grandparents' house to get on the road before six and had hustled to arrive in a little over three hours. He might have been eager to explore the campus, but the events of the past few days troubled him deeply. He carried the artifacts with him to Dublin, though the stone slab remained locked in his car.

Ian was determined to arrange some kind of meeting with Professor O'Rourke as soon as possible, but nobody had returned his calls the past couple days and the nature of the artifacts still perplexed him.

A young male student wearing a Gaelic Athletic Association t-shirt strolled his way. Ian stopped in front of him and put up a hand. "Hey, can you help me a second?"

"Come again?"

"Look, I need to know where I can find a history professor. Do you know Professor O'Rourke?"

"Not a chance, chap. I'm a computer science major. We don't mix with the art crowd."

"Can you point me in the direction of the arts building at least?"

"No worry. It's straight ahead." He pointed at a building with large rows of solar-panel windows. A circular, cobblestone patio that cut into the finely manicured lawn led up to the building. A sculpture of twisted black metal that vaguely resembled a desert cactus adorned the cobblestone.

"What's that sculpture out front on the stone circle?" Ian asked.

The kid turned around to look at it. "It's called 'Cactus Provisoire.' Been there since the late 60s."

"Hey, I thought you were a computer science major?"

The kid shrugged his shoulders and walked off.

At least Ian had a direction. He decided to try the number listed for the professor on the campus website once again. If he rang the number often enough, maybe he could entice someone to answer.

After four rings, a generic, pre-recorded voice requested the caller to leave a message. Ian dropped another one and hung up. He knew he sounded desperate, but time was of the essence given his grandfather's health and the trouble with his own job brewing at home. Moreover, if Papa's dreams were right about the great revival of Christianity, what lay ahead was so fantastic that no defeat, or even delay, could be tolerated. On the other hand, if Papa, was simply a deluded old man, Ian had to know that as soon as possible as well.

Undaunted by his lack of success so far, he pushed on toward the arts building. The sun had crested over the campus buildings to the east under the cirrus clouds that spread like thin feathers in the sky. Students swirled in a dozen directions, a busy intersection of the campus.

The first-floor lobby swarmed with students, most of whom were headed up a flight of stairs. He joined the line, trying to meld with the flow. A security checkpoint manned by a hefty, uniformed guard loomed ahead. Ian adopted the casual nonchalance of a student and turned to make small talk to the fellow next to him in hopes of pushing through the line without being singled out for special scrutiny. Blue jeans and a sweatshirt would have blended more seamlessly than his dress slacks and shirt.

"Do you have a student identification?" the guard asked when Ian made it to the front of the checkpoint.

"I didn't realize—"

"You need a student identification or a visitor permit to get beyond this line."

"Uh ... I'm looking for a professor."

"Sorry, mister."

An argument, or even a further explanation of his purpose, would be futile. "Never mind," he murmured, walking back down the stairs.

LORCAN DUIHBUR HAD A SINKING FEELING IN HIS STOMACH as he made his way to the second-floor hospital room of the cancer ward where his sister lay. She was his only sibling and his junior by two years. At 40, she was too young to die. He wiped a tear from his cheek as he walked, all the while picturing her bony frame, languishing from the kidney cancer that had metastasized and spread to her liver. He made his way past the nurses station and nodded to the lone woman on duty at the desk. He had never seen her before during any of his prior visits and wondered if the woman had recognized him as the important government official that he was. As Minister of Foreign Relations, he wasn't often recognized in public as much as the taoiseach or the high king would be. And, honestly, that's the way he preferred it. So much of what he needed to accomplish in the days ahead would depend on secrecy.

He straightened his tie as he approached the partially closed door of the room. He'd left his penthouse so early in the morning he hadn't had the proper time to attend to his appearance. It'd been a couple of weeks since he had been by to see his sister. There'd been so many government meetings to attend to—and then, hearing of the discovery of the chalice had set off all sorts of alarms for him.

It was definitely time for even bolder action now.

He took a deep breath and entered her room, securing the door closed behind him. Propped up with the bed raised just enough, Fiona sipped liquid through a straw from a cup. Flesh taut over pointy cheekbones and the sunken area below them, she peered at him, eyes larger than they used to be, almost like saucers. New age music charmed the air as bells chimed in harmony with the wistful melody of harp strings.

"You look good, sis." He lied. But what else could he do? The reality seared his soul. He did have a plan, though. Maybe sharing it with her would lift her spirits enough to get her through this stretch until he could fully execute that plan.

"I feel like a million," she said, her voice only a wisp.

He placed a gentle hand over her delicate fingers, and with the other, touched her forehead, both to feel if she had a fever and to comfort her. Tears welled in her eyes to match his. He swiped his face and crouched to sit in the chair already pulled next to the bed.

"Listen," he murmured, "I figured out why this has happened to us. And what we can do about it."

She looked almost too weak to talk, but her eyes beckoned him to continue.

Both hands around one of hers, he leaned toward her. "This came upon you because of father."

She shook her head.

"Hear me out, Fiona. You know our family was always faithful to the Goddess until just before dad died. Hell, he was going to build her a temple. We still have land near Tara that he purchased for it. She deserves to be honored again as in former times. If we don't bring her ways back to Eire, who will?"

"Not his fault. He went to explore a different road but—"

"You call converting to Christianity merely *exploring a different road?*"

"Not a true believer in Maeve's powers as much as you or I. Not the witchcraft but the folklore. Oh, how he did love the history, though."

"That was the problem—if he had honored her rightly, he would never have ended up the way he did—a chap who owned a store full of old relics, who could out talk the wind, but who never made a real difference in the world and ended up dying tragically young because of his folly."

"An accident. A drunk driver hit him, nothing anybody could have done."

"The Goddess had him on a short leash. A single cycle of the moon was all she allotted to him to come back to her after he turned away from her."

"I never thought that."

"Yes, I told him he wouldn't live out the month if he didn't return, but he wouldn't. With you, there's still time."

The revelation seemed to weaken his sister even further. It wasn't his intent to be harsh with her. "The Goddess is the way. She'll brook no defection." He said it as softly, lovingly as he could.

"I've never left my devotion for her."

He locked his eyes on hers. "But we have to do more now."

She stared back at him a long moment, before shaking her head.

"It has to be," he said.

"You can't mean what I think you mean."

"Yes, it has to be this way."

"You could use *me* to be the sacrifice."

Lorcan shook his head. "Don't be silly. I'm trying to *save* you. Besides, the sacrifice has to be perfect. Physically perfect."

"I don't want you to do this," she said, as she looked away toward the woolen grey sky visible through the small window. "Some days I feel so bad I *want* to die."

He squeezed her hand. "I know. But I can save you. Sacrifice releases power. It's an elementary principle of the universe. And with it comes good fortune from our Queen. I will find the perfect somebody. When all is accomplished, you will get well."

"I don't want you to."

He waited for her to say more, but she fell silent.

"It's not just about you," he said. "There's been a discovery."

"What are you saying?"

"A chalice with a promise of a prophecy."

"Like the legends surrounding Maeve warned of."

"Yes. You know how the legends warn of a prophecy that could possess the power to keep people from rediscovering her?"

She bobbed her head. "A false prophecy will come causing people to reject the path back to the Goddess."

"Exactly. Now consider this. The Old Latin words on the chalice we found read, *He who uncovers this cup and the related mysteries will unlock the hidden prophecy of Patrick to lead the people back to God in the hour of Braden's reign.*"

Fiona pursed her lips. "It has to be stopped," she said, with more strength in her voice than she had yet shown.

"It will be. The sacrifice will release the power to stop its fulfillment."

There was a knock at the door and then it opened. It was a cardiac trauma nurse called Eva Morgan, part of Lorcan's inner circle. He had asked her to meet him at the hospital room.

Eva checked Fiona's vitals then said, "I'm all ears, Mr. Duihbur."

Twenty minutes later, Lorcan watched Eva leave Fiona's room with her orders clear: Put George Shaw in just enough of a decline with some untraceable drug cocktail so that he would be unable to help his grandson.

EVA PICKED UP A MAGAZINE SHE'D BROUGHT TO READ AND thumbed through the pages as she sat next to George in the living room of the Shaw farmhouse. The old man had just dozed off. Eva waited for Aryana to exit the room, leaving Eva entirely alone with the patient. The Shaw family knew Eva only as Maureen the nurse, filling a gap in the hospice care.

As Aryana occupied herself with picking pumpkins from the garden, Eva took her syringe in hand. She moved to George's bedside and slipped the solution into the IV bag that would administer the untraceable drug into his bloodstream. It was going to put the old man in decline all right. It would probably knock him out for a week. "No need to kill the old man yet," Lorcan had said. "It would only engender needless suspicion." But the words on the chalice were troubling. And more time was needed to weigh the options, without interference from the old man.

IAN SAT IN A CAMPUS CAFE STARING AT A COKE AND hamburger he'd ordered. An hour had passed since he'd been turned away by the security guard, and Ian's appetite was on sabbatical just like the professor seemed to be. Some further inquiries of students had yielded the fact that Professor O'Rourke had indeed been seen on campus that morning. Still, he had no idea how to locate her without a return call.

Ian closed his eyes and began considering the Dublin antiquities dealers on his list when he heard a lively female voice. "Will ya be havin' some humble pie with your burger, sir?"

His eyes darted open. A girl in her early twenties with a pixie hairstyle dyed a unique silver grey hovered over his small table. Nose rings adorned her nostrils, dangling down to just above her smiling lips. She might have been attractive if not for the hair and nose rings. Heck, she was probably attractive even with, but the image she presented was too distracting to consider the thought further.

Ian just gaped at her, not sure what to say. "No, I like my humble pie a la carte," he said finally.

She giggled. "My name's Myrna. I saw you over at the arts building getting turned back by security. Are ya some kind of threat?" she asked with a smirk.

He wondered what it was about him that caused women to think he was either in the espionage business or a threat to public safety. "Ah, definitely no threat. My name's Ian. I'm an attorney from California, visiting family here. But I need to talk to a particular professor about some unusual things my grandfather found. I need more insight. An expert would be a big help and—"

"Tell me," she said, "what did you find? The next technological breakthrough that promises to change the world? Are you another American Zuckerberg or Steven Jobs or something? I bet you've come up with the innovation that will shake the world. Facebook III. Change all our lives, huh?"

He flashed a smile that belied his bewilderment over her quirkiness. The bewilderment only lasted a second, though, when he considered the madness he'd seen in the California surfing world. "Ha, well, I don't have anything against Silicon Valley, but no, it's nothing like that. We found some artifacts. We're in need of more information."

"I can help you," she said with what seemed like real confidence.

He tried not to laugh in her face. "What I need is to get in touch with a certain professor."

"Like I said, I can help."

Ian was silent.

She sighed. "No one ever takes me serious. I'm in graduate school, would you believe it?" She danced a short jig then broke form by finishing with her arms flailing out.

Ian simply watched. She must have taken his lack of speech as a sign of encouragement because she jabbered non-stop for the next ten minutes, giving Ian a tutorial about the college, interspersed with her own personal history. He still didn't know if the girl would be able to help him, but she sure had the gift of gab and was bursting with facts and information.

"Did you know I started out as a gender and women's studies major? That explains my look, huh?" She fluffed her spaceship silver hair and crinkled her nose like a rabbit munching a blade of grass, causing the rings at her nostrils to dance. "I switched to Irish history and Irish studies and got my undergrad degree in that."

Ian was wondering when she would catch her breath and started to tune out.

Finally, she asked, "So, where are you from?"

"San Francisco Bay area now, a number of places before that."

Myrna's eyes widened. "You're jesting! I am sure of it! I've been accepted to the doctoral program at Berkeley for next year. This is unbelievable!"

Ian didn't want to divulge too much about his mission, but his options were dwindling. "Yes, that's amazing," he agreed, "the campus isn't too far from where I live. I've been working in the city for three years now. But let me ask you something, you said that you could help me?"

"Yeah."

"I found some artifacts on my grandfather's farm about three hours north. I made a promise to investigate further. I thought that Professor Saorla O'Rourke could help."

Myrna threw her head back, let out a loud guffaw, then checked her smart watch. "She's giving a lecture at one o'clock in an early Irish history course. I think they are somewhere in the fifth century right now. I know I can get you in to see the lecture, and maybe I can arrange for you to meet the professor afterwards. I'm her assistant."

Ian gawked, all the while searching her eyes. A light flickered in his soul. Years spent as a criminal defense attorney had trained him to spot falsehood. It was absent now. God's hand was in this. Gratitude welled, and he said an audible "Thank you, God."

"What?"

"Uh ... I'm grateful."

CHAPTER TEN

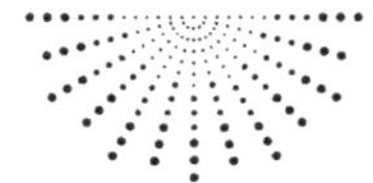

Sophie Zaworski pulled her Volkswagen onto the road leading into Phoenix Park, a sprawling 1,750 acre walled garden located about two miles west of the city center of Dublin. After passing the largest obelisk in Europe near the entrance, stunning green squares of manicured lawn and a cavalcade of flower displays sparkled into view as shafts of sunlight pierced down between the retreating grey clouds. Further on, she sighted her destination—the eighteenth century Farmleigh Estate—originally owned by members of the Guinness family. It was now the site of the high king's mansion. It was also the site of her next cleaning job.

She rehearsed in her mind what she had been learning. The term *rí Érenn uile* meant *king of all Ireland* in the Irish language, and people of Ireland applied the term to their new high king, the billionaire David Braden. He traced his lineage to the high kings of old and this allowed him to make his full-time residence at the mansion, which would have otherwise been reserved for the taoiseach who served as the head of the government in the function of a prime minister.

"Tee-sha," Sophie pronounced out loud. Such a simple pronunciation for taoiseach, a word Sophie still had trouble spelling.

Post-pandemic, the Irish government allowed Mr. Braden to serve as royal liaison to the people, but support of both houses of parliament, or the *Oireachtas* as it is formally called, is necessary for him to remain in that capacity. There was even talk about making his position an elective one subject to the democratic electoral process. Her citizenship classes were proving to be an invaluable way to learn about her newly adopted country, and honestly, she didn't know what she would do without them.

Sophie's employer, Maids of Warsaw, obtained the contract for the mansion sometime last year. Her good fortune of landing the responsibility for cleaning the site was due to happenstance. After filling in for a sick maid, the high king himself requested Sophie be used for all future cleaning at the mansion. These days he always seemed to catch her alone. Often, he would proceed to tell her about all the possibilities that could be opened for her future, implying that he could make all the right connections for her.

The reason for the high king's special interest in her gradually became apparent. She'd become convinced at first that he simply wanted to sleep with her. But now she thought that maybe it was more than that. From the way he often spoke to her, it was as if she'd become Queen Esther to him with an unspoken plan to make his wife the vanquished Vashti.

Despite the advances, she steeled herself against the dread she felt and forged ahead to remain upbeat and keep the job she couldn't afford to lose. She prayed often that God would give the high king wisdom to lead the nation and, most of all, that his life would turn around. Maybe he could sense her prayers. How else to explain the favor he'd shown her even in the face of her repeated rebuffs to his advances?

Still troubled by the sorrow she saw in Professor O'Rourke, she continued to pray for her too. The professor's soul remained clouded, and breakthrough dallied. Sophie sensed God's heart was stirring, and so, she was eager to contend in the battle.

She passed through the security gate and parked in the space designated for her in the back of the mansion. The home, easily the most impressive on her list, had been renovated over a decade ago at a cost of over six hundred thousand euros.

Carrying her supplies in both arms to the back entrance, she stumbled over a raised crack in the cobblestone walkway about ten feet from the doorway. A bucket spewed from her arms. She bent to pick it up, and a cheap cell phone plummeted from her shirt pocket. A shadow emerged from the door and lingered over her. Then, long arms reached past her and snatched her cell phone and a bottle of window cleaner that had fallen from the bucket.

"Beautiful day, eh, Ms. Sophie? But dare I say not as beautiful as you, and, unlike the weather, your beauty never changes." *Rí* David Braden's six-foot-five-inch frame stooped before her. He was in his late forties, his thinning brown hair neatly parted to the side.

Sophie felt her face grow hot. Seizing on the weather-related portion of his comments, she said, "Yes, little bit like my home in Warsaw this season of year."

"Ah, you've been in this country too long now to still be thinking about Poland. You must be lonely for some male companionship?"

"Less than one year. Not enough time to learn English better, I am sorry."

"Nonsense, you are doing very well."

"Thank you."

"On behalf of the Irish," he said, "I declare you an honorary Celt and would love to show you just how sincere I am about that. We could have a drink together, perhaps." He gave her a slight wink, while he fidgeted with her cell phone, punching some numbers into it. "There, I've plugged my personal number into your phone in case you get lonely and decide to take me up on my offer."

Sophie had heard Mr. Braden say similar words to her on previous occasions and ones that were even more overt. She didn't always know how to take them.

"That is very kind. I am the one most honored to be working here."

"If you feel that way. I was wondering if you and a friend of your choosing would be our personal guests for dinner—just the queen and me. No press. No cameras. I would be so grateful to have the perspective of how a newcomer to Ireland sees us. And I must insist on meeting the lucky man who stole your heart." He paused to wink at her again. "Mrs. Braden has also expressed an interest in meeting your *male* friend."

The security detail had finally caught up to the high king and eyed her suspiciously, probably because of some rumor that had spread about her and Mr. Braden fueled by his penchant for attempting hushed conversations with her.

Her stomach churned not only from the presence of the security, but also from the high king's twisted logic. Nevertheless, she found herself saying, "Yes, of course. I would be honored."

"How about a week from this Saturday?"

"Yes," she said, knowing that the dinner would have to take precedence over anything else that might be on her schedule that day. Security, in their dark blue suits, looked on, unsmiling. "I must get started now. There is much to clean." She began to push past him with her broom and bucket flapping from her arms.

"Oh, one more thing," he said.

She turned to face him.

"I hope that male friend of yours knows as much about politics as you say he does. The event will be picture perfect for allaying suspicions." He chuckled, then stepped close to her out of the earshot of his security. "And then you and I can get down to working together on giving people something to be truly suspicious about."

The outer door that Sophie had been eyeing burst open, and a raven-haired man pranced out into the daylight. "A beauty fit for the goddess," he exclaimed, looking at Sophie. "Remind me to thank the human resource department for such a vision."

"Don't mind him, dear," Mr. Braden said to Sophie. "This is my Foreign Relations Minister, Mr. Lorcan Duihbur. Mr. Duihbur, meet my *most valuable* government employee."

Mr. Duihbur smirked. "I can see that. And I can also see that the high king has become his own *domestic affairs* minister."

"Pay no attention to him, Ms. Sophie." The high king laughed. "Lorcan is after my title, and he just may have it someday."

"I can assure you I don't want his job." Lorcan chuckled. "I've bigger fish to fry. Like getting him to see the wisdom of joining the UN effort to censure Israel."

"If you will excuse us, my dear, we've an important meeting with the taoiseach and some key members of parliament to attend to at Leinster House. Please make yourself comfortable inside."

As Sophie parted company from the men, she pondered Lorcan's words that she was a "beauty fit for the goddess." This was a phrase she hadn't heard before, but then again, she was learning new Irish phrases every day.

THIS TIME IAN BREEZED PAST THE SECURITY CHECKPOINT at the arts building and up to the lecture rooms. Myrna had somehow come up with an identification card for him. He didn't know how she'd obtained it, and he didn't ask. She'd continued to regale him through the noon hour with stories of campus life, only stopping to excuse herself by telling him she would be back in a few minutes. True to her word, she'd returned several moments later and dropped a temporary visiting student ID into his hand.

They walked into the lecture room together and took a couple of seats in the back. A dozen students sat in the classroom with a seating capacity for thirty.

Eager to observe the professor in action, Ian hoped the small enrollment wasn't due to her presentation. Her qualifications suggested that the class should have been full. Plenty of intelligent attorneys Ian knew struggled to keep a jury's attention. The academic world must operate in similar fashion.

"Is this a typical class size?" Ian asked Myrna.

"It's on the picayune side of the scale," she said. "Early Irish History is a new class offering that just came on this semester, plus it's an elective undergrad course. I guess there's not that much interest yet."

Promptly, at the stroke of the hour, Professor Saorla O'Rourke strode into the classroom. She wore a black leather coat that highlighted her un-styled, full-length, black-brown tresses. She placed a shoulder-strapped briefcase onto a desk next to the podium and slipped off her jacket, revealing a tannish body-tight sweater that showed off an athletic figure. Ian sized her up: five-foot-five inches and a hundred and twenty pounds of graceful elegance.

She took some papers from her briefcase, perused them for a few seconds, and then shoved them back inside. "Last time we ended, we were somewhere in the fifth century looking at Saint Patrick's coming to Ireland." With those opening words, she captivated the room.

"So let me pose this question first: Why are we studying the life of Patrick?" It seemed to Ian a rhetorical question, but a hand shot up from a boy in the first row. Professor O'Rourke indicated the student could answer.

"Because we are Irish, and he's responsible for a national holiday, and we can sell more Guinness in America around that time."

A few chuckles. "That's more insightful in some respects than you might think," the professor kindly responded. "Even the greatest heroes and legends can be coopted by commercialism. Winston Churchill called Patrick the 'greatest soul in a thousand years' in his five-volume History of the English-Speaking Peoples. He said there would not arise a soul on par until the French Joan of Arc came on the scene in the fifteenth century. Their stories of supernatural guidance and victory, Churchill determined, would be beyond credulity if they were not, in fact, true. Another famous historian has called Patrick the strongest 'voice' in history up to the seventeenth century.

"Let's see if we can get to the bottom of the intrigue and fascination surrounding him and perhaps sever the fact from the fantasy. To recapitulate some of the basics—which you can get in more detail from both the required and suggested readings in the course syllabus—last time we touched on how Patrick was born in Britain near the last decade of the fourth century. Roman in culture, outlook and appearance, his family was part of the landowning aristocracy. He would have written and spoken Latin as well as a local British-Celtic language related to the inhabitants of Gaul who had come to the British Isles in previous times. He also, no doubt, would have heard many other languages in town from people coming from throughout the Roman Empire to engage in the virile trade that was popping up at this time. These languages would have included the native Irish tongue.

"His Latin name was Patricius, meaning 'noble.' The idea here was that he was to be a nobleman, living comfortably atop the ruling class. But that was not to be, of course."

The student who'd made the earlier comment about selling Guinness in America shot up his hand and blurted, "Happy Nobleman's Day doesn't have the same ring to it as Happy St. Patrick's Day."

Saorla pressed forward with her lecture undaunted by a few lingering giggles. "We know his father was Calpornius and his grandfather was Potitus, who was a priest. In those days, priests could marry and have children. Now, as I said last time, Patrick was captured by pirates and taken to Ireland around the age of seventeen. Thus, he likely lived on the western coast of Britain. Britain, at this time, had been part of the Roman empire for hundreds of years. If Patrick had been born in earlier decades, he might have had a more tranquil go of it. But he found himself in a time where thousands were being led away to slavery to the then barbaric land of Ireland. The Roman Empire was beginning to unravel, and Britain was on the outer edges. Barbarians from without, social rot from within. As one of our own poets put it, '*things fall apart, the centre cannot hold. Mere anarchy is loosed upon the world.*'"

Recognizing the reference to a Yeats poem he'd heard his grandfather quote, Ian's heart warmed. It brought to mind the good times he'd had with the old man, despite the dire subject the poem spoke to.

Even with the sweet reflection on his grandfather, Ian found the professor so profoundly interesting that he was right back tracking with her. The students likewise appeared to be hanging on her every word.

"Ireland was a land completely beyond Roman rule and custom," she said. "Irish slave traders began to make raids into Britain, and Patrick was swept up. It is possible he saw his own capture as divine judgment in his life. Scratch that, not only was it possible, that was, in fact, how he saw it. He said in his confession that '*we ignored the warnings of our priests, who, again and again begged us to watch out for our eternal souls. Therefore, God's anger burned against us, and he scattered us to the barbarians at the cliff's edge of the planet.*' Now, he, in particular, may have felt he was being punished for a sin he committed as a youth. We know that he committed a certain sin during his teenage years, actually two years before his capture at age fifteen, that was so serious he confessed it privately to a friend when he began studying for his ordination many years later. But as happens, secrets are not always kept, and we know about it to this day. What we don't know is what the sin was."

Myrna poked Ian in the side with her fist. "I bet it was a girl next door."

Ian rolled his eyes. "Please."

"What do you think it was?" Myrna asked in a whisper.

"I don't know," he said, louder than he meant to. "You're making me nervous. Maybe he killed someone."

The professor continued with her lecture. Nobody in the classroom noticed the distraction in the back, except Ian, of course. He returned his eyes to the professor and watched the words roll from her lips. Hopefully, Myrna was done with the interruptions.

"Now we know that Patrick was taken as a slave by a king named Miliucc to the Antrim Hills. I say king, but there were many kings in Ireland, so he was more like a petty gang lord, who engaged in cattle raids to build his wealth instead of drug deals. Patrick is given the lonely job of tending sheep in the hills. He probably went many weeks at a time without any human contact and suffered agonizing deprivations while living outdoors with little food. By his own admission, he did not believe in God at first. But he was forced to turn heavenward during this time and became a praying man, saying hundreds of prayers a day. There is this beautiful quote from his Confession that says, '*In those days, I would awake the dawn and pray through frost, snow, rain; the love, the rapture, the fear of God swallowed me, my faith grew and my spirit was strengthened and there was no laziness in me, for the spirit in those days was all burning fire within me.'* By the way, his Confession and his Letter to Coroticus are the only surviving works we have from his pen and basically provide all we know about his life."

"Patrick labored on in this manner for six or seven years until, on the last night he was ever to be a slave, he heard a supernatural audible voice informing him that *'You have fasted well; you are going home.'* The voice went on to tell him that his hard labors had ended and that his ship was waiting for him at the sea. With that, Patrick left the next day, traveling hundreds of miles to the coast. He was not recaptured and was indeed able to gain passage on a trading vessel bound for mainland Europe. He was likely easily identifiable as a slave, probably had an iron yoke around his neck, and punishment for escape was death."

Amazing, Ian thought. He never really knew the story of Saint Patrick and was more familiar with how most Americans celebrated his birthday on March 17 with parades and drinking fests. Now Ian felt his heart strengthening to hear this story. Despite his trials, Patrick resisted bitterness, rising above his depredations to the betterment of himself and others. Ian considered his own current trial, so minor in comparison to Patrick's, yet here he now stood, summoned from his own life in America and brought to Ireland, while his job remained in jeopardy at home.

"So Patrick trod two-hundred miles to the coast where he found a trade ship ready to set sail. Patrick approached the sailors and told them he had the means to procure his passage. No one knows where he would have obtained it, another miracle perhaps. The captain, however, turned him down flat, saying *'Get the idea out of your head. There's no way you're getting on with us.'* Hearing that response, he turned to find a place of prayer. During the middle of his entreaty, he heard one of the crew yelling to him, *'Come, they are asking about you!'* They invited him aboard, and he sailed with them to what some think was Gaul, the coast of modern-day France.

"A strange thing happened upon their arrival: neither people nor food could be found. For several weeks they walked in pitiful lack. The absence of food and people may have been due to a Germanic invasion of the area that occurred in 407 AD, as some historians have speculated. Whatever the cause, desperation gripped the men. They began to taunt Patrick and his God. Patrick stepped forward with the solution. '*Give your hearts to the Lord my God,*' he said, '*and trust in him, for all things are possible with him and he will give you food in great stock.*' The starving sailors, feeble as they were, heeded his call and decided to call on the God of Patrick. No sooner did they finish praying, when a herd of pigs made its way down the road."

Ian was thrilled by the account. Experience had taught how hard it was to be out in the wild low on calories. He didn't think that any of those men with Patrick would ever be the same again after that day. No wonder this man was able to convert an entire people to his view of the world. Never one to study much history, Ian vowed that next time he was out on one of his grand adventures, he'd have a book on Patrick's life to pass the lonely time in his tent if the weather took a turn for the worse.

"It wasn't until several years later that Patrick actually made it back to his family in Britain. When he arrives, there is no doubt much joy. It must have been as if one had come back from the dead. We know that his parents begged him not to leave them again. Eventually, one night in his parent's home, a man named Victoricus, who he knew in Ireland, visited Patrick in a dream. He held many letters, and he handed one to Patrick that said, '*Vox Hiberionacum,*' translated from the Latin as the 'Voice of the Irish.' In that instant, he heard the voice of a great multitude gathered in an Irish forest, crying out '*Holy boy, we plead with you to walk among us again!*'"

As the professor continued on with her lecture, Myrna interrupted periodically. The interruptions became even more pronounced when the professor began to describe how Patrick baptized thousands after he returned to Ireland as a bishop.

"In those days, the one baptized was immersed in the water

completely in the nude," the professor explained. "It was a symbol of a new birth, becoming born again like a naked baby."

Myrna poked Ian in the arm. "I wonder how many people would want to become Christians if they knew they would have to let it all hang out in public. No secrets from anyone, eh?"

Ian fought off a vision of Myrna being struck mute.

As he watched the professor beginning to wrap up, he felt his heart tap a bit faster at the thought that he was actually about to meet her.

"The sum of it," she said, "is that Patrick went to the very edge of the known world, to an island steeped in greed and violence and, some would say, without the knowledge of God. This was all at great danger to his personal safety and freedom, knowing from six long years of captivity what potentially awaited him when he returned: slavery, death, and all kinds of schemes against his life. Even witchcraft, for those who believe in that sort of thing. Yet, with a love that burned within him, he went, and the result was that within one hundred years of his death, Christianity was so firmly planted in Ireland that it became a base for it to go forth to many distant lands. Some have also pointed out that Patrick may have been the first missionary of the Christian church, after the close of the first century, to go beyond the demarcation of a world constrained by Greco-Roman influences. And, as you will see from your reading of the 'Letter to Coroticus,' he arose as one of the most ardent voices in the history of the world to plead against slavery.

"I see the time is up. I am going to add one thing to the syllabus." The professor pulled out some copies from her briefcase and passed them out. "I would like everyone to read the '*Lorica*,' that's the Latin word for *breastplate*. It's a morning song of praise and invocation, often referred to as the 'Breastplate of Patrick.' Most historians think that it was written a century after Patrick died. Regardless of the putative authorship, it certainly captures what must have been the spirit of the man."

IAN SAT LISTENING TO MYRNA BLATHER ABOUT HOW SHE would have been too modest to have been baptized in the fifth century. After the final student filed out of the classroom, Myrna jumped out of her seat.

"Come on. It's your lucky day."

Ian followed her to the front of the room where the professor was putting papers back in her briefcase.

"Professor O'Rourke, this is Ian Shaw," Myrna said, "a bona fide campus security threat." Myrna winked at Ian. "Ah, what I meant to say is Mr. Shaw is from America, California. His grandparents live in Northern Ireland, and he would like to talk to you about some archeological discoveries he's found on his relative's property. He thinks you could lend some insight."

Ian had been watching the professor's eyes carefully. Glints of enthusiasm flashed in her retinas, but something else was there too.

A sadness?

"Hi, Professor," Ian said. "Amazing lecture, I'm so honored to meet you. I've researched your background and left a few messages—"

"You've just showed up in my classroom? Should I consider myself a stalking victim?" Irritation etched on her face, the sadness gone.

"Excuse me?"

Ian immediately wanted to take the question back. Having his artifacts examined was his central purpose, and an ugly scene would only dismantle his efforts. "I'm sorry, I should have explained that I came to Ireland at the request of my ailing grandfather who had been finding some strange artifacts on his property and is very curious to find out more than we know. We realized we needed expert help, and we ... I ... decided you were the best."

Her face softened. "I have an important conference call scheduled in less than fifteen minutes. Perhaps you can meet me down in my office, and I can take a quick look."

"Sure," he said with a nod.

SAORLA SCOOPED UP HER BRIEFCASE AND ANGLED directly toward the classroom door. The nerve of the American was a wee bit much. He was probably used to getting his way, maneuvering himself into places and before people for opportunities the ordinary person couldn't make happen. The manly good looks and silky speech had served him well, no doubt, all his adult life. And why was he here anyway, wasting her time? Folks all over Ireland always thought they were digging up something of historical significance, like it happened every day, but Saorla knew better.

But he is handsome, like Stuart, and polite and, he called your lecture 'amazing,' didn't he?

The fleeting thought was sacrilege to the memory of her beloved, dead partner, and she swiftly batted it away as she grabbed her briefcase tighter with one hand and flicked her hair back over her shoulder with the other.

Nobody could compare with Stuart, certainly not this shallow American. And if he had liked her lecture, it was only because of Stuart. She'd taught the class today like her husband would have taught it—with reverence and devotion and something more: blind and persistent faith.

But it was all a lie to hold on to that during the lecture, darling pretty.

She realized that now. Stuart was the true believer, not her. He was the one who attended St. Teresa's every week, a place that was refuge of peace tucked away as it was out of sight and sound from the nearby chaos of the shopping on Grafton. As she pictured the tranquil setting of the church, she realized she hadn't darkened the doorway there since Stuart …

"Could you slow down," Myrna shouted. "You're moving like a faerie through the forest making off with my jewelry."

Saorla stepped a wee slower. "Oh, was I up to ninety?"

IAN FOLLOWED THE PROFESSOR AND MYRNA AS THEY descended a flight of stairs and then meandered through a few hallways. They finally came to a green metal office door with the professor's name on it and entered. Ian watched his new expert hang her coat on a hook on the back of the door and then settle in at her desk. Taking a seat next to Myrna in one of the chairs across from the professor's desk, he figured he was in the right place when he noticed the books stacked in every cranny—on the shelves, desk, credenza, and in various piles on the floor. Books and more books. They were everywhere, forming a veritable sea waiting to be surfed.

He handed the professor several photographs. One had been taken of the chalice before it was stolen. The other photos were of the stone slab, the silver cross, and the satchel he'd found. He fumbled through his pocket for the silver cross after the professor grabbed the pictures and glanced at them.

"Where did you find these?" the professor asked.

Ian held the silver cross in his hand now. "On my grandfather's farm in a stretch of bogland. The old man had dreams … about where to dig. That's how the mystery all started."

"Mr. Shaw. I don't have time for hoaxes." She rose to her feet and headed for the door.

"But if I can just show this shiny sil—"

She was at the doorway now with her hand ushering him out. "I really don't have time to waste. Now if you will excuse me."

Ian looked at Myrna. She was speechless for the first time all day and appeared as baffled as him. Myrna left the office first. Ian followed her out. The office door slammed behind him.

"Is she always so friendly?"

"I've never seen her so rude. Look, I'm late for class. I have to sprint. I'll think of another idea. What's your mobile number?"

CHAPTER ELEVEN

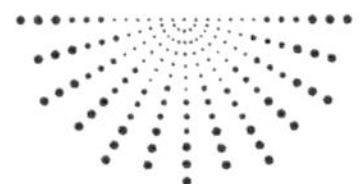

Ian left Professor O'Rourke's office in such a hurry he'd forgotten his photographs on her desk. Unfazed, he was already on to a new plan that involved another history professor at the university—Dr. Claire Curran. Her name display on an office door down the hall from Professor O' Rourke's office had caught his eye earlier, while en route from the lecture room. From his research, he knew that she was an Irish history professor but also had some experience in archeology. Maybe she could help him or at least point him in the right direction.

Ian found Professor Curran's office door closed and locked. He decided to leave a message for her. He scribbled a note indicating that he was a barrister that had found some items of archeological significance and needed to talk to her as soon as possible, as he was only in town for a short stay. He would pay for her time. Proofing the note, he scratched out the word "barrister" and replaced it with "attorney" when he recalled that the professor hailed from New York City. He jotted his name and phone number at the bottom, folded the note in half, and slipped it under the office door. A prayer tumbled from his lips that Dr. Curran would prove to be more friendly than Dr. O'Rourke.

Ian left the building and wandered the campus before looking for a spot to kill some time while he waited for a reply from Professor Curran. He settled on a bench looking out over a green quadrangle in front of the entranceway to the Book of Kells exhibit. A strange mix of students and tourists wandered about in the afternoon sun, which hung low in the pale-blue, mid-October sky.

A queue formed in a bay across from him to see the Book of Kells. It was a line he almost joined but, in the end, he decided the ticket was a bit too pricey for his level of interest. He opted instead to make an overseas phone call to Mike back in San Francisco. When Mike didn't answer, he dialed Jeff, who answered on the first ring. It was only then that Ian considered that it was before 8 a.m. back home on the West Coast.

"Hey, bro, just checking in. Hope it's not too early?"

"Naw. I'm up studying already. Everything all right? You left in such a hurry last weekend."

"It's crazy. My grandfather is dying. I'm on a wild goose chase in Dublin, getting nowhere, trying to get to the bottom of some strange stuff going on with a chalice that was stolen from him. Then there's a whole big mess at work I got into. On top of that, I'm AWOL from the action at Mavs, and I'm getting a little stir crazy, like I need to climb a mountain or something. Other than that, it's all good. But, hey, I called to find out how things are with you. How was the meeting at the Cantina on Saturday?"

"Whoa! Are you trying to change the subject?"

"Actually, yeah. I wanna get caught up, so let's forget about me for now.

"All right." Jeff sighed. "Turnout was smaller than expected. But it was a fantastic afternoon. Your friend, Shark, came. And guess what? He got it big time and wanted to be baptized that very afternoon. We took him back out in the water and dunked him under."

"Oh my goodness! The Shark? A believer now?" Ian was up off the bench, pacing back and forth as he held the phone to his ear.

"Yeah, it's true."

"No kidding? I've got to call him. I'm surprised he went anywhere near the water after what happened in the morning."

Ian quit pacing and went back to sitting on the bench.

"That's just it, Ian. The trauma of that morning really shook him up. His story gets bigger and better. He insists that when he was unconscious—"

Ian didn't hear what Jeff said next. From behind, two hands slapped him on the back and a voice yelled in his ear. "Hey there, Mr. Humble Pie."

Myrna. How had she found him?

Ian ended the call with Jeff and put his phone in his pocket.

"Do you always have to be so dramatic?" he asked.

"Drama free? Is that the way you like to roll?"

She really had no clue. His life had never been drama free.

"I wouldn't say that."

"Look, I have an idea."

"Uh-oh."

"I'm logging you in for a micro-aggression."

"Huh?"

"Smart-aleck American, you're lucky I'm not easily offended." She was smiling playfully. "I'm going to make this work yet. Thursday is the professor's birthday. I've already arranged to take her to Milton & Murphy's Pub where I tend bar twice a week. It's just to the north of here and to the east of the Temple Bar area, near Temple and Essex. She thinks I'm meeting her there for a low-key dinner to talk over some things having to do with my living arrangements. I will get her there at high tea."

"High tea?"

"That's 7 pm, you Jackeen."

"Okay, what's wrong with this plan?"

Myrna ignored his question. "It's going to be a surprise party. A few of her friends and some of the faculty will be there when she arrives. You need to be there too."

"I don't drink tea."

"Neither do I."

"What makes you think she'll want me there? I have this tiny suspicion that I'm one of the last people on the planet she would want to see on her birthday."

"She's never acted like that before. I know you're not trying to pull a hoax. I've always been a good judge of character, except the time … never mind. I'll work on her. I have great hopes for you two—that it will be just like Bogie and Bacall or Tristan and Isolde. Are you married?"

Ian just shook his head. This could go wrong in so many ways.

Myrna locked into his eyes. "So would you take me on a date?"

"Are all the Irish women this pushy or just the Women's Studies majors?"

"Thursday night?"

"No way."

"You are a micro-aggressor. I meant you can see the professor Thursday."

"Oh yeah, that."

CHAPTER TWELVE

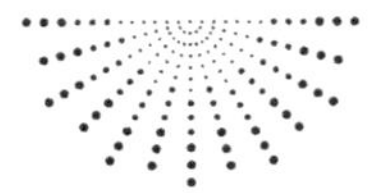

Wednesday afternoon was the time faculty from the History Department usually congregated to chat about campus issues, world events, their own personal lives, or just about anything at all. A little camaraderie among academics that Saorla couldn't afford to miss. Not unless she wanted rumors to fly that she was avoiding social contacts because she was hopelessly depressed.

Sometimes the Wednesday group went out to a pub, but more often they simply gathered in the faculty lounge, a comfortable room with a refrigerator, a couple of brown leather couches, and a few lounge chairs. Today, it was the faculty lounge.

Saorla arrived early, poured herself a cup of tea, and joined the lively discussion that was already brewing among the other early arrivals. Michael Mac Cionath, a modern European history scholar, opined that Rí David Braden should either abdicate or take a stronger position on Ireland's commitment to the European Union. "We must stand united with all of Europe," he said. "We don't want to end up like the Brits. The first thing we should do is raise a larger common tax. We need to get our poor socialist comrades from Greece on a more secure footing. A more open-hearted approach to taking in Middle Eastern and African refugees, especially the women and children. More unity in all respects. Braden should make a strong stand for participation in any future military coalition to march against Jerusalem. I would also say that we make entry into the EU irrevocable for all member states. That would take care of any waffling based on the political winds blowing at any particular time in any given constituent state."

Many heads nodded at Mac Cionath's critique of the high king. A reasonable progressive consensus usually developed on almost any issue discussed.

After Ireland's role in the European Union and other political matters were thoroughly bantered about, Saorla moved to another group of a half dozen professors who had arrived and were now mingling by the coffee counter. The group included Claire Curran and Raicheal Meegan, a medieval history lecturer whom the faculty all called by her surname, Meegan.

Meegan greeted Saorla with a quick hug and asked, "How are things in your world?"

Saorla never knew what to say to that, so she just said, "Fine." Nobody could possibly know how painful the past couple of years had been, or even how rough this week had been. Always a good listener, Meegan had the most charming anecdotes about her current projects and the places she planned to visit on holiday. Saorla considered it a bit of sporting competition to come up with something interesting. The actual truth of Saorla's painful existence would no doubt spoil the happy mood of the occasion, so she settled on a story about the American who'd paid her a visit.

"An unusual incident happened yesterday," Saorla said. "An American man came into my office with a batch of photographs of some artifacts he claimed to have dug up. It was quite an elaborate hoax, really. The photos looked to be of fifth century antiquities that would be priceless if they were authentic. It started me thinking that we should all come up with a hoax to stir interest in the university, get enrollment up, and everyone can keep their jobs."

The other five academics all laughed. "Now you're thinking," Meegan said, joining in the spirit. "It happens more often than you think it could with our media. Some big story hits the wires, it turns out to be false in the main, and no one ever sets the record straight. They just move on to the next, dare I say, fabrication. In the meantime, the agenda that the story set is advanced, and hardly ever does anyone find out that the narrative was wrong to begin with. So hoaxes have often been useful in ideological wars."

They all chuckled enthusiastically.

"So, what's so urgent, Red?" Lorcan asked, amused by the cloak-and-dagger tone of Claire Curran's request to meet with him. Darkness had fallen on the city now, and they huddled on the quay east of O'Connell Street out of the path of all foot traffic by a stone railing overlooking the inky black River Liffey.

"This could turn out to be a game changer," Claire said, as she handed him a manila envelope containing the photos she'd heisted.

Their two voices spoke softly in the dark. He looked into her eyes the way he used to do when they were lovers. The look back from her said they might rekindle the fire. He thought now of how the flame had burned hottest when he first ran for parliament and less so during his tenure as curator of the National Museum, but now, deep into his service as Minister of Foreign Relations, the embers were suddenly glowing again. He tousled her hair with his fingers.

"I'll be the judge of that, Red."

"Our bridge to the future."

He pulled her close, wrapped his arms around her, and kissed her lips aggressively. A moment later, he nudged her away. "What makes you think we have a future?"

"We could make the world a better place."

"It's going to take a lot of euros."

A look of disgust crossed her face. "I hate the capitalist turds that have it all."

They'd covered the same ground dozens of times. He knew Red cared little for his motivation of getting-rich quick. Rather, she simply saw the money as a necessary evil in furtherance of politically transforming the world and purging it of Christianity. But these shared aims were consistent with his highest objective in life of pleasing the Goddess Maeve, who would make all his lesser desires possible. If things worked out as planned, he could live the most lavish of lifestyles while making the world a better place for everyone. If he obtained enough wealth, he might be able to buy the kind of world he envisioned by helping leaders in other nations with similar views. He'd slowly come to realize that it would be much easier to work behind the scenes, and therefore, he really had no desire to go any further in politics. He would get out of the public eye as soon as he had the wealth, and he would shroud his net worth from public knowledge. The kind of visibility attached to high political office would only hinder his ability to take the risks needed to bring about the type of society he dreamed of—one free of Christianity, of course, but also one increasingly open to the more native, more organic, paganistic Celtic roots of the island. One open to worshiping the Goddess herself.

Lorcan flashed a grin. "Don't ever change, Red."

She nodded. "I'll meet you again tomorrow night. By then I should know more. The American called my office and wanted to set up a meeting about his artifacts."

"And you'll meet with him and keep me abreast?"

"Of course. And I can stay with you tomorrow night ... if you want."

"Excellent," he said, nodding to her as he placed the envelope with the photos inside his jacket pocket. "By the way, I think I found a sacrifice for the Samhain."

"You're really intent on going through with it?" She seemed genuinely surprised.

"It's what the Goddess demands. The better the sacrifice, the better the blessing."

"Where did you find the prospect?"

"A Polish immigrant girl who cleans at the king's mansion. She's flawless."

Red may not worship the Goddess as he did, but he could trust her. And trust meant everything. Too many people were ethereal waifs who begged to be deceived by the strong. Not Claire though. She could handle his truth. And he had started to see a crack in her atheistic-humanistic philosophy with a turn toward his pagan view of the world. She'd be on board in the end. He could feel it. Call it instinct. A lot of life was like that for him, he just knew things simply by sensing them.

Red looked down at her boots and said, "Are you sure you—"

"Yes, that part isn't going to be a problem." He reassured her because it was true. The sacrifice would release spiritual power and approval from the Goddess. Fiona would get better, make a full recovery. A lot of things would get better. He'd finish mending his father's fallen legacy. But Red might as well know there was something worrying him.

"The message from the chalice is what has me bothered," Lorcan said.

"The chalice?"

"The American's grandfather brought an ancient silver chalice to a shop in Belfast. He found it on his farm in Antrim. I have eyes everywhere, and before he even left the shop, I had arranged to co-opt it."

"You're scared of an artifact?"

"The Latin inscription on it. It was a prophecy."

"And you believe in it?"

"Not a question of believing it. There are opposing forces in the world. Everyone can sense that. An ebb and flow to these things, a yin and a yang, a good and a better. Tides can turn quickly. I'll do all I can to prevent the prophecy from happening."

"Could be a fable."

Lorcan shook his head ever so slightly. "The Old Latin on the chalice translates as *'He who uncovers this cup and the related mysteries will unlock the hidden prophecy of Patrick to lead the people back to God in the hour of Braden's reign.'*"

Claire's eyes widened. "It can't be legitimate. David Braden is the high king now!"

Lorcan nodded. "The style dates the chalice to the fifth or sixth century. It's been in the ground for fifteen hundred years."

"But ... you don't think it relates to ... David Braden? It couldn't—"

"I ... *we* need to watch this closely. Much damage could be caused if the masses hook on to this. It could start a resurgence of Christianity that we would be hard pressed to reverse. Potentially set us back a thousand years on all we've worked so hard to accomplish."

Red sighed. "I see. But perhaps not as clearly as your other adherents, especially the ones that have been with you since the days of your father's folklore store. They do a great job of promoting your views on magic."

"You're *starting* to see, you've come out of the dark ages, through enlightenment, modernism, post-modernism. Soon you'll see that the ancient Celtic ways were always best."

"Even if all the worst you mention about the chalice is true, I just don't see it as much of a threat to you."

"Preparing for the worst is always the smartest option." Lorcan turned to the water, rested his arms over the stone rail, and peered out into the blackness of the river. Claire, by his side, did the same. "There's something more I haven't told you," he said. "The grandfather, George Shaw, had a dream of a great treasure that was to be uncovered. From my eyes and ears out at the farmhouse, I'm told this could refer to a literal treasure."

"Surely you're not putting stock in the dreams of an old farmer?"

"One of his dreams led to the discovery of the chalice. We have to pay attention. If a hidden prophecy shows up claiming to be from Saint Patrick, we have to make sure it's destroyed so people never hear of it. And if there's a treasure to be found, we'll be the ones to claim it."

Lorcan parted company with Red on the quay and made his way to the black Mercedes waiting for him at the curb. Once seated in the back of the vehicle, he ordered his driver to take him to his penthouse suite, located on the top floor of a high-rise on the edge of the leafiest part of Dublin. As they pulled away, he watched the woman who still stood on the bridge and considered how much he had invested in her over the years. He could trust her to find out what she could. After that, she'd have to prove she wasn't a liability.

FOR HIS STAY IN DUBLIN, IAN HAD CHOSEN TO BOOK A room at the Shelbourne Hotel—an expensive five-star palatial Victorian—because of its central location just minutes from Trinity College, Grafton Street, and the National Museum of Ireland, and because the nearby less expensive hotels were all booked up. The next morning after his unsuccessful encounter with Professor O'Rourke, he was about to grab a quick breakfast at the hotel before he caught a cab to an antiquities dealer north of the city, when his cell phone rang. It was a local number he didn't recognize but he answered anyway.

A voice on the other end introduced himself as Frances Flannagan, an archeologist on staff at the National Museum of Ireland on Kildare Street. "Claire Curran asked me to give you a call and look at your finds."

Ian felt a smile creasing his lips. "How soon can we meet?"

"Half an hour, at the national museum."

Ian hung up and hoofed his way through thick fog to Kildare Street carrying his artifacts with him in a large briefcase. Throughout the ten-minute walk, he had an uneasy feeling that someone was slipping into the foggy shadows whenever Ian looked back.

Entering through the main doorway twenty minutes early, he passed into a large rotunda. He paused to look behind him. Nobody had followed him. He took in the scene before him. Zodiac signs depicted on the flooring greeted him, surrounded by Greek columns rising a hundred feet to the dome-shaped ceiling. Ian had read of the museum's boast that it held the greatest treasures of Europe outside of Athens, with artifacts dating to 7000 BC. Its collection included the most important Celtic and pre-Celtic pieces in the world.

Early for the meeting, he decided to enter the museum proper to compare any exhibits similar to the items his grandfather had found.

Thanks to the instructions in a brochure he'd snapped up in the rotunda, he spotted a number of the world-famous objects on display, including the Ardagh Chalice, the Tara Brooch, and the Cross of Cong. He marveled at the vast collections of bronze-age gold.

He spent most of his limited time studying the Ardagh Chalice, learning that the silver vessel dated to the eighth century, its primary use, a communion cup. Intricate patterns carved into gold filigrees surrounded the outside of the chalice. Its crafter had inscribed in the midst of the gold the Latin names of two of the apostles. In many ways, the Ardagh Chalice reminded him of the one Papa had found. Papa's chalice wasn't as ornate as the one here in the museum, but it had the same shape and silver look. This, more than ever, convinced Ian that the similarity marked his grandfather's missing chalice as an old artifact of great value.

A few times during his study of the chalice, Ian felt eyes boring through him. Men in suits stood like sentries and stared coldly at him from various and sundry positions, but mostly near the edge of the second-floor balcony in the museum. Was it normal security protocol? Or was he being specially targeted? He wasn't sure.

Ian departed the exhibit area and came back toward the rotunda where he caught an elevator to the top floor and then made his way down to Flannagan's office. Flannagan carefully examined the stone slab, the satchel, and the silver cross, and then he said, "They're modern ... of no interest."

Disappointed, Ian politely thanked the man. But he already planned to get another opinion. He took the elevator down and ended up in the rotunda.

Over by the cash register of the bookstore, he spotted a familiar face. Cheryl Miller, the American Airlines flight attendant who'd given him her phone number, was purchasing a book. Another layover, Ian decided.

He couldn't resist having a little fun with her.

He took his cell from his pocket and her phone number from his wallet. From thirty feet away, he could hear her cell ringing. She flipped her purse strap off her shoulder and fished for her phone.

Oh yeah. This was going to be beautiful.

"Hello, this is Ian Shaw. Do you remember me? The guy on your flight last Sunday?"

"Ah, sure. How could I forget 007?"

Ian grinned. "Glad you remember. Listen, any chance you might be back in Dublin on another layover?"

"As a matter of fact I am."

"Just so happens I'm in Dublin too. I don't suppose you'd be interested in heading out with me on this fine foggy morning to the National Museum?"

"On Kildare Street?"

Ian could see her eyes growing wide. "That's the one." He headed in her direction and clicked his phone off.

He could hear her say, "Actually, I'm—"

"—There now?" He finished the words for her as he stood facing her.

Her palm covered her mouth, and then she dropped her hand to tuck away her phone. "Yes," she said, her face reddening. "I was right. You are a spy!"

They were both smiling now. "Uh, I saw you from over there," he said. "Are you coming or going?"

"I've been through once. But I missed one of the most important exhibits—an exhibition called Kingship and Sacrifice."

"What's the draw with that one?"

"It has a number of human bodies that have been found over the years in Ireland's bogland. The bog has a fierce preservative nature, they say."

Her accurate assessment of the bog's preservative nature intrigued him. The chalice his grandfather had unearthed lacked traces of tarnish, but could the bog really preserve human flesh? "Let's go take a look at it."

LORCAN WATCHED THEM ON A HIGH-DEFINITION SCREEN set up in the security room of the museum. He'd long admired the Kingship and Sacrifice exhibit; it had always been his favorite at the museum. Turning up the volume of his listening device, he tuned into the couple's conversation as they came to a glass-case exhibit of the upper torso of a man. He'd been torn in two by a peat harvester that unearthed him in 2003.

The American, Shaw, had called his female companion Cheryl, who recoiled at the sight of the torso as she cuddled her arm into Shaw's. "What happened to him?" the woman asked.

Shaw seemed to tense at Cheryl's touch. Foolish man. Lorcan admired the woman's beauty for a moment from the privacy of his perch in front of the screen.

She too would make a good prospect for the demands of the Goddess.

But then he was reminded that he already had a perfectly good candidate he would tap at the appropriate time for the appeasement.

"It says he was a victim of human sacrifice around 300 BC," Shaw said, after perusing the explanation displayed on the placard below the corpse. "He was a tribal king who was killed in a ritual, they think. The belief then was that the king was somehow responsible for the poor harvest, and his killing was meant to appease the Goddess of Fertility."

Lorcan felt a rush of pride at hearing those words. He'd essentially written them himself.

"Unbelievable," the woman said, frowning, her face pale now.

"Yeah, can you imagine if people still believed that way? There'd be a lot of dead leaders whenever the economy tanks."

"You can still see his reddish hair in a pompadour style and the reddish whiskers on his chin. And is that a bow tying his hair back?"

"He was in his early twenties," Shaw said, gleaning from the placard. "He used a 'hair gel' made of plant oil and pine resin imported from southwest Europe. The gel was still in his hair when they found him."

"Some things about humans never change," Cheryl said.

"Like the tendency toward violence?"

"Actually, I was thinking about vanity."

"I'm not going to touch that one," Shaw shot back. "But I doubt you have a vain bone in your body."

They both chuckled. Shaw seemed to relax, and Cheryl had released his arm by now. The couple moved on a bit.

One exhibit, sure to disturb most people, featured a Druidic ritual killing of a man. Shaw studied it carefully, read the placard, and then turned to Cheryl. "In addition to their admirable qualities as poets, musicians and wordsmiths, the Druids seemed to have had a fondness for human sacrifice."

Cheryl shrugged a shoulder and smirked. "Well-rounded individuals for their times."

She moved on to the next display and stopped to stare at a two-thousand-year-old corpse.

Shaw came to her side. "Do you want to get some lunch?" he asked. "My stomach's growling.

"I kinda lost my appetite with the ritual sacrifices, but maybe it will come back. I know a good vegetarian place not too far away called Cornucopia."

"Are you a vegetarian?"

"Not really, but if I'm going to eat anything after seeing the victims in these exhibits, I'd rather it be a plant."

"I'd like to say, 'good point,' but I'm a hopeless meat and potatoes guy."

"Maybe it's time you broadened your horizons."

The woman slipped in close to Shaw's side as he walked for the exit. Lorcan noted that despite the distraction of the woman locking her arm around his, the American glanced up at the two security guards stationed to watch him from the balcony above the exit.

CHAPTER THIRTEEN

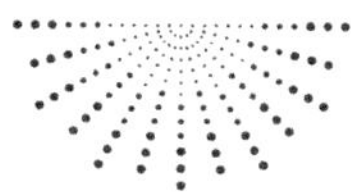

The last time Saorla had crossed through the brown-wood, Viking-style doorway of Murphy's Pub was nearly three years ago with Stuart. They used to stop in often, mostly on Thursday evenings to mark the near end of a school week. With Stuart, anywhere was fun, the center of the party.

Entering now with Myrna, she resolved to at least smile through the evening. It was her birthday after all. And Murphy's was just the place for it. It had a well-earned reputation as a go-to hangout for locals to socialize away from the sea of tourists that occupied the Temple Bar scene.

Saorla considered herself lucky to see her thirtieth birthday given the incident last weekend. Maybe she would even have a glass of wine. But under no circumstances would she repeat the fiasco of last Friday night. She'd learned a lesson, and the timely aid of her housekeeper had given her some small measure of hope. Still, she doubted if God really existed despite the otherworldly nature of her encounter that day.

Something spiritual, or at least mysteriously intriguing, occurred when she was preparing her lecture on Ireland's patron saint and then telling his story to her students. At times, she fiercely wanted to believe what Patrick had believed. She just couldn't make the jump, however, because she saw too much evidence to the contrary. On the wall opposite the bar was a picture depicting Saint Patrick in regal bishop attire. "How did you do it?" she whispered.

As they ambled into the bar area, Myrna clipped ahead, striding toward the back.

"What's the hurry, sister?" Saorla yelled.

Myrna turned back and flashed a grin. "Just because you're old now at the big three-zero, and nearly a pensioner, doesn't mean you have to shuffle around."

"People ought to be able to keep personal information like their birthdates a secret."

"No such luck with a researcher as good as me. Come on, you're moving like a turtle through the brush in the mountains of Wicklow."

"I thought we came here to have fun, not workout our arses and—"

"Surprise!" the table in the back erupted as one.

Between the dim lighting over the tables and fussing with Myrna, she hadn't noticed her friends. If she had known it was a surprise party, she probably wouldn't have come. But honestly, she welcomed the sight of familiar faces.

Her eyes searched the room. Seated at a table were professors Michael Mac Cionath, Claire Curran, and Raicheal Meegan, along with Kelly Burns, an administrative assistant at the college. Saorla considered them all close but hadn't shared the pain of her inner sanctum with them over the past couple years. Saorla continued to scan the table. There was Jim—a grad assistant and friend of Myrna's that Saorla knew only by his first name.

"I had no idea ..." Saorla said to the group.

And then she saw him.

The American, Mr. Shaw.

How in the world had he found her? Had he been following her? Why was he sitting with her friends?

She turned back to her colleagues on the faculty. "I didn't think—"

"Didn't think we could keep a secret, eh?" Michael Mac Cionath asked.

"Speak for yourself," Meegan said. "She knows the rest of us could keep a secret, but heaven knows you're a hopeless blabbermouth."

"I'm going to ignore that this once," Mac Cionath said with a straight face. "Let's not get distracted from our mission. It is a fine day, and a wonderful thing that happened thirty years ago. Fill your glasses. I want to propose a toast to our esteemed colleague."

Mac Cionath poured glasses of wine for Saorla and Myrna. He turned to Meegan as he did. "A little collegiality from some on this fine occasion would be appreciated."

He raised his half-full glass. "To Saorla, a fine professor. A better lover of knowledge there has never been, and a greater human being you'd be hard pressed to find. Like the spring gorse, the flower and horse, the keeper of flock and the sun on the dock, you bring a warm smile, you're a friend we can dial, in snow or in rain—"

"Does this have a point?" Meegan asked.

"Hmm, let me see. A *point*, yes, I'll get to the point, right here in this Dublin joint."

"You're a doppelgänger of a mental patient," Meegan cried.

"You are projecting," Mac Cionath retorted. "And you know I'm an academic. I'm paid to talk, not make points."

"Everyone, you are so kind to surprise me like this," Saorla said. "Thank you, really. Can you excuse me for a second? I need to discuss something with Myrna just a moment."

Saorla yanked Myrna by the hand and tugged her from the table to the bar area. "Can you tell me what he is doing here?" She turned her eyes in the direction of the American. "I thought I'd made it clear that I wasn't buying what he's selling."

"I think you should give him a chance—"

"You planned this behind my back?"

"But you got too busy and—"

"I've heard enough already."

Myrna glanced over at their table. "There's something spectacularly keen about him, don't you think?"

"Yeah, he's tall and solid with movie-star looks, but you can't let that fool you."

"He just wants to show you one more thing. Heck, maybe he'll even ask you to dance. The good Lord knows you need to loosen up."

"Is that what this is about?"

Myrna shook her head. "Like I said, he just wants to show you something."

"More photos? Please."

Mac Cionath's booming voice called Saorla and Myrna back to the table. "I have some more words for the occasion, if I may."

"You most certainly may not," Meegan said.

Mac Cionath ignored his critic. This time he dumped the sing-song and gave an epic Irish toast that was poetic, comedic, and completely appropriate for a birthday celebration.

When the toast was finished, the group sang *"La Breath Shona dhuit!"* A rousing rendition of "Happy Birthday" in the Irish Gaelic language.

The American seemed comfortable speaking with Claire, Jim, and Meegan through dinner. He ordered fish and chips and was more interested in conversing than eating and drinking. His dark green sport jacket and body-tight black shirt gave him a neatly dressed appearance of calm, thoughtful collectedness. He used his hands to converse, and those listening to his cocoa smooth voice at the far side of the table seemed sufficiently engrossed. Whenever, he looked Saorla's way, she avoided eye contact and wanted to ask him in private if he planned on stalking her all over Dublin. But she didn't have a chance, and the evening settled into a nearly normal night out with friends.

Saorla was thinking that maybe he would ignore her altogether, and she would be able to avoid an unpleasant scene when he finally spoke to her.

"Excuse me, Professor O'Rourke. I have something for you to open for your birthday. I want you to know how very thankful I am to be privileged to share the occasion with you."

He reached under the table and hoisted up an awkward package.

He handed it to her, his blue, blue eyes dancing. She felt the eyes of the other guests trained on her. They each had presents in their hands now and were no doubt biding their time to hand over their gifts.

She took the package and carefully began unravelling the wrapping. Sheep leather?

Her heart tapped faster.

Real sheep leather?

Yes. And the leather was old but well preserved. Dark brown, with intricate patterns carved into it. She tore the rest of the wrapping away and held an ancient satchel in her hands.

Her heart galloped against her chest now.

This sort of antique should be displayed in the national museum. Kept under lock and key.

She studied the contours and intricacies of the artifact. A miniature inscription engraved into the leather near the knobs of the top cover. She dug a pair of supermarket-reading glasses out of her purse that she used only for extra-fine print and put them on.

"Do you find it interesting?" the American asked.

Her voice caught in her throat. "Yes," was all she could manage.

She squinted through her lenses. "It has an inscription. It's Old Latin."

"Can you read it?" the American asked.

She was seeing but hardly believing as she translated the words. *It is the glory of God to conceal a matter, and the glory of kings to search it out.*

By the time she read to the last word, the room went misty on her.

Saorla faced the American. "Is this ... where did ... I mean, did you just find this?"

"Yes, this week."

She tucked her hair back over her shoulder. "How could you have known? We have to talk, later."

"Sure."

The words on the inscription? How could Sophie ... anyone, have known? The atmosphere turned august as she pondered the questions.

She continued to examine the satchel, amazed, torn between

credulity and incredulity. She opened the cover. Was something inside? She slipped out a single leaf of deer vellum. Delicate and smooth, she felt its contours in her hand, while she searched the page for writing. A single sentence was encrypted in Latin. The same as on the satchel itself. *It is the glory of God to conceal a matter, and the glory of kings to search it out.*

Everyone at the table seemed oblivious to what had just transpired. "A nice facsimile of a pre-Medieval treasure," Mac Cionath said, obviously assuming the American had purchased a cheap knockoff.

Claire suddenly stood up and flicked a strand of red hair from her forehead. "It's getting late for me. Big morning ahead. Sorry to wilt on you while the night is still in bloom." She hugged Saorla, handed her a birthday card, and left.

CHAPTER FOURTEEN

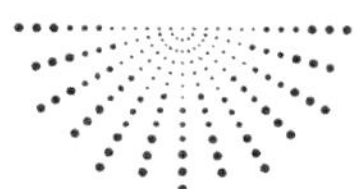

Later that night back in his room at the Shelbourne, Ian clicked the deadbolt of his door. Had he been followed from Murphy's? Men seemed to sift in an out of the shadows as he walked the streets back to the hotel. But he couldn't be sure.

He flopped down onto the king-size bed and checked his email. He saw one from his secretary, Joan, at the law firm.

Dear Ian,

I have some bad news. I heard this morning from the partners that after an investigation, the State Bar filed formal charges against you. There is going to be a hearing on the matter next week. If you don't return, it is likely the State Bar Court will expedite the case and hear it in absentia. Also, Jarvis lost the hearing on your motion to dismiss in the Calderon case. They are setting the matter for trial next month. Sorry to hear about your grandfather. I hope he makes a speedy recovery, and you can get back to the grind soon.

Very truly yours,
Joan

Ian sank his head into the pillow on the bed. With five thousand miles separating him from home and no solutions, his career seemed to be crumbling by the day. Perhaps even worse, José would face prosecution now. Would the motion have been successful if he had argued it instead of Jarvis? His clients were suffering, that much was clear.

He should go back now to plead for his job. Apologize. Throw himself at the mercy of the system. But he just couldn't bring himself to do it. Was the reason rank pride?

He searched his heart and was struck with a moment of clarity.

No, it wasn't pride, he decided. An apology would give the wrong message about what he had felt compelled to do. Instead, he would write a letter to the men he'd harmed in defense of the innocent and let them know unequivocally that what *they* did was wrong. It was the only option he could live with. He would make it clear that he held no ill-will and desired peaceful relations. He would point them to the same love of God that he had recently found. If this didn't satisfy the partners at the firm, then so be it.

What about the disciplinary charges now pending against him in the Bar Court? This problem weighed more heavily. To be unemployed created one level of concern, but to be disbarred would dismantle his ability to work as an attorney anywhere. He could hire someone to appear on his behalf to get a short continuance until he made it back. But when would that be? The commitment to help his grandfather dominated his time and attention. Bailing on the work here was out of the question.

Finances loomed as another impending problem. A room at the Shelbourne ran $375 a night. He couldn't hold on much longer at that rate. And the farmhouse was too far out from Dublin and the help he needed from the still fragile relationship he'd forged with Professor O'Rourke.

The meeting had gone remarkably well with the professor. She'd agreed to help at no cost. The cause for her change remained a mystery, but a marked transition in her countenance emerged when she translated the words on the satchel. With a distant gaze in her eyes, she'd kept repeating, "There's no way you could have known about those words." She left him in the dark, however, as to what she'd meant. The mysterious phrase about *the glory of kings to search out a matter* obviously conveyed some great significance for her. To find out more would top his to-do list.

Ian turned on the television and watched the weather report on the local news. Cloudy and a high of 16 °C, 61 °F, chance of rain. Nothing new.

As he flipped the channel and a commercial for a London law firm filled the screen, an idea snapped in his head that might ameliorate his financial situation. His dual Irish-American citizenship would allow him to work. Perhaps he could qualify for an inter-jurisdictional law license that would afford him the opportunity to practice as a solicitor or a barrister. In the morning, he would make an inquiry into the application process now that it looked as though he would be staying in Ireland for the foreseeable future.

He would also keep a keen eye open for figures shifting into the shadows.

CROWDS ALREADY FILLED GRAFTON STREET BY MID-FRIDAY morning. Thick pale grey clouds hung in the sky with no indication of the sun trying to poke its way through.

Saorla headed past the shops, the windows no longer instruments of self-destruction. She'd made it past her birthday, and the black dog of depression had been chained up if not euthanized. Even better, she started this side of thirty with a new mission: to pursue the admonition *to search it out*. For the first time in a long time, a sense of adventure swept over her. Where would the road lead? She'd be a fool not to explore it.

Maybe it would all come to an end, leaving her at the exact same place where she started on the night of her anniversary: that God was either non-existent or, worse, an unconcerned being she could label *The Cosmos* for lack of a better name. But for now, anyway, she was leaving her uneasy status quo from the past and heading out on a new road, searching.

Like a hobbit on a quest.

A new road and a new mission required music, so she listened to Irish folk pumping through her headphones as she walked. Her favorite growing up in the hills in County Donegal in far western Ireland, folk music of all kinds where the Irish language spoken as a first tongue told a story, and it reminded her of riding horses with her father through the glens and fishing and swimming the streams.

Oh, how she missed her mother too. No parent had ever read more books to a child. Saorla could still hear her kind voice, "O dear, one more time for this story and then we shall go on to ride the wind of another tale."

"Thank you, Mommy. And then we can read them all again tomorrow, yes?"

"Yes, dear," she said as she swallowed Saorla in her warm arms.

Saorla snapped out of it and considered that the first order for the day included having pieces of Mr. Shaw's sheep leather and deer vellum tested. A lab nearby at the National Museum could run the carbon-14 analysis. The results would be ready within forty-eight hours if they weren't busy. She'd sealed the discoveries in an air-tight container when she got home. Also on her agenda for the day, she planned to lecture Mr. Shaw again about the proper steps to preserve artifacts.

As she crossed through the flowered grounds at St. Stephen's Green, a sudden and unexplainable urge to turn around grew into a sense of foreboding. She dismissed the feeling and treaded on, making her way onto Kildare Street to within a few meters of the entrance to the National Museum. She paused to wipe the cool sweat from her forehead.

The foreboding increased.

What was wrong? No explanation came.

She would have the piece of vellum tested at the lab inside. A simple matter of signing in and paying the fee. A routine business transaction.

A bus stopped along the curb in front of her. An advertisement on the side of the vehicle featured the Swiss Alps and beckoned would-be travelers to book a resort vacation.

And then the bus faded away, her memory of the Alps eclipsing her current surroundings. The same creeping notion of impending dread she'd experienced there years ago, hiking on a remote, little-used trail came on her now like a horse in full gallop. Alone and on holiday from her university studies in her early twenties, she'd hauled a thirty-pound backpack full of camping supplies and some books to pore over each evening by aid of her headlamp after a day of hiking. She'd already trekked ten miles that day. She was looking to set up camp and came to a clearing suitable for a tent.

Out of the forest, two men had surprised her, one wearing a green army coat and the other a black hoodie. High on the neck of the man with the army coat, almost at the jaw line, she could see the tattoo of a snake, striking out at the profile of a naked female body.

"Hope you don't mind if we camp with you," the green army coat said. "We're kinda lost."

They weren't saying where they were headed, though. So how could they be kinda lost?

"If you just follow this trail for another twelve miles, you'll be at a lake," she said, pointing down the trail. "It's on all the maps."

"Wouldn't be as much fun as camping here with you though, would it?" the black-hooded one asked.

The men glanced at each other and grinned.

Cold beads of sweat swam down her forehead. Moving in close enough for her to smell the whiskey on his breath, the army coat pulled out a fifth and offered it to her.

Aside from the fact that the man's lips had touched the swill, only one swig remained. It was doubtful that even a hundred proof could kill the germs from that mouth. But she had an idea.

Like any good girl from Donegal, she carried a pint of Jameson. She unfurled the pack from her shoulders, opened the pocket and retrieved the pint. She handed her whiskey to the hoodie. "I don't mind sharing," she said, "but you better save me some. I gotta pee."

"Hurry back, we're looking forward to some fun, sweetie."

She yanked her dinosaur of a tattered tent out of her pack and flung it on the ground at the feet of the two men. "Be a dear and get started setting that up for me."

She grabbed her pack in one swoop, swung it over her shoulder, and headed into the forest. The instant she gained the cover of the foliage she began sprinting and didn't stop for another five miles. Exhausted and unable to get another breath, she finally collapsed. Tall grass off the trail beckoned and she fell into it, panting into the dusk before gathering the strength to climb into her sleeping bag and pray to the saints for a rainless and snowless night.

The Alps on the side of the bus now moved across Saorla's path of vision. The vehicle rumbled from the curb and spewed black smoke in Saorla's direction. No way would she go inside the National Museum today. The same sense of foreboding she'd had in the Alps hovered over her. Even though it couldn't be explained, it had saved her once. She's made it through that night on the mountain unmolested. It was worth harkening that same feeling again, and if she were honest, she'd felt it on the day Stuart had died, just moments before it all came down.

Taking the four blocks back to Trinity College at brisk pace, Saorla arrived at her office. She had a class to teach in half an hour, and then the sample would be tested at a different lab, one that didn't remind her of whiskey in the Alps.

CHAPTER FIFTEEN

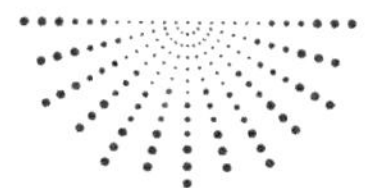

Lorcan Duihbur leaned over the desk in his plush office on the top floor of the Leinster House and glared at his chief of security, Hogan Kirby. "It is imperative that nothing can be traced to the museum. Tell the others that any lapse in our protocols will be punished severely. Do you understand?"

Kirby nodded his thick skull. The hammer-shaped scar in the center of his forehead bobbed. "Have I ever let you down?"

Lorcan froze the powerfully built Kirby with another glare. "You know what it would mean if you did."

"Yes."

We're getting close to victory—important things are about to be uncovered. We will take control of that prophecy and snuff it out of existence. No errors can be tolerated."

The private office line rang. The call was expected. He picked up and heard the voice of his appraiser. "I've got that buyer from the Netherlands with me. The one interested in your stash from the midlands dig and anything else you want to add from your reserves from your time at the museum."

"Excellent," Lorcan said.

"But there is a problem with the price of one of the items you signed off on. Listen, we're here now. A half hour ahead of our scheduled meeting, I know. But can we come on up to your office now?"

Lorcan indicated that they could, and a few minutes later, the appraiser along with the buyer walked through the door. The appraiser introduced the man with him as Hue Kendricks, but Lorcan already knew who he was. His real name was Asim Nassar, and he lived in Turkey, not the Netherlands.

"There must be some mistake about the price of the scroll," the appraiser said to Lorcan. "You signed off on a figure that is just about one-third of the fair market value."

"Wait outside for a moment, please," Lorcan said to the appraiser. "Give me a moment alone with Mr. Kendricks and leave the scroll with him."

The appraiser handed the scroll to Asim and left, shutting the door behind him. Kirby sat in a chair in the corner of the room.

Lorcan pointed to the fire blazing in the hearth built into his office wall. "Do you want to do the honors, Asim?"

"My pleasure, Mr. Duihbur.

Asim walked toward the fire, gripping the scroll. He tossed it into the flames.

Lorcan grinned. "If we keep this pace, friend, the legacy of Saint Patrick will barely be a memory for the next generation. All they will know is another holiday for drinking."

Asim nodded as he watched the flames consume the last of the scroll. "One day, you'll be honored for your work, Mr. Duihbur, and thanked for purging this island of Christian superstition."

"You have likewise made great progress in your sphere," Lorcan said.

Asim nodded. "We fight the same enemy."

"My people will be in touch," Lorcan said.

Lorcan ended the visit by showing Asim to the door. Lorcan could share his desire to please the Goddess with only a select few. He discounted Asim as one of those. But the organization Asim represented, the Art of Death, Lorcan considered an ally in the fight. As the old saying went, *the enemy of my enemy is my friend.*

Lorcan turned to Kirby. "The day is off to a good start. But I've no time to waste going forward."

"Except for our chess move for the day?"

"Yes, of course, but even that teaches useful lessons about mental determination and artifice."

He thought about how in his years as curator, he'd siphoned nearly sixteen million euros into his account from selling artifacts on the black market, many of the items of great significance to the Christian religion. His last project while still at the museum involved the excavation of a site in County Offaly in the Irish midland. Two reports from his men at the dig site waited unread. He hoped they would continue his good fortune. That is, if his men could make the rarest Christian relics disappear from the dig.

Lorcan turned to Kirby. "I want you to continue to keep a close eye on the American Shaw and the professor he's working with. We'll step in if they stumble onto something big."

Lorcan slid a partially played chess board across his desk toward Kirby. "Your move." They always had a game in progress, and each was allowed no more than one play a day.

Kirby looked over the board. He'd had twenty-four hours to prepare, same as Lorcan. Several minutes ticked off before he moved a knight. He kept his finger on it for thirty seconds and released it.

Lorcan moved his queen into position. "Checkmate."

"Bloody game!" Kirby cursed, spraying spittle.

Lorcan chuckled. "You could have declared checkmate three days ago. When you fail to seize opportunities, don't be surprised when it costs you. Now, if you'll excuse me, I have a Samhain to prepare for."

Kirby grunted and rose from his chair at an impressive speed for a man so large, and in another instant, he was almost out the door.

"Remember, if there is anything out of the ordinary with the American or the professor, you will alert me immediately."

Kirby nodded and left.

Lorcan placed his hands behind his head and leaned back in his chair, thinking about his red-head from last night. Educated, sophisticated, ambitious, she was at least compatible, but she lacked magic.

Ultimately, he would need a queen worthy of sharing a throne of behind-the-scenes power. She would have to be a goddess.

SAORLA MET MYRNA AFTER CLASS, AND THE TWO TOOK A bus to University College Dublin, a Catholic university founded in the 1800s to provide an alternative to the Protestantism of Trinity College, that housed a well-respected science lab. From a bundle of money Ian insisted on giving her for expenses, Saorla handed the cashier five-hundred euros as payment for the carbon 14 testing. The assistant at the desk said it would take a couple of business days to run, and they would be in contact as soon as they finished. Unlike at the museum on Kildare, Saorla didn't experience cold sweating, nor did any more images of the Alps pop into her head.

After they arrived back at Trinity College, Saorla busied herself in her office, preparing for her Monday lecture. A light knock at the door interrupted. In walked the handsome attorney from America, holding a large piece of stone and smiling, revealing perfect teeth that shone milky white juxtaposed to his strong, tanned jaw.

"Hi. Sorry I'm late. I know I said last night that I was going to stop by early afternoon."

Saorla remembered herself and glanced at the wall clock. Almost 4:30. "What's your excuse?"

"You sound like a teacher."

"Uhm. Professor."

"I detoured over to the legal aid clinic downtown on O'Connell Street. They do mostly *pro bono* work. Help the poor."

Saorla grinned. "Now you're into poverty law?"

"Part-time work will help me stay afloat. The pay, of course, isn't good. But they're not picky about who they hire as long as they have the minimum legal credentials."

"What about your position at your law firm in California?"

"I ... uh ... have some time off. But the clock is running. Roughly three weeks left. Better if I get back sooner, though, but there's no way I can break the promise to my grandfather."

"How's he doing?"

"Still alive. Sleeping a lot, Nana says. Thanks for asking."

With two hands, Ian hoisted the stone he had tucked under his arm. "I was going to show you this last night, but it was getting late."

The American placed the stone on her desk. She rose to her feet to get a better look. It appeared to be half of a piece split in two, an oval shaped monument if intact. A grave marker most likely. She ran her fingers over the simple lines etched into the stone. Simply amazing. "This is Ogham script."

"Huh?"

"A cumbersome written language, a forerunner to early Irish, common on monuments and grave markings. It was used in the third, fourth, and fifth centuries."

"Is there a way to know how old it is exactly?"

"We can't test the stone itself to find a date for the writing, of course. Unlike the deer vellum, it's not something that has been alive like a plant or an animal, which decays with a half-life for radiocarbon-dating purposes. But the writing on the stone—the Ogham script—that speaks for itself. It's obviously old."

The American had a puzzled look. "Those lines mean something more than a number or a quantity?"

"Sure. Think of it as prehistoric language. The lines carved at different angles can be translated into actual words. Actually, the written language on this island moved from Ogham script to Latin after the coming of Patrick and the Christianization of the island, and then, by the middle of the eighth century, the native oral Irish had become a written language too. From then on, the Irish language predominated as the written medium of thought and expression. Homilies, devotionals, and books on the saints by the ninth century were all being written in a form of old Irish. Basically, Ogham was not used much after the end of the fourth century, perhaps into the middle of the fifth century at the latest."

The American continued to look confused. He shook his head

slightly.

"Is everything keen?" Saorla asked.

"Yeah, I was just thinking what a great witness you would make in a courtroom, if you ever had to testify."

She felt herself blush, and it irritated her. "I'm not clear what that has to do—"

"Can you decipher what the lines mean?"

"Of course. They form just two words."

"Seems like a lot of effort for two words."

"The first set of lines is the word 'take.'" She pointed at a grouping of several slanted lines. And pointing again at the other grouping, she said, "The second word is the article 'the.' So it merely says, 'Take the.' As you can see, the monument itself appears to have been broken in half. Likely split over the centuries or perhaps on removal."

"I dug it up with a shovel, not hard enough to break the stone. I couldn't find the other piece to it. A deluge hit, and I had no time to explore further. Then I was in a hurry to get this half looked at."

"No need to be defensive."

"I'm not defensive."

"I didn't mean to imply you did anything wrong."

He shrugged his shoulders. "You think there's more to the writing?"

"Those two words by themselves don't seem to make much sense. Like I said, it's a difficult way to communicate but not entirely unsuited for the purpose it was used—for example, as a brief message on a monument. Ogham is probably how the monks who created the Book of Kells came up with the idea for carving the large letters that formed the initial capitals that start the first sentence on each page of the book."

"I saw the Book of Kells many years ago with my grandmother. I was in grammar school. We waited in a long line. I don't remember much about it, except it's a ceremonial book."

"The four gospels," Saorla said. "Used for special liturgical services in the early Irish church."

"What language is it written in?"

"Latin, around the year 800 AD, and the reason you had to wait in line is because it's considered the most beautiful ancient manuscript in the world. A priceless piece of history and art, the nation's greatest treasure, and on a short list of the most splendid relics in the western world. The stunning full-page miniatures of Christ on his throne and the portraits representing the gospels and its writers in symbols caused some to say it was the work of angels and not of men. You really should take some time to learn the history of your forefathers, Mr. Shaw."

"Please call me Ian. When you call me Mr. Shaw, I feel like I'm one of your slacker students you're scolding after class."

"How do you know I don't think you're a slacker?" She said, as she felt a grin creasing her lips.

Ian chuckled. "Because I can see right through you. And a slacker wouldn't be so persistent in getting your attention, would he? Besides my fellow attorneys at my firm would get a kick out of you calling me a slacker."

"Okay, so maybe you're a stalker, not a slacker."

"Like I said I can see right through you."

"You don't know anything about me."

"I know you love a good challenge, but something caused you to irrationally decline this one at first."

Time to change the subject. She studied the stone and noticed a spot in the lower right corner. A layer of grit half covered a faint symbol. She brushed it with her finger. Roman armor? A shield and breastplate?

"Did you notice this in the corner?" She inspected it closer. "It looks like some sort of a symbol."

The American stood next to her, nearly a foot taller, while they examined the stone. He smelled clean like soap with an evergreen scent. A long sleeved, tin-cup grey shirt clung to the contours of his strong, toned shoulders. "Wow. I had brushed it off as best I could, but I didn't want to damage anything in the process."

"Your instincts were right."

"What's the next step?"

"I'd like to take the vellum from the satchel to a lab in Belfast for some additional testing. Also have them examine the monument and see if they can restore it, sans grit. Of course, we need to find the other half."

"Consider this an official invite to my grandparents' farm. We can take the items to Belfast and then swing down to the Antrim Hills where they live."

The room was suddenly too warm, and the conversation came to a pause.

"Yes, it has to be done," she finally said, looking down at her shoes, avoiding those blue, blue eyes of his.

"Do you want to grab a sandwich, take it outside?" he asked. "I haven't eaten all day, and the sun is making a rare appearance."

Saorla looked out the window and confirmed the accuracy of the weather update. "I haven't eaten either. I had to run that sample over to the lab today."

"So is that a yes?"

"It's not a no."

"I'll take that as a yes."

"If I say no, are you going to show up at the next party with all my friends?"

IAN WAS INDEED HUNGRY. SAORLA ADVISED THAT THE quickest option was to get a sandwich at the Arts Cafe just outside the building. They both ordered a chicken sandwich, with bacon and sage stuffing, and a couple of bottled waters to go.

Saorla carried the food bag and led him to the back of the campus, to a place called College Park.

"Sometimes I like to come here and sit by the football field. You'd call it a soccer field in the States."

"I know what you meant."

"I like to watch them play, to see how they react so instinctively. That's a form of intelligence I admire."

They sat on a bench overlooking the field. Leaves on aged trees glistened a golden carnelian in the autumnal sun, while a soccer scrimmage raged in progress. As they ate their sandwiches, Ian critiqued the play on the field.

Munching her last bite, Saorla said, "Sounds like you know a lot about the sport?"

"I used to play," Ian answered, his words slow and measured. "It was a big part of my life, but it caused a lot of friction between my dad and me."

"How did that happen?"

"I gave it up. The last time I played was the state championship game in high school. Scored three goals in the first half and decided that was it. I left the field at halftime. Never played another minute. Looking back, I see it was my way of getting back at my dad."

The professor frowned then raised an eyebrow. "Are you some kind of lunatic?"

"Why do you ask that?"

"I'm just wondering why anyone with that kind of talent would quit."

"Besides the thing with my father, I found the sport too boring to devote all my time. There are other things I like more."

"Such as?"

"If I tell you, you'll really think I'm a lunatic."

"Try me."

"Okay. Adventure sports of all kinds—mountain climbing, cliff jumping, paragliding. I love surfing the best. Check that. I'm not sure you could call what I did last weekend surfing. You ever hear of Mavericks?"

"Isn't that an American cowboy show?"

Ian chuckled. "Well, it's kinda like what the bull riding cowboys do. It's actually a location in the Pacific off the northern coast of California that produces huge waves. Last weekend I hooked up with a fifty-foot bull ride that almost killed me."

Ian realized he sounded way too enthusiastic about the prospect of his own death. He searched the professor's face for a reaction. She didn't seem turned off. "A friend of mine hooked into the same wave. The paramedics were able to revive him. Thank God, and I say that sincerely because I was sure praying that he would make it."

Saorla shook her head. They both chose silence for a moment.

"You said—"

"Tell me—"

"I win," the professor said. "My question started first."

Ian nodded.

"What did your father do that was so terrible that you quit football?"

Ian wasn't sure he wanted to air his family's dirt, but he decided to be honest with her. "My dad's a professional soccer coach in the States. He was a former pro player too with the New York Cosmos but was born and raised in Ireland."

"Wait a minute. You're dad's Rory Shaw?"

"Guilty as charged."

"Incredible. He's a legend here. Everyone knows of him!"

Ian nodded. "He and my mom split up when I was in high school just before that championship game. My father stayed in New York, my mother left for Oregon, and I came to Ireland for a while. I quit soccer to make a statement because that was the one thing he cared about the most. When I came back to the States, I ended up in Colorado for college where I learned to climb mountains. During the summers, I stayed on the West Coast where I learned to surf."

"And then you went to law school?"

"Enough about me. It's my turn to ask something."

Ian looked at her hand and didn't see a wedding or engagement ring. Did she have someone special in her life? "Do you have family in the area?"

Ian watched the color drain from her face. Likely, she knew just where his line of questioning headed. That's the way it was with geniuses. They were hard to cross examine even if you were subtle about it.

She hurriedly gathered the water bottles and sandwich wrappers. "It's time for me to go."

CHAPTER SIXTEEN

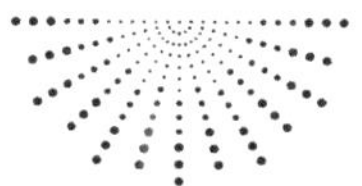

Lorcan rode in the back seat of his Mercedes down Lower Leeson Street when the call came on his cell.

"Hello, Mr. Duihbur," said Torna Mag Vidhir, second in command of his security staff behind Hogan Kirby.

"Where's Kirby?"

"Had to tie up some lose ends. Left me in charge. I've something you might find important."

"What?"

"The professor did not bring her item in for testing at our lab at the National Museum where we had a bad accident planned for her. We followed her to the outside, she looked like she would enter, but then left without coming in."

Lorcan cursed.

"You will like this, though. We managed to get a spy in at the lab at University College, and we have the test results."

"This soon?"

"Yeah, and the item dated to the mid-fifth century. It's legitimate."

Lorcan felt a rush. A big pay day was coming. "Contact Kirby and have him call me, *now*. Pass the word on to our man on the ground at the lab that the results must disappear at once without any report back to the professor. I want her and the American placed under electronic surveillance, with someone monitoring their activities at all times. No more private spaces for them. And, of course, continue to have them followed. Report back regularly."

Lorcan hung up the phone and ordered his driver to take him by the cigar shop.

"Good news, Mr. Duihbur?"

"Yes, Max, it looks like our two treasure hunters are on to something hot, even if they don't know it. And I, of course, will be there to take it off their hands."

Early on Saturday morning, Sophie arrived with her cleaning gear. Saorla welcomed her with a hug, and then they sat at the table, drinking tea and eating American blueberry muffins.

Saorla told her about the meeting with the American attorney and the mysterious satchel engraved with Sophie's words about it being the glory of kings to search out a matter.

Sophie's sky-blue eyes glistened. "This makes me so encouraged. It was prophecy then. I am now learning so much."

"Thank you for caring and the courage it took to share. I've been better since you showed such concern for me."

"I will keep praying. God has special plans for you."

"God or the cosmos," Saorla muttered.

"What is cosmo?"

"Oh, nothing, really. I want to believe the best days are ahead, but it's still a struggle." Saorla took a sip of tea, wanting, needing to change the subject. "So, tell me, how was your week?"

"I am cleaning at Phoenix Park mansion where the high king lives. I have been only in this country short time, but now I am specially invited to lunch with king and his wife. Not because he is interested in how I see this country through fresh eyes. But because he make many tries for an affair ... he wants more than cleaning from me. And

I am also to invite male guest to keep his wife from having suspicions."

Saorla shook her head. "That must be awful. You should quit, and there's got to be a way to expose him for what he is doing."

"I am told by one of my Polish friends that he could have me deported if I complain, and I need the money."

"We can find you something else. I don't think he can deport you. Let me make some calls."

"No, I will be fine. I have my boyfriend to help me."

Saorla studied Sophie, whose face imbued nothing but calm confidence. "I didn't even know you had a boyfriend."

Sophie blushed. "I have special friend at church. His name is Killian. I never meet anyone like this man. From him I learn so much about following God and how to love people. But he is older."

"What's the age difference?

"I am twenty-eight, and he thirty-nine."

"That's not bad, and I'm speaking from experience. Stuart was ten years older."

"Really," Sophie said, looking relieved.

"What's Killian like?"

"His parents were missionaries in Bolivia. He coach tennis and is businessman and investor. He prays so much, always praying and very kind."

The cell phone on the kitchen table buzzed. "I was able to sublet my apartment last night," said Myrna, sounding anxious. "The problem is they want to move in tomorrow."

Saorla didn't expect to have her space invaded this soon, but Myrna needed financial help. It was either now or never. "I'll be out all day, but I'll leave the back door open. You can move your stuff over whenever you like."

"Thanks. I don't have much. See you tonight."

Saorla ended the call, and then the doorbell rang and the door knocker on her Georgian clanked a couple times.

"Oh rats, I forgot to tell him about the change in plans," Saorla said.

"Who?" Sophie asked.

"The American, Mr. Shaw. I made plans with him yesterday to go to Belfast and then to his grandparents' house where the artifacts were discovered. But that was before I spoke to Dr. Greenwald last night."

Saorla opened the door and let Ian Shaw inside. They stood in the hallway, his blue, blue eyes sparkling, his smile a halogen spotlight. "You're prompt. Listen, Mr. Shaw, I mean Ian, the plans—"

"Beautiful morning. We've got a great day to travel—."

"—I'm sorry I forgot to let you know. There's been a change in plans."

"Change?"

"Look, I should have texted you. I got busy on some things, and all of sudden, it was morning."

He chuckled. "Oh, I get it. You're the absent-minded professor type."

"Like I said, you don't even know me."

"Right. So what's up?"

"Why don't you come to the kitchen, have a muffin, and I can explain? You can also meet a friend."

She sensed his eyes on her as he followed her to the kitchen. Saorla introduced him to Sophie and invited him to sit, which he did.

She poured him a cup of tea and slid it in front of him. "Last night I arranged a meeting with a Dr. Martin Greenwald. He's a retired professor who has an unusual theory about the Book of Kells and its connection to a mysterious message about the future of Ireland. He's leaving the country shortly and could only meet with me today. So, as I said, there's been a change of plans."

"A message for the future, like a prophecy?" Ian asked.

"I'm not sure, but his theory sounded so similar to what you told me of your grandfather's musings and dreams about artifacts."

"Is the similarity that they both see a spiritual awakening for Ireland?"

"That's doubtful, but it's one of the things I can rule out only after we visit."

"When do we leave?"

"We? I was planning on doing this myself."

"Are you kidding? I wouldn't miss this for all the fresh powder on Snow King."

Saorla's head tilted. She'd rather go alone for a number of reasons but could see that it wouldn't be easy to explain to him. "Is that American slang for 'there's no talking me out of it?'"

Ian laughed. "I'm tempted to say you hardly know me. Tell me more about this theory."

"Years ago, Dr. Greenwald claimed to have come across a writing or a book, which of the two is a wee unclear to me. But the information he found dates to the seventeenth century and even earlier. It details the McCoyne family and their connection to the Book of Kells.

"McCoyne Family?"

"There was a time, many centuries ago, before the book came to Trinity, when it was kept by a single family devoted to preserving it. Greenwald believes the McCoynes found a code hidden within the Book of Kells. According to him, the code leads ultimately to a message about the future of Ireland that is simply fantastic."

"How long has he known this? Has he written about it?"

"He's not written about it but has been working on it for years. Last night's email said he'd just had a major breakthrough in his research. Didn't say what it was, but that it was the most extraordinary thing he'd seen in his career. He wants to meet me at his place on the coast after lunch and explain. I tried to pump him for more information, but he didn't want to talk about it over the phone."

"So where are we going?"

"Wexford."

"I hope that's in Ireland."

Saorla laughed. "You are a hopeless Yank. We have a two-hour train ride down the coast."

CHAPTER SEVENTEEN

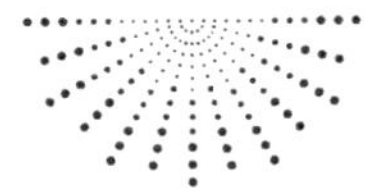

Sophie dropped Saorla and Ian at the O'Connell Street station, where the two boarded a crowded train bound for Wexford. Saorla rebuffed Ian's attempts at conversation during the ride south, claiming she had research to do for an article she hoped to publish.

The train arrived in Wexford about 2 p.m. There, they hailed a cab to 2257E Gorse Street, the home of Professor Martin Greenwald. Located just north of the town upon a cliff overlooking the Irish Sea, it was an impressive property. The rush of sea tide moving in greeted Saorla as she walked to the front door. Not bad for a retired academic on a pension. As prime coastal real estate, it could easily carry a two-million-euro price tag.

For the last ten minutes, she'd been trying to call the professor to let him know that they'd arrived. No answer. With Ian at her side, she stepped onto the welcome mat and looked at a plaque in the brick exterior next to the door. *Welcome to Greenwald's World.*

She rang the bell. "Dr. Greenwald, we're here." Another ring.

Silence.

All we can do is wait," she said. "Perhaps he's indisposed.

"Maybe he's out surfing the waves."

"He just turned eighty."

"Maybe he's in good shape."

"Are all Americans like this or just surfers from California?"

"Just surfers from California."

Saorla wandered around the outside of the house and across the backyard with Ian following. They stopped at the edge of a cliff. The sea below sparkled an emerald-hue.

"So what do you like to do for fun?" Ian asked.

The question hit her hard. The loneliness of the past months flooded her mind. "I, uh, I guess I haven't had fun … for a while." When was the last time she'd gone shopping or hiking or even home to see Papa? She couldn't even remember.

Ian's eyes, tender and kind, peered into hers. "Do you want to tell me about it?"

"About what?"

"Look, I saw the wedding picture on the mantle in your house. I might have guessed anyway. Beautiful Georgian home. Not easy to afford on a young professor's salary. *Two* expensive cars out front. But you aren't wearing a wedding ring? Divorce?"

"If you get tired of being a barrister, you can always work at Scotland Yard, Sherlock." A tear threatened the corner of her eye, and she lashed out at him. "You should mind your own business."

"I'm not trying to pry. If we're going to work together, we should get to know each other a little. I shared a little of the pain over the relationship with my dad, didn't I?"

"You don't know…"

"True. Why don't we start? Tell me what happened. How long were you married?"

She had to talk about it, needed to air it out, and honestly, maybe it would be best done with a relative stranger like Ian Shaw.

But could she?

She hadn't been able to open up to anyone—not her Papa, not her friends, not her colleagues. And she flat out refused to see a professional psychiatrist. They'd probably just prescribe some stupid pills like the last ones that had almost killed her. And every time she made an appointment, she always ended up canceling it. She didn't even know why. Shame, fear, pride? Who knew? The Cosmos denied her an answer.

The topics Ian talked about at the edge of this small cliff increased its emotional height. She felt like she was walking along the Cliffs of Moher with a thousand feet of air to the rocky shoreline below. Exhausted from holding it all in for so long, she decided to see what lurked over the emotional ledge.

She pulled out her wedding ring from her pocket and looked down at it. "I don't wear it because I don't feel worthy. I met Stuart when I was a graduate student at Oxford. He was a visiting lecturer, and I was in one of his classes. We fell in love and had to be together. We both came to Trinity College. He took a position on faculty, and I finished a PHD."

Saorla put the ring back in her pocket and lifted her head. She'd expelled some of the basic facts between calming breaths, but the feelings remained locked below the surface. Ian held her eyes with his. "He must have been very special."

"It's ..." The words died in her throat as she tried to speak. Looking down, she tried again. "It's been over two years since he ... passed away. Sometimes I think I see him walking out of what used to be his office. Or I imagine that he's going to be standing outside a certain restaurant on Grafton Street, waiting for me. And sometimes I dream at night ... The dreams are so real. He's hurt, and I can't get him to be better."

The tear crawled down her cheek, and she ran her finger over it. Ian placed a hand on her shoulder. It felt comforting, secure, strong. "I'm so sorry. No one should have to go through something like that."

"I feel like his death was my fault."

"Your fault?"

She looked away, then took out a handkerchief and wiped her eyes. "The sun's getting lower. We need to find Professor Greenwald."

Ian's eyes fixed her in her tracks. "Death hurts so much because it was never meant to be. In the garden, in the beginning, the human race chose wrong, and death entered into the equation. But that was never God's desire."

Could that be right? She was familiar with the theology of original sin, and Saint Patrick certainly would have agreed with Ian's take. But Ian's words were so simple and down to earth they caught her off guard. It couldn't have been a *good* God's prime intent to create something that hurt so much, provided he was indeed good. "We should try knocking again."

"I really want to hear your story."

"Maybe later."

They walked back to the front, and this time, Saorla grasped the ornate doorknocker, clacking it. The door creaked open. Saorla exchanged a concerned glance with Ian, and they crossed the threshold into the home, and began calling for the professor.

Still no answer.

"Why would he leave his door open but not greet us?" Saorla turned toward a hallway.

He knew I was coming.

Saorla moved through the hallway into the main living area. Items littered the hardwood floor, every drawer hung ajar. A ransacked mess. Her heart pounded, and her stomach curdled. She inched one way through the house and Ian the other.

She stumbled over items scattered on the floor. Amidst the chaos, her eyes registered an eight-by-eleven paper drawing of a Celtic cross and an ancient Roman breastplate, shield, and sword.

"Did you find him?" Ian shouted from the other side of the house. "I'm in the kitchen."

"I think you should get over here," she muttered as she proceeded on through the house and then shoved open a door of what appeared to be the professor's study. A desk with a computer on it, screen lit, chair empty.

Down on the floor. Spilled liquid.

Red Wine? No.

A pool of blood. Shivers spread down her neck to her spine. She howled a guttural scream.

IAN RAN TO HER AND FOUND HER IN THE STUDY MOVING toward the body on the floor. A grey-headed man, it had to be the retired professor. A knife protruded from the old man's neck, probably hit a carotid artery, causing him to bleed out.

Ian bridged the space to Saorla and held her, shielding her eyes from the gore. They'd been outside of the house for at least fifteen minutes, waiting and talking. He'd been bleeding at least that long.

Ian ushered Saorla away from the blood, briefly retracing her steps. He told her not to touch anything, dialed 999, and reported what he saw.

Saorla rubbed her head into Ian's chest, while his eyes swept the scene.

"Whoever did this was looking for something," he said to Saorla as he stroked her hair that matted near his chest, "and I pray it has nothing to do with us."

SAORLA SAT ON DR. GREENWALD'S FRONT PORCH STOOP WITH her hands wrapped around her knees and her head buried beneath her arms. How would she ever erase from her memory what she'd just seen? She wanted to erase so many things. Erase the sight of her dead colleague. Erase the horrific amount of blood. Why was there so much of it?

Then warm hands cradled her face. The American.

"You're cold and clammy. Probably shock. I'll get a pillow so you can lay down."

"I'm okay," she lied, but he had already disappeared. A wave of nausea washed over her.

She resumed her near fetal position but then heard vehicles screeching up to the curb. The Gardai—the police force of the Republic of Ireland—had arrived with their lights flashing. An ambulance with paramedics pulled up seconds later.

The first Garda out of the vehicle began barking orders. More officers arrived with each passing moment. As Saorla hauled herself to her feet, the yard swirled and she nearly fainted. Ian returned with a pillow and steadied her.

A Garda approached. "Madam, I'm Garda John Brennan. May I have your name?"

"O'Rourke, Saorla O'Rourke."

He turned to Ian. "And you, sir, are the one that called us?"

"Yes, I'm Ian Shaw."

A flurry of Gardai passed them, entering the home with the paramedics.

"Stay here."

Brennan went inside for a moment and then returned with another Garda. "Jack, we need to get Ms. O'Rourke off her feet. I'll take her to the car. You interview Mr. Shaw."

Saorla hobbled to the squad car with the aid of Garda Brennan and took a seat in the back.

"Can you tell us who found the body?"

"We did ... I mean, I saw him first."

Brennan recorded her answer on his notepad.

"How well did you know the deceased?"

"Not well, professional basis."

"What was your business for coming to his home?"

Her vision clouded. She tried to focus by staring at the back of the seat in front of her. "We spoke on the phone last night to set up a meeting."

"About what?"

"Research he was doing in Irish history."

"Will your phone records show that you spoke last night?"

Where were these questions going? A murderer was on the loose out there.

"You don't think I had something to do with this."

"Calm down, madam. These are routine questions I have to ask. Are you positive the phone records will show you spoke?"

"Yes, of course, and we emailed too. I'm a professor at Trinity in Dublin. Dr. Greenwald is a retired professor."

Garda Brennan scribbled on his pad. "For approximately how many minutes did you speak?"

"I don't know. I don't see the point. A couple of minutes maybe. He seemed in a hurry.

Said he had something he wanted to show me."

"And what was that?"

"Unclear."

"You came all this way, you can't say why?"

"Academic curiosity."

"Do you know of any reason why someone would want the professor dead?"

"No."

Brennan rubbed his mustache. "Maybe an intellectual conflict? A philosophical difference of opinion?"

Saorla regained her full vision. She stared impassively at the Garda and waited.

The Garda blinked first. "I've seen people killed for less. I've got to ask the questions. Is there anything else you can tell me?"

"I considered him a colleague even though he was retired. We were on friendly terms, but I didn't know him well. I'm sorry I don't have more for you."

"I'm done with the questions for now." He handed her a pen and paper. "Write down your phone number and address. You're free to go … we'll be in touch."

Furious over learning how Dr. Greenwald had been killed, Lorcan arranged a meeting of the inner circle of his security staff for late Saturday night. Seated around Lorcan's office desk were Hogan Kirby and Torna Mag Vidhir, along with a half dozen others of his staff.

"Idiots," Lorcan screamed, "you knew I sequester and interrogate for information first. Abduct, question, torture if necessary, silence them, and hide the body. The usual protocol. Why are such simple instructions so difficult?"

"Can I explain?" Hogan asked.

"I don't want to hear it from you. Who screwed up?"

Torna slowly raised his hand. "It was me. I can ex—"

"—It better be good."

"The old bat was deleting information from the computer. No question about it. I yelled to stop, but he kept hitting buttons."

"Your brilliant idea was to kill him on the spot?"

"No. It was just a reaction. I used to be better with a knife..."

"*Used to* is an old man's excuse, chap," one of the men around the table quipped. A sprinkling of laughter swept the room.

Torna's face reddened, and he glared at the man. "Pray you never find out what I can still do." Torna turned to Lorcan. "When I flung the knife across the room, I intended to hit him in the shoulder blade to stop his typing motion. My aim was off, I plucked him in the neck instead."

Lorcan couldn't help but smile at the comedy those words presented. "And the blood gushed."

Silence draped the air for a moment.

"What happened after that?" Lorcan finally asked.

"We recovered the computer," Torna said. "I think what we need is on there."

"Sir, if I may?" Hogan Kirby interjected.

"So long as your *may* doesn't include more mistakes." Lorcan nodded.

"We've downloaded the contents of Greenwald's laptop, which we left at the scene. Our tech boys have the items he recently deleted. And there is one thing in particular you've got to see. It's some sort of symbol—a cross, shield, sword ... appears over and over in the recovered documents."

CHAPTER EIGHTEEN

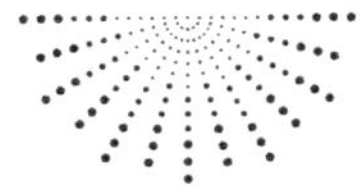

Back in Dublin late Saturday evening, Ian tried his best to comfort Saorla, who still reeled from the gruesome events of the afternoon. Too frightened to return to her home at the moment, she walked with him down the streets of Temple Bar, and Ian hoped her nerves would calm enough for her to get some rest eventually.

They passed one noisy pub after another. Revelers swaggered arm and arm down the cobbled-stone walkways. A street band played a U-2 hit. Try as he might, Ian couldn't shake the feeling that they faced serious danger. Someone murdered the retired professor. And maybe that someone didn't want the old man talking, at least not to his guests who had made the trip from Dublin to Wexford for the afternoon. All the indicators—from his grandfather's accident to the missing chalice to the murder of Dr. Greenwald—suggested that someone tracked them. In a flash, it came to him that their private spaces may have been bugged.

"Can we stop by your office to … uh … investigate something?"

"What?"

"I hesitate to tell you."

"I'm a big girl."

He hated to worry her further, but he saw little choice. "All right.

I need to check your office for any sign we're being watched. If everything checks out okay, then maybe I can get some sleep tonight."

"And if it doesn't check out, then what?"

"Lincoln used to say the key to crossing the Fox on horseback was to never cross that river until you got there."

Saorla nodded her understanding. They arrived in a couple of minutes, passed a security guard, and crossed the campus, dark and quiet. Their forms cast long shadows as the waxing moon parted through the gridlock of clouds.

Making their way to the third floor of the art building, they climbed a faintly-lit flight of stairs.

"Do you really think we're being watched?" Saorla whispered.

"I don't know. But if it turns out that way, you should stop helping me, and I can handle it from here."

"What are you saying?" she snapped, brow furrowed, the irritation in her voice very clear.

"I don't want to place you in harm's way."

"Who do you think you are to make that decision for me?"

"I got you into this mess. I should be the one to get you out."

"Ahh, the illogic in that. I thought you were a barrister capable of rational thought. You must know it's too late to get me out of anything. I'm all in whether I want to be or not."

Why hadn't he taken his grandfather seriously from the start? He never would have asked for Saorla's help.

God, don't let the office be bugged.

Ian waited for Saorla to unlock her office door, and then he herded her inside. He eased the door shut behind him, and they stood facing each other in the near dark, the only light filtering through the window from the campus square.

"Don't turn on the lights," he whispered in her ear. Her hair smelled like lilacs after a rain. He lingered a moment before hopping cat-like onto the top of her desk, and then rose to run a hand along the ceiling. A small, rounded object protruded from a vent, and he pulled it out. A bugging device used to record sound. He was about to place the tiny object in his pocket but thought better of it and placed it back in its position.

He flowed off the desk toward Saorla. His lips again brushed her ear. "I found something but put it back."

More lilacs, and the wisp of her breath, a peach-mandarin-tea scent. She whispered, "Okay," back at him, her lips glancing his ear.

He smothered the tug of attraction. *Stifle it in the bud. You're not ready for this.*

A relationship in normal circumstances would be enough trouble, given his job thousands of miles away and his extreme-adventure lifestyle, but it would be impossible given the threat level of this new mission and the constant state of high alert it would require.

He checked himself with a dose of reality. *There's no way she would ever fall for you anyway, dude.*

"I need to investigate one more place besides your phone and laptop."

He angled to the corner of the room and climbed on a chair to reach a vent. He removed a tiny camera and a miniature transmitting device, and then placed them back carefully.

He made his way to Saorla and took her hand, noticing its softness, before he led her out the door.

"Very high tech. Straight from my neck of the woods in Silicon Valley."

"You're joking, right?"

He shook his head. "I wish. These thugs are using expensive technology. Must be dead serious about keeping an eye on us."

She clenched her fists, her knuckles glowing white in the dimness of the hallway. "I'm not going to let—"

"—Let's get out of here."

They traversed down the stairway and into the improved lighting of the first-floor lobby. The shock on Saorla's face from the afternoon had been replaced with something that looked like resolve. It was a look he'd seen on the faces of elite surfers when they were about to catch a wave in a competition.

"Wait, won't they be able to check the recording and see you checking the camera and putting it back?"

"No, the camera is activated by light and sound. We were too quiet and it was too dark."

"It was brilliant, then, that you left the equipment there," she said. "We can lead them down lots of dead ends that way."

"I suppose," he said after a slight pause.

"We have to find out who these people are and what they want."

Ian said nothing. The change in her mood surprised him. He'd been considering calling it all off for her, making her understand that she had to think about her own safety. As for himself, he was all in no matter the cost.

"Ian, what about my home? Do we need to go there and make the same check we just did of my office?"

He nodded, rubbing his forehead. He'd dragged Saorla in this mess, and he was going to get her out of it.

Once they exited the campus gates and crossed over to Westmoreland Street, they hailed a cab to Saorla's home. During the ride, Ian brought up the photographs he'd left in her office.

"What did you think of the pictures of the chalice?"

"Well, I didn't really look at them before I threw you out of my office. Listen, I'm sorry about that ..."

"That's all right. I just thought you might have seen them there on your desk and gotten curious and taken another look at them."

"Wait, you left them on my desk? My desk was empty, and I never saw them. I thought *you* took them.

"Whoa. You're serious? I left them right on your desk hoping you would change your mind and take another look."

"Someone took them. Who?"

"We're going to figure that out. Anyone else have a key to your office?"

She shook her head. But then said, "I think the dean's office has a key."

The cab dropped them off, and they went inside the house. Saorla turned on the speakers. Irish folk music pumped out and reverberated off the walls. Their conversation would be safe now.

Myrna bounded down the stairs. "A party? You didn't tell me you're having one."

"Shhh ..." Saorla caught her in the middle of the stairs. "There's been trouble." She turned back to Ian. "Myrna just moved in with me today."

Ian walked them to the front door. "Take a stroll," he said softly. "Better tell her everything now that you have a houseguest."

The women went outside. Ian walked through the home, checking for electronic eyes and ears. He found listening devices in all the rooms, and a tiny camera was recording in the kitchen from a perch in the corner of the ceiling. This time he disabled everything. Whoever was behind this would know that they were on to them, at least as it pertained to Saorla's home, but they would need the privacy, he figured.

Before he left, he advised them to keep the doors and windows locked. "If they wanted us dead, they would have already done it. We're still alive for a reason. I intend to find out what that reason is." He added that if they saw or heard anything unusual, they should dial 999.

On the way back to his room at the Shelbourne, he planned his course of action. He would hire a private investigator to watch over the professor's Georgian at night while the women slept. Next, he'd wire his bank at home, drain the rest of his account, and open up a new account in Dublin. How long would it be before the bank foreclosed on his condo? He didn't know. California had lax foreclosure laws. Perhaps he'd be able to get caught up with the bank in the end.

There was no escaping that conserving cash would be important from here on out. Relocating himself from the pricey Shelbourne Hotel would be a high priority, even though he loved the location and comfort. A nearby hostel offered a private room at a fraction of the cost.

Back at the hotel, he checked his room thoroughly for any sign of surveillance devices. Finding nothing, he prayed for the safety of Saorla, Myrna, and his grandparents.

AFTER SHE RETIRED MYRNA FOR THE NIGHT IN THE GUEST bedroom, Saorla poured herself a glass of wine from a bottle Myrna brought as a house-warming gift. A gentle internal nudging told her not to take comfort in liquor, but she ignored the prompting. A stiff drink was the only way she was going to get some rest. Even so, it was three in the morning before she drifted off into an unsettled sleep.

CHAPTER NINETEEN

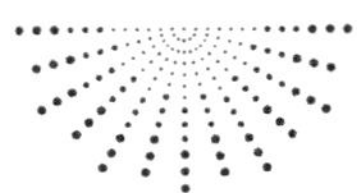

The BMW made its way down Merrion Street under a gun-metal grey sky. From his spot in the passenger seat, Ian couldn't help but notice the simple elegance of the driver. Soft white skin and perfectly matched teeth set off the professor's dark hair and peach-colored lip gloss. Her earthen-colored shirt and jacket gave her a look of comfortable ease, like she was a seamless part of nature itself, and her black leggings revealed runner's legs.

He needed to get his mind off the driver's appearance. They had a long drive ahead—first to Belfast and then to his grandparents' farm. What he really needed was to share some spiritual connection with other believers in the worship of God. They had all day and no time constraints. But he wasn't sure how Saorla would react to the idea of stopping for church.

Ian settled on a bit of an indirect approach. "Do you go to church?"

Saorla kept her hands steady on the wheel, but her eyes diverted to her lap before she got them back on the road. "I haven't been, not since ..."

"Oh, I see. I'm sorry."

"No need to apologize."

The car pulled to a stop at a traffic light. Ian admired her profile. "Are you Catholic?"

"I never missed a Mass on Sunday until I got out of high school. How about you?"

"It's a long story."

"We have a long drive," Saorla said.

Ian cleared his throat. "The short version is I've been going to an evangelical church near my condo since July."

The light turned green, and Saorla accelerated through the intersection. "Sophie, you met her yesterday. She has a church, even invited me to go."

Perfect. "Do you know what it's called? We could go."

"I don't think I want to."

"Why?"

"I'm not a real believer anymore."

"How can that be true? The Bible verse on that old satchel sure meant something to you."

Ian saw from her face that he had her on that one. "Come on, it will be an adventure."

They drove in silence for two blocks.

"It's Rivers in the Desert Church," she finally said.

Ian punched the name into his smartphone to get an address. "Great name for a church on such a green island."

They crossed the River Liffey and headed northeast, passing Croke Park, a ninety-thousand seat stadium that hosts the biggest sporting and music events in Ireland. In a couple of minutes they arrived at a rundown storefront that was the church.

"Not the best neighborhood in Dublin," Saorla said, as they got out of the car. "Lots of robberies. A woman was recently raped near a canal that runs just to the south."

"Is this Cecilia's neighborhood?"

"Uh, her name is *Sophie*, not Cecilia, and she doesn't live far from here."

Ian nodded. Sophie's name was a fact he knew. It just came out wrong when he said it. But Saorla delivered the correction like he was a kid back in grammar school, and it made him smile. If only he had had a teacher that looked like this one in the car with him now, he might have been the teacher's pet.

The church service had not yet begun when they entered the building. A Bible study of about ten people seated in a circle was in progress but winding down. The blonde polish girl Ian had met yesterday sat next to a tall man with glasses who was doing most of the talking. Ian stared at the blonde and repeated the name "Sophie" to himself to get it ingrained so that it didn't ever again come out as Cecilia.

Sophie whispered something into the ear of the tall man, who then dismissed the gathering with an invitation to read chapter eight of Romans for next week's study.

Sophie, smiling wide, bridged the distance to Ian and Saorla and met them with a hug. "I am so surprised you came. I want you to meet Killian."

The tall man walked over and introduced himself as Killian Murchu. He started to shake Ian's hand but decided mid-stream that a firm bear hug was a better greeting. "I'm so pleased to meet you. Sophie tells me you're friends. I know this may seem awkward so soon after just meeting you, but can I pray for you?"

"Sure," Ian said.

Saorla remained silent.

Killian placed a hand on each of their shoulders and began to pray. At first, he offered a fairly typical prayer—one that any Christian might pray for another … until … the room started to mist over. Ian had to admit it wasn't an actual physical mist, but there was no other way to describe it. It was like a fine Irish morning in the misty hills of Atrim where you could barely see through the moist crystal grey, as it muted all sound. The mist in the room now was an unmistakable peace over the minds and spirits it fell on. Ian had experienced it before with his new pals at home, but it was more pronounced here. As Killian prayed that a weight of glory would descend, Ian became even more immersed in peace.

Ian peered through the supernatural mist toward Saorla. Her eyes were closed, and then she suddenly slumped toward the floor. A church team member caught her from behind and eased her to the carpeted floor.

"I feel so heavy," she said, "but in a good way."

Killian stood in front of Saorla and spoke directly to her. She was sitting yoga style now, looking up at Killian who stood crouching toward her.

"Is it okay if I share a Scripture with you."

Saorla nodded.

"It's from Isaiah 61. The Spirit of the Lord is binding up the brokenhearted and proclaiming liberty to captives ... comforting all who mourn ... to grant to those who mourn in Zion, giving a garland instead of ashes, the oil of gladness instead of mourning, the mantle of praise instead of the spirit of fainting, so they will be called oaks of righteousness, the planting of the Lord that he may be glorified. I think the Lord wants to show you just how good he is."

WHEN SAORLA HEARD THE WORDS ABOUT MOURNING AND God showing her he was good, she began to softly weep. And honestly, she didn't understand why. Maybe it was all the stress washing off her now. So much had been happening in the past week.

Her mind flashed to the horrific scene from yesterday. Such a contrast between the goodness of God and the work of evil men. Here, there was a presence—a calm, a serenity, a comfort. But maybe God was just good inside these walls. What about outside in the real world?

Killian excused himself after he prayed, explaining that he was a member of the worship band and had to set up for the service that was about to start.

Sophie slid down to sit next to Saorla. "That was amazing prayer. I told you that he is special man."

"How did he know to say those things?" Saorla asked.

"I told him that you are good friend, that you have been through tough time, and that I work at your house two days every week."

"I really have no words to describe how I feel. I am even more confused than I was yesterday about what is happening with me."

Behind the wheel of her vehicle again, after church, with Ian as her passenger, Saorla tried to cling to the now fading peace that had visited her with Killian's words. Under the surface, an incongruity reared between that peace—fading now as it was with the moments that passed—and the unsureness of whether she even believed God was real. There was a vague uncertainty that gnawed at her. The uneasy status quo might shift one way or the other if she just had some real answers about the validity of the artifacts.

An hour after leaving Dublin, they arrived at the town of Newry and rolled up the Antrim Coast Road. All of nature seemed sparked with a touch of the divine as her gaze alternated from the glens on her left and the Irish Sea on her right with Scotland beyond. The dark haze from earlier in the day had lifted, and the gold blossoms and the green grasses meshed with the grey stones and the cottony puffs of resting sheep to warm the eyes and calm the heart.

The twenty-five-mile stretch of road never ceased to amaze her. Blasted into the foot of the cliffs along the sea in the 1830s, it had challenged its creators at conception and to this day ranked as one of the greatest tourist routes in the world.

Ian remained quiet for much of the drive, but he too seemed taken by the beauty. "The Pacific Coast Highway has nothing on this little gem," he said at one point, as he gazed out his window at the sea. Saorla had never been to California but couldn't imagine anywhere more scenic than this simple, no-frills Irish highway, so she agreed.

They drove a few more miles before Ian spoke again. "So you're a believer now, right?"

"How to precisely answer that?" she asked, stalling to collect her thoughts.

"You're the professor. I thought you had all the answers to everything."

She felt her shoulders shrug. Answers? They were more elusive than a leprechaun, more fleeting than the sun in the cloud-strewn skies over Ireland. It seemed like she was only *beginning* to ask the right *questions*. And she knew that there had to be more to this whole faith-in-God thing than a mental assent to the historic facts, moving from non-believer to believer. The sermon at church that morning had conveyed as much when it talked about a radical giving up one's life for the cause of following Christ. And there was certainly something uncanny, even mysterious, about Christianity, or at least the brand she'd been exposed to this morning. This left her comfortable for now in the acknowledgment that God probably existed, and that there was a possibility that he was even good. But she didn't know as much as she should, she decided, about other spiritual modules.

"The little jury in my mind is out deliberating. The inner debate is still being conducted," she finally said.

"You're kidding, right? After all those words spoken over you today?"

"I'm a slow operator."

"Like an earthworm crossing a road."

"I prefer to see it as prudent due diligence. Once I'm convinced, I'm all in."

"I don't question your loyalty, just your eyesight. You can't see what's right in front of you."

Ian didn't seem angry in his pressing of her, and the playful repartee made her nearly laugh out loud. "Are you always this good of company?"

"Don't worry. I'll be nothing but sweet hospitality when we get to my grandparents' place."

"They know you're bringing a guest, right?"

Ian laughed. "I knew I forgot something."

"You're terrible."

"I told them not to expect to socialize with you. That you would probably be too busy with your nose in a book. But that they should get an extra good bedside lamp for your bedroom, so you didn't have to strain your eyes."

"You are a complete monster."

"Is this where you ask if all surfer attorneys from California are like me?"

She actually chuckled at that. "Ah, you're getting to know me a wee bit."

"Uh-oh, a concession. And now you're going to stop saying I don't even know you, right?"

"I wouldn't bet on it. Some say I'm hard to get to know. And you might not like what you find out if you did."

"Sounds like surfing the waves at Mavs. You never know where they might land you."

"Hopefully, spending time with me won't be fatal like you say Maverick's can be for some. But there's still time to back out."

"Are you kidding? This is a set I can't miss."

In another forty minutes, they arrived at the lab in Belfast where a friend of Saorla's named Amy worked. Even though the lab was closed on Sundays, Amy had agreed to meet them and check in their samples. Ian had wanted to snoop around at the antiquity shop where George had brought the chalice for inspection. It was only with great difficulty that Saorla was able to talk him out of the idea. His appearance there would likely only draw attention to the fact that they had left Dublin, if whoever had been watching them didn't know already.

When Amy had the items properly entered into the system, she told Saorla that the lab would start the testing by the accelerator-dating method first thing in the morning and have the answer for her sometime this week. And if she had anything more she wanted tested, she could have it sent special delivery to Amy's home. The lab in Belfast would be able to run additional tests to verify authenticity that the lab in Dublin could not.

Pleased with the process, she and Ian headed for the farm of George Shaw. So far there were no signs they had been tailed.

ARYANA SETTLED SAORLA INTO THE GUEST BEDROOM AT the farmhouse after a late arrival and an even later dinner. Saorla read in bed for an hour from a historical novel called *Strumpet City*—describing the poverty and tragic lives of workers in 1913-era Dublin. She was about to turn off her light when Ian knocked at her door with news that George's vital signs had worsened. Probably too much excitement for him, they both agreed. He didn't have long, regardless. She would have to hurry her investigation. Perhaps they could report some good news to George before he passed.

After Ian left, Saorla climbed in bed, turned out the lights, and considered her own future. If they found some notable artifacts, it might bolster her own reputation and the enrollment at Trinity College. Right now it seemed to be her last desperate shot to avert the cuts in her department.

The thought came to her that she should pray, but she dismissed the idea as being for true believers, not inquirers like herself. She had to be careful of extremism.

Yeah, right, she mocked, maybe she should make a pilgrimage next and kiss the blarney stone for good luck.

She turned out the light and realized that she hadn't thought of Stuart in ten hours. She couldn't remember the last time that thoughts of him hadn't intruded upon her day like storm clouds out over sea at the Cliffs of Moher.

CHAPTER TWENTY

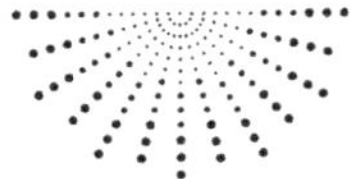

Saorla woke to sunlight drenching her face through yellow curtains she didn't recognize. She yawned away the remnants of a heavy, peaceful sleep. On the wall hung a reproduction painting of Michelangelo's *The Creation of Adam*. This one simply showed the iconic fingers of God and man almost touching. She sat up in bed, soaking in the stillness and gained her bearings. Yesterday, her finger must have been that close to God's. It seemed farther away at the moment.

The quiet allowed her to formulate a plan for the day, which included calling the lab in Dublin for the radiocarbon test results and then going to the field where Ian and his grandfather had made their finds. Although not an archeologist, she'd studied the discipline in some depth and could judge the relative importance of whatever curios they might unearth from Irish soil.

Her thoughts turned to George's dream and its similarity to what Dr. Greenwald had described. He had mentioned a book to her years ago, but what was the title? She had a near photographic recall for facts, but a lot had happened in the last couple of years since the professor had mentioned the title.

Peeking outside the window, her eyes feasted on rippling green slopes under partly cloudy skies. She dressed for a day outdoors. The temperature range didn't vary much this time of year, ranging between twelve and fifteen degrees Celsius. She would be comfortable in a light jacket if it didn't rain. She dialed the number of the lab in Dublin and was placed on hold. She hit the speakerphone and put on her shoes.

The smell of breakfast cooking wafted into the bedroom. Saorla grabbed her phone and marched to the kitchen. An enormous breakfast of scrambled eggs, toast, rashers, potatoes, tomatoes, and baked beans steamed from the countertop near the oven.

Aryana greeted Saorla with a smile and placed an empty teacup in her hand. "Fix your tea however you like it, dear."

Saorla poured in the milk first—one-fourth of a cup and then added the strong brew of tea. Slipping into a seat at the table, she asked, "How's George?"

"The old dog sleeps a lot but his life signs seem stable for now," Aryana said, as she set a plate of steaming hot food on the table in front of Saorla.

Saorla's stomach growled, and she took fork in hand and had a bite of the scrambled eggs. It was so good she began attacking the plate with real gusto. The hunger surprised her. She hadn't been able to eat much for breakfast in the last couple of years.

"It is such an honor to have you here, dear. Ian says you're brilliant."

Saorla had just taken a bite of toast and nearly choked. "He does?"

"You sound surprised?"

"Uh ... sorry. It's just that we've been working together, and I hadn't considered ... by the way, the food is delicious."

Saorla was relieved when Aryana didn't revisit the subject of what Ian thought of her and asked instead if she'd had a good night's sleep. It wasn't that she didn't care what Ian thought. It was more the odd feeling, which she couldn't shake, that she was really on a trip to meet a good friend's family instead of a business trip.

A good male friend.

And even more unsettling was the fact that she enjoyed the feeling whenever she slipped into it.

"Did you grow up in Dublin?" Aryana asked.

"County Donegal," Saorla said softly. Ian had described his grandparents as Protestants loyal to the British crown. A crown that had welcomed Rí Braden's claim to a throne that had the potential to unite all the Irish counties under it. Still, she wasn't sure how Ian's grandparents would react to hear that she was a Catholic girl from Donegal, a place considered to be a hotbed of Irish nationalism.

"Oh my, that must have been wonderful. You're from the land with the slogan, *Up here things are different*."

Saorla laughed. She'd seen the phrase plastered on billboards and had heard it repeated ad nauseam on radio when she was a kid. It was the county's marketing slogan to lure tourists. Donegal, had maintained a distinct cultural identity from the rest of Ireland that was more in tune with its Celtic roots.

"Haven't heard that in a while."

"Ian tells me you speak the Irish language?"

What else had Ian said about her? Had he mentioned her loss?

Loss?

The word conjured up images of misplaced car keys. When in reality, what had happened to her was more like open heart surgery where her beating one was replaced by an empty cardboard box.

"Irish, not English, was the first language for me. That's what we mostly spoke in the house, if not at school. It was certainly different."

"We have something in common," Aryana said, a broad grin lighting up her countenance. "I too grew up speaking a language that was not English. A dialect of Italian known as Genoese."

"Amazing, I would have never guessed. You have no accent."

"I came here as a little girl and in a few short years—*Voilà*!"

Saorla chuckled. "I am curious about so many things about your family."

"Ask anything you like. I love to talk, and I don't get much conversation out here anymore other than when we go to town for church."

"What was it like raising a football legend? Ian told me his father is Rory Shaw."

Ian came into the kitchen, and Saorla regretted asking the question, given how he felt about his father. Ian hugged and kissed his grandmother. Hopefully, Aryana would talk about Ian's father some other time when Ian wasn't around.

Aryana filled another plate with steaming hot eggs and rashers. "The professor was just asking about your father. I forgot to mention that we expect him to arrive later today."

So much for that.

She placed the plate on the table in front of Ian and turned to Saorla. "To answer your question, it all came about quite naturally. Rory was a good worker on the farm—always saw to the sheep and his chores, but he loved football more than anything. We knew from the start … before he even began school … when he got his first ball, that he was special."

Ian, head down, poked at his rashers with a fork but not eating.

Aryana poured Ian some tea. "Rory was always organizing football games with other farm children and going wherever he could for a game. But the thing I remember most is that he would kick balls for hours against a circle he'd drawn on the barn. He alternated legs, kicking right for a few hundred then left for a few hundred. Did this for hours on end every day. He ran sprints and did all manner of workouts, until he was one of the best players on the pitch in the British Isles as a teenager."

"Nana, I'm afraid we're going to have to get rolling. We need to get digging and take a look at some things."

"But she hasn't even finished her breakfast yet," Aryana protested.

"What I ate was delicious," Saorla said. "I'm not usually one to have a big breakfast. I've eaten more than usual already."

"I'll keep it warm for you both in case you're hungry when you get back."

A voice suddenly crackled through Saorla's speakerphone. She'd forgotten she was on hold with the lab in Dublin. It was the lab manager, claiming that they had lost or mislaid her sample. Saorla couldn't believe what she was hearing, and immediately her suspicions were up.

"How can this be?"

"I really don't know. Nothing like this has happened before I can assure you. We do apologize. We can run another sample for you if you bring one by."

"Send me a refund," she said and hung up.

First the murder of Professor Greenwald, and then the eavesdropping devices they had found, and now this. Somehow, someone had infiltrated the lab in Dublin. All her hope now rested with the lab in Belfast.

FROM THE TRUNK OF HER BMW, SAORLA GRABBED HER tools for the job—a couple of shovels to cut through the thick peat and a special brush she'd bought at a store on Grafton Street to remove grit from whatever they might find.

"Do you want to see the horse stable?" Ian asked.

She nodded, and they walked toward a wood structure that was about a hundred meters behind the farmhouse. Halfway there, George's dogs launched out of the house after them. "Whoa, boys," Ian shouted. "I almost forgot about you." He bent down to pet them.

When they came to the stable door, the dogs pranced up and down in a circle. Ian made them sit. "My grandfather has two good horses." He beckoned Saorla inside. "I think it would be fun if we rode out to the site on them. They need to be ridden. A neighboring farmer's been taking care of them, but he can't give them much time."

The last time Saorla had been on a horse was ten years ago on an outing with her father. The pungent odor of the stalls filled her nostrils. "The smell reminds me of my papa," she said.

"Your dad smelled like a horse stall?"

"Smart aleck." She grinned and punched him on the arm. "We used to ride a lot, especially on our way out to fish for salmon."

Ian opened the stall. Two healthy and eager sorrels greeted them. Ian gave each one a carrot. "I was going to ask if you need some lessons until I heard you telling grandma about being a country girl from Donegal. But if you do need any help—"

"Help? Ha! I bet I can show you some things about riding."

"Maybe."

"And why were you eavesdropping?"

Ian shrugged his shoulders. "We don't have far to go. We'll take the long way around to give the horses some exercise."

"They're beautiful," Saorla said, rubbing one of the sorrels above the nose.

"His name is Sundance." Ian smirked. "He's pretty calm. Why don't you ride him? Maybe he'll rub off on you."

"Ouch. The American has jokes, not funny ones, but at least—"

"—I know, at least I try."

With Ian pointing out various landmarks, they rode for about thirty minutes along a lengthy stretch of a stream. Ian pointed ahead. "That's Mount Slemish."

"Legend has it that Slemish was the mountain where Patrick was a shepherd-slave for King Muirchu. It was supposedly there that he prayed all day long while living outdoors in fifth century Ireland."

"My grandfather spoke of that often. He believes it to be historical fact."

"Patrick's autobiographical *Confession* refers to the Woods of Fochoill as the place of his enslavement. But who knows where that was? There's lots of sheep to be shepherded and lots of room for one to commune out here, as Patrick must have done."

They finally arrived at the large native oak. "Why do you keep looking behind you?" Saorla followed the direction of Ian's glance.

"Making sure we aren't being watched. Can't be too careful. I think it's all clear."

"It makes me nervous to be out here alone," she admitted. "After what happened Saturday."

"I considered bringing George's rifle and his .357 but decided to just keep a close lookout instead."

Ian found the place where he'd dug into the bog last week and pointed it out for Saorla. "Most of this George cut, but I had a go at it too."

They dismounted and tied up their horses. The dogs meandered off by the stream to have an adventure of their own.

Saorla took one of the shovels. "All right, where are you?"

"Who?"

"The other piece of stone slab to match yours."

They began picking through the cut-out section of peat. Saorla warned him to be careful not to swing the shovel too hard.

SAORLA HAD BEEN DIGGING FOR ABOUT TWENTY MINUTES, drifting farther and farther to the right of where the other piece had been found, working on the theory that the stone had been placed on the ground with the words face up and had simply become detached by some means over the years. Because it was the right half that was missing, Saorla had assumed they needed to dig to the right. But now she considered a different theory, one that would take it to the left due to trans-surface shifting in the soil over the centuries. Twenty minutes into the new location, which required cutting out a new area of bog, her shovel struck something hard.

Stone?

She continued to dig around it until an oblong shape took form.

"I think I hit the mother lode," she yelled.

Ian came near and began scraping and digging around the object. In a few minutes, he hoisted the other half of the oval-shaped stone out of the ground. Something else was in the soil around it. A leather strap? She rushed to the spot and tugged on the strap, pulling out another ancient looking leather satchel like the one Ian had presented her with on her birthday. She didn't know which to look at first, the satchel or the stone. Covering the satchel with a junk of peat, she opted for the stone. She brushed it off and confirmed it was the other half of the monument.

"Can you read anything on it?" Ian asked. He sounded a wee impatient. Another American used to fast food restaurants.

"It looks like an exact match for the other half."

"Is anything written on it?"

Saorla felt her heart race. It was too fantastic to believe. "It's Latin. *Quaesitio Gloriosum.*"

Ian frowned at her. "Huh?"

"This is why you need a linguistics and history professor, Mr. American Attorney."

"Are you going to tell me? Or make me beg?"

Her mind scrambled to make sense of it all. It couldn't be, but she could see no other explanation. Someone from the past was trying to communicate with them.

"I should make you sit like Lance and Yeats for a biscuit."

Ian cupped both of his hands by his face looking like a dog begging for a treat.

"No need for that," she said. "The writing on the stone gives me pause because it seems more complicated, or maybe more fantastic is the word I'm looking for, than it first appears. The words looked at in isolation would mean 'glorious search,' or 'glorious investigation.'"

"But you think there's more to it?"

"Well, certainly if this slab is the other half of the first, and it certainly looks to be the case, then we have to consider the words that were written on the other side."

"But you told me that the etchings on the other side were in Ogham script, and that the lines merely represented words."

"It is indeed puzzling. But many scholars believe that the template for Ogham is Latin. Ogham was only used in a short window of time around the fourth and fifth centuries, at least that is the time period when most all of the examples we have today are from."

"So you have a theory?"

"It's more of a feeling or intuition than anything scientific."

"A non-scientific feeling? Maybe I need to get a philosophy professor to look at it instead."

Saorla smiled. She had to admit he did have a sense of humor. "You are being difficult. I think I liked you better when you were sitting and begging like a dog. What I am trying to say is that it is almost like something spiritual is going on. Like real communication with the divine. You know, like Sophie and Killian are into."

Ian's teeth were clasped down on his bottom lip. He looked down and nudged a clump of peat with his shoe. "I thought you weren't a believer. At least you wouldn't admit to being one yesterday."

"Listen, it's just a feeling I have. Putting the two sides together would literally read 'Take the glorious investigation.' But the word 'Take' at the beginning makes it an admonition or a command, but in our case, it seems to be more accurate to say that it's an invitation. It's like someone is inviting us on a journey. Perhaps I'm crazy, but it almost seems to me to be personal encouragement for us to take this quest we are on. The fact that it switches from one form of writing to another halfway through, from something primitive to something that can be more readily understood in all ages, suggests to me a connection between the past and future. And the fact that the slab was split in two, given its thickness is, well, remarkable."

Ian slowly nodded his head. "I see your point. Especially considering the Scripture words from Proverbs 25:2 etched into the first satchel about it being the glory of God to conceal a matter, and the glory of Kings to search it out."

Tears formed in her eyes, and she blinked them back to keep them from escaping down her cheeks. "I never told you why those words impacted me the way they did."

"I wondered about it."

Saorla drew in a breath. "Sophie gave me that scripture the Saturday before I met you. I was a mess, I almost tried to ... I almost died. She found me unconscious, prayed for me, and gave me those words. That's why I agreed to help you. And now we find this."

Ian's eyes brimmed too, and he started to say something then stopped.

Silence fell between them.

He glanced down at the leather satchel caked with peat and then turned his gaze back to Saorla. "We need to have a good look at the satchel. Do we need to take it somewhere? Have it preserved?"

"I know I should immediately put it in an air-tight container," she said, "but I'm tempted to examine it right now."

Ian pointed at the half piece of stone monument. "If someone is personally challenging us to pursue these things to wherever they might lead, then I think we are entitled to look inside that satchel right now and find out what's in it. The question is who's behind all this?"

"It seems far-fetched to think that God himself placed these items here for us."

"I agree. But the question remains. Who?"

Saorla barely heard Ian. She lifted off the peat she had placed on the leather satchel. Delicately, she brushed the satchel and began examining the exterior. "The style looks to be from the early medieval period, somewhere between 400 to 800 AD."

Her perusal continued as she spun the item around. The sun poked through the clouds, illuminating the grains in the leather. A shift of her head to the side offered a better angle yet.

A drawing? A symbol etched into the leather?

She retrieved a magnifying class from her handbag. "There's a drawing on it I can't make out because it seems to be in miniature."

She squinted through the magnification of the glass. Familiar shapes formed before her eyes. "I can make out a Celtic cross and a sword. A Roman legion breastplate and a shield maybe."

Not a common symbol from antiquity, but she'd seen this at least once before. She was sure of it.

Where?

The filing cabinets of her brain opened to a memory. Amid the clutter of Dr. Greenwald's ransacked home, the strange symbol had barely registered in her sub-conscious. But she had glimpsed it there, drawn on a piece of paper scattered on the floor. Processing it all now, it struck her like lightning from the sky. Hadn't George described the same thing last night in their conversation about his dreams? How were they connected? Another revelation hit her even harder. She'd seen a breastplate under the grit of the first half of the monument that Ian had dug out by himself. When she had the stone restored would it reveal the same symbol, complete with Celtic cross and Roman armor? The symbol didn't appear to be one that she had ever seen before the events of the past couple weeks. It must have been one of the things Dr. Greenwald had wanted to talk to her about on the day of his murder.

As she continued examining the exterior of the leather, it dawned on her that there was something inside. The other satchel had been empty except for the small piece of vellum. She had to have a look at the contents now, despite the established protocols that were screaming in her head to take extreme caution to preserve the artifact.

She opened the pouch and peered inside. Vellum leaves of calf hide clustered neatly to form a collection. She slid it out into the open air and turned to the beginning. The first page of an ancient manuscript.

CHAPTER TWENTY-ONE

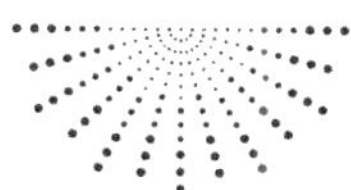

Lorcan had another busy day scheduled of promoting Ireland's interests and values to the world. He'd just finished going over a speech he needed to deliver later in the day at an "All-Island Civil Dialogue" at the Royal Hospital Kilmainham in Dublin, where he would wax long on the topic of "a constructive response to the challenge posed by the UK's exit from the EU." Later in the evening, the cabinet was scheduled to meet with the high king and the taoiseach on the Jerusalem question.

On Mondays, Lorcan had the museum closed to the public while he reviewed any new items brought to the on-site lab. He had without notice moved out of storage and off the books several items relative to medieval Christendom. A client in Sicily paid handsomely for the relics and had promised to keep them as part of a strictly private collection. The price was right—a million euros a piece for a psaltery and large Celtic cross that both dated to the thirteenth century.

He was about to delve into the inventory with Torna when a call came on his cell. The private line of Hogan Kirby came up on the caller ID, and Lorcan answered immediately.

"We're keeping a close eye on them at the old man's farm," Kirby said. "From the high ground I'm on right now, I can see them at the site they've been digging. The nurse inside the house is keeping us informed should there be any new developments."

"Are they digging at a site we've already swept through?"

"I'm afraid we didn't know about this one. The old man had lots of areas he'd dug from, and there's probably a hundred and eighty acres or so of bogland out there. It would have been like finding a five-leaf clover."

"Let them do all the hard work for now. We can collect from them in the end. How's the old man?"

"He's hanging on—must be a strong one. Do you want to speed things up?"

"No. It's enough that he's not able to help. We can learn more with him alive now that he's incapacitated and his grandson is reporting back to him. Did the grandson and the professor find anything?"

"We should know more when they get back to the farmhouse."

"Great work," Lorcan said. "Have the area where they are digging swept through right after they leave just to make sure they didn't miss anything. But be discreet. Shovels only. Continue to keep a close eye on them."

THE WRITING WAS LATIN AND CLEARLY LEGIBLE. SHE translated for Ian.

I arise and shine today
With strength and power from above, inviting the Trinity
Believing in the Three
Confessing the Oneness
Of the Creator of All

RECOGNITION TRIGGERED FROM SAORLA'S GREY MATTER, rifling to her heart, causing it to beat wildly. "Janey Mac, will you look at this!"

"What?"

"It's amazing." She couldn't choke out more. The words of this manuscript were … well, honestly, there were no words to describe what this all meant for them.

"What is?"

Saorla kept marveling at the tender old leaves of calf skin, their condition astounding. She ignored Ian's question and continued to translate aloud.

I arise this day
In the mighty power of Christ's birth and baptism
In the mighty power of his crucifixion and burial
In the mighty power of his resurrection and ascension
In the mighty power of his final judgments on the nations

SHE PAUSED FROM HER READING TO LOCK INTO IAN'S EYES. "This is unbelievable. It's a version of Saint Patrick's *Breastplate*. Different from the earliest known versions—"

"—How?"

"—we have of it. The meaning of the words is the same, but this version is written in Latin."

"That's significant?"

"This is profoundly astonishing because the other versions are in the old Irish language and were probably written a century after Saint Patrick. Most scholars have thought that Saint Patrick didn't actually write it because Irish wasn't a written language during his lifetime. But this is written in the old Latin that Patrick wrote his other surviving works in. What if it was written by Saint Patrick?" She couldn't believe she was asking the question. "But it can't be an original," she said, trying to bring some reality back to the world.

"Of course it is," Ian said. "This explains why my grandfather carries such a burden in his heart that we follow this trail wherever it leads."

"I don't know, Ian, if this turns out to be a hoax …" It will destroy the little bud of faith that has sprung from the ashes.

Yes, darling pretty, it will snuff the last bit of life right out of you. Send you back to where you were before. Before you met Ian and you had only the crumbling ashes of your memory of Stuart.

"From your class I remember you said the 'Breastplate' was also called the *Lorica,* is that word Latin?"

"Latin word for body armor."

"As in Roman breastplate, shield, etcetera?

"Yeah, just like the symbol at Greenwald's and on the satchel."

Saorla looked at the manuscript again. "It must have been a dangerous world he lived in if indeed Saint Patrick wrote this. It's a daily prayer to be sure, but more potent and war-like ... like a bomb detonated into the atmosphere. Kind of like yesterday when Killian started making those Scripture declarations over us. It gives me the same kind of feeling of strength. Look at this."

God's shield to guard me.
God's angels to save me
From traps of demons
From all temptations
From all who wish me harm
Abroad and near
Alone and among the people
I invoke today power to protect me from every evil

AGAINST EVERY MERCILESS FORCE THAT MAY ASSAULT MY BODY AND SOUL
Against incantations of false prophets
Against ungodly laws of pagans
Against the false laws of heretics
Against the greed of idolatry
Against the spells of witches, wizards, smiths and druids
Against every philosophy that corrupts body and soul

CHRIST TO SHIELD ME TODAY
From poison and burning and fire
From floods, from drowning, from wounding

So that I might attain the abundant reward

CHRIST WITH ME, CHRIST BEFORE ME, CHRIST BEHIND ME
Christ in me, Christ below me, Christ above me
Christ on my right, Christ on my left
Christ when I sleep, Christ when I sit, Christ when I stand
Christ in the heart of every man who thinks of me
Christ on the lips of everyone who speaks of me
Christ in every eye that looks at me
Christ in every ear that listens to me

SAORLA CAME TO THE END AND SAW A FINAL SURPRISE. A notation at the bottom claimed that it was penned by the hand of *Patricius*. She marked that area of the notation with her finger and showed it to Ian. "It purports to be written by Patrick himself," she said struggling to keep her voice even.

Ian's eyes grew wide. "There's more then, and this is just the beginning. You've answered my question about *who* is communicating with us. Now we know. Is there anything in there that suggests where to look next?"

"Look for what?"

"The treasure Papa talked about, of course. His dreams revealed that there were a lot of mysteries to be solved to get to it. And are you forgetting about the treasure chest?"

"Whoa, hold on," she said, raising her palms to him. "Do you realize that if we didn't find another thing, and if this really is the 'Breastplate' written by Saint Patrick himself, it would be one of the most important archeological discoveries ever made? She let her words settle, and then added, "It would be on par with the discovery of the dead sea scrolls just off the top of my head."

Ian didn't seem to be listening, though. He was staring off in the direction of the higher elevation of Mount Slemish.

Saorla turned from him to glance back at the site of the dig. She examined the satchel again and pondered the strange symbol on it: breastplate, sword, shield, Celtic cross. She had seen this symbol somewhere else, somewhere else besides the paper on the floor of Dr. Greenwald's house and on the satchel and the stone monument.

"There is another place that I saw—"

"—Come on." He started gathering up their belongings in a frenetic flurry. "We have to go now," he ordered.

"Why?" Saorla asked, annoyed at the sudden rush.

He pointed to a hill off in the distance. "We're being watched, and I think they're headed this way."

CHAPTER TWENTY-TWO

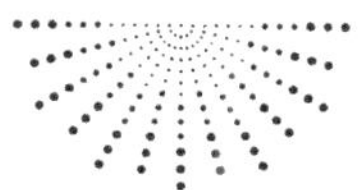

By late Monday afternoon, Ian was back in Dublin behind a small desk at the legal aid clinic in a recently vacated office they'd given him. The clinic had four small offices with dingy linoleum floors and walls painted a hideous shade of light green.

"Can I get you anything before I leave, Mr. Shaw?" Gretchen, the office manager, asked him. "The truth is I'm knackered, and I'm going to leave early."

"No, I think I have everything I need," Ian said, as his eyes scanned around the office at a dark metal desk, a green filing cabinet, and a large bookcase propped against the back filled with outdated legal codes and periodicals.

After Gretchen left, Ian took a break by kicking back in his chair and remembering the road trip with Saorla. They'd decided to leave the Antrim farm sooner than he might have liked both because of the unwelcome news that his father would likely arrive in the afternoon and because there was no time to lose. Extreme diligence would be necessary if they hoped to have any chance to provide an answer for Papa before it was too late. For better or worse, he, at least, was committed to his new mission. *Take the glorious quest* was an instruction he intended to heed.

Upon leaving the farm on the return trip, he'd noticed an SUV was following them. He'd been driving at the time, not Saorla. When they came to a caravan of four cars traveling ahead of them at the speed limit, Ian maneuvered into the right lane to pass just as a caravan of ten vehicles—including a couple of hefty trucks—approached from the opposite end of the narrow single lane roadway. He made it back to his lane just in time to miss a head on collision with the oncoming lead vehicle.

"Why are you acting the maggot?" Saorla screamed at him.

"Huh?" he asked as he sped out of sight from the formerly tailing SUV now stuck behind the traffic. "Now I'm a maggot? Or is that some kind of Irish idiom I'm not familiar with?"

"Yeah, the latter," she said. Her hands trembled, he could see, as he exited from the arterial road down a side thoroughfare.

"We just lost our tail. You can lean back now, take a deep breath. So you don't really consider me a disgusting larva?"

"Not really." She was able to laugh now, and her hands weren't shaking anymore. "*Acting the maggot* means you're causing some fierce trouble for others or acting in an irritating manner."

Ian let out a hoot. "Some opposing attorneys have probably thought I was acting a maggot in the courtroom before."

She grinned. "Maybe all American attorneys are maggots."

Thanks to the evasive driving techniques, they scheduled another meeting with Amy in Belfast. They met at a crowded restaurant where they entrusted her with the satchel and its contents. Saorla seemed to visibly relax once they'd divested themselves of their treasure. The consensus among the three was that it would be safer to leave it with Amy, a woman who was not on anyone's radar. She would see that proper testing procedures were followed and that a strict chain of custody was maintained.

For most of the drive back to Dublin with Saorla behind the wheel, Ian couldn't stop thinking about the strange symbol on the satchel that matched the picture that Saorla had seen on Dr. Greenwald's floor. He asked her about it again, for what seemed like the third time. "Are you sure you don't remember where you saw it?"

"No," she answered, "but I know I've seen it elsewhere, in a book for sure. I just can't quite place where, other than a vague recollection about it being in a tome that Dr. Greenwald had shown me years ago when I first came to Trinity College."

"I know it will come to you. Your mind latches on to facts like that shark in the Jaws movie from the seventies. None of its victims swimming near the beach ever got away. That's you with information. And that's not just for the short-term minutiae but for the long-tucked away stuff too."

"Awe ... I think that's a compliment."

"Oh, believe me, it is. And I only give them out rarely."

"You're funny. Everything with you is about the ocean. Anyway, you're not too bad yourself for remembering things." She reached over with her right arm to punch him in the shoulder while she kept her left hand on the wheel and her eyes on the road.

The symbol, however, was not the only thing that had been brewing in his mind on the drive back. Captivating was the only way to describe his newly hired expert.

"You're staring at my legs, *again*." she said.

"Uh, it was your *hair* last time."

She chuckled. "At least it wasn't my breasts. Not much to see there."

Ian felt his face growing flush, but recovered in time to say, "I wouldn't say that." But then made the tactical choice to tone it down a bit. "Sorry, Miss PHD, I'll keep my eyes on the scenery *outside* the car from now on."

Enough of the flirting, he told himself. *I'm not ready to give up dreams of a big salary and even bigger waves waiting for me back in San Francisco.*

He doubted he would ever be ready to do that.

And it was probably all a moot point anyway. She gave no indication she had any feelings for him. A pathetic joke was what he must seem like to her in comparison to her late husband.

Ian sat in the fake leather chair at his desk and powered up the small desktop computer. What was the best way to search the meaning of a symbol? Certainly, he could describe it and attempt to run a search that way.

He landed on a website run by a Christian group that had researched hundreds of symbols from all over the world, with an explanation for their history, use, and meaning. Ian waded through a myriad of images used throughout history, and fascinated, he fell into the erudite world of online symbology.

There were Celtic crosses and there were swastikas. And a Christian fish symbol and the Darwin fish and the eye of the pyramid on the American dollar. And pentagrams and the star of David and symbols of fertility cults and symbols of Egyptian gods and symbols representing love, eternity, life, the sun god, mother earth. And all kinds of Christian symbols and all kinds of crosses. There were many symbols with shields and swords. But there were no symbols with a Celtic cross on a breastplate with a sword and shield.

Frustrated, Ian flicked off the computer and leaned back in his chair. A bell sounded to indicate that someone had walked through the front door. The office closed at 5:30, but the staff, including Gretchen, had cleared out early. Ian went to the front and was surprised to see Sophie. Then he remembered that he'd given her a card for the clinic and had told her to pass the word around at church.

Sophie brought a couple downtrodden souls with her—a disheveled looking man in his early fifties and a thirty-something woman with black bags under her eyes. They both just looked sad and tired. Neither of them spoke English. Polish was Ian's guess when Sophie began to seamlessly interpret. She explained that the older man faced eviction because he had complained about the lack of heat in his apartment at night. Ian wrote all of the man's information onto his legal pad, and after a quick legal search, he told him he could defend the eviction and would file a counterclaim for triple damages under a statute that allowed tenants to recover for insufficient heat. He explained he would need to send an investigator out to document the inside air temperature at various times.

The woman with Sophie had a much different problem. Her former boyfriend had just been released after a long jail stint. He had recently thrashed her around, giving her two black eyes and was threatening more violence. Ian promised to file an emergency order of protection the next day.

When his newest clients left, Ian's mind seized on just how far he'd fallen from his lofty perch at Horowitz, Dunlap & Connor. The coveted west view of the Pacific seemed a dream floating away with the wind.

The phone on his desk rang. Saorla. "I remember where I saw the symbol in the book."

CHAPTER TWENTY-THREE

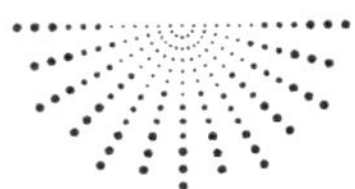

The wood floors creaked as they entered the main chamber of the Old Library known as the Long Room. The bookcases on both sides of the main walkway were roped off from use. The site closed to all but faculty at 5:30 p.m. They now had the place to themselves.

Since Ian had last spoken with Saorla, Myrna had been brought into their inner circle. Saorla had given her the details of the past couple days, starting with Papa's dreams and moving on to the artifacts they had found so far, including the manuscript of the *Breastplate* and the strange symbol that Saorla had finally remembered seeing years ago *in this very library*.

Ian languished at the sight of thousands and thousands of volumes to choose from, most of them apparently dating to the sixteenth or seventeenth century, and computer-assisted research had yet to convert these dinosaurs into digital form. "I don't like our odds."

"That was my sentiment exactly," Myrna added. "I think we're going to need more coffee before we get started."

Saorla turned to face them. "Would you two show a little optimism? And you, Ian, whatever happened to the old-fashioned Norman Vincent Peale positive-thinking can-do kind of American?"

Ian pretended to draw a six-shooter from a holster. "He went the way of the open range and rode off into the sunset. Now we have a lot of whiners and complainers in the States. Doesn't usually jump on me, but I don't like libraries, and I don't care much for research either. Just put me in the courtroom with a jury."

"Why don't we make a wager?" Myrna asked. "If we don't find what we're looking for in a week, the professor has to buy us dinner at the Winding Stair."

Saorla shook her head indignantly. "No way. What's the incentive in that? It has to be that the person who finds what we're looking for gets a free dinner. The two losers buy."

"Why do I feel I'm going to be buying one of you two dinner?" Ian asked, as they stood at the foot of a long, rectangular walkway that separated two sides of the successive rows of bookshelves that characterized the Long Room.

"I plan to order three courses," Myrna said.

Ian shook his head. "Maybe we should say the loser pays for just one."

"Get used to it. It's going to get expensive now that you have a girlfriend," Myrna blurted.

"What are you talking about?" Ian asked.

"The two of you going away on holiday last weekend."

Saorla's face blushed the color of a cooked lobster. "You know it wasn't like that."

"Louie, I think this is the start of a beautiful friendship," Myrna quipped, channeling her best Humphrey Bogart impression.

"Can we get back to the job at hand?" Ian asked.

"Okay, where was I?" Myrna continued. "Oh yeah, the three courses. I'll start with the seafood chowder with Fingal Ferguson's chorizo and treacle bread. Followed by steamed cockles and Roaring Bay mussels with Clogherhead crab, brown shrimp mayo—"

Ian interrupted, "Sounds like you committed the menu to memory—"

"Toast and chips," Myrna resumed. "I'll top it off with the white chocolate and cherry brownie with white-chocolate ice cream."

Ian watched Saorla, who followed along with her eyes closed as if imagining the food being set before her. When Myrna ended her description of the cuisine, Saorla added, "Don't forget to match that dessert with a glass of Domain Madeloc Grenache."

"You girls act like you haven't eaten all week," he said, walking away from them to admire the splendor of the Long Room.

He came to a halt at the first of a number of bust sculptures that lined the central walkway. A tap on the shoulder caused him to turn to find Saorla smiling, Myrna nowhere in sight. "Do you want a tour before we get started?"

"How'd you guess?"

"Full tour-guide mode, you sure?"

"Why not?"

She pretended to tighten an invisible tie. "This walkway is over two hundred feet long, though, it's only about thirty-six feet wide. The building was erected between 1712 and 1732 and contains two hundred thousand of the library's oldest books. In 1801, the library gained the free right to every future book published on the two islands. The storage problem this caused resulted in a decision to raise and repair the roof and add a second floor of bookshelves."

Ian's eyes drifted up to marvel at the barrel-shaped ceiling and symmetrical rows of shelving on the upper floor. He turned to Saorla. "You are good. If you ever tire of being a professor, I'm sure there's a job here waiting for you."

Saorla grimaced a split-second and then nodded. "Too bad Myrna disappeared. She used to be a real campus tour guide."

"Perfect. Somehow that doesn't surprise me. She lives to talk."

Saorla laughed at that. More and more she'd been doing that—laughing at his analyses and jokes, even though he must seem like a Yankee rube to her. She was nothing if not polite. That was all it was, though, simple politeness, maybe to make up for the rude way she'd treated him in the beginning. But it was nothing more.

Ian heard some creaking noises coming from somewhere up on the second floor. Perhaps the place was haunted by specters from the past. The history in the building overwhelmed him.

Saorla walked ahead and pointed to a series of marble busts. "They're of famous philosophers, scientists, and writers of the western world—Homer, Shakespeare, Aristotle—Forty-eight in all, some famous, some not-so-famous."

As Ian strolled along, he thought of the many generations of Irishmen who'd taken the same path through this iconic library. When he got to an old wooden harp set up in the walkway, Saorla said, "It's one of the main attractions here. A fifteenth century harp made of oak and willow with twenty-nine brass strings. It's become a symbol of Ireland itself."

Ian studied the harp for a moment then strolled on. Saorla matched his stride. "The other item I have to mention," she said pointing to a glass case in the center of the walkway, "is a rare copy of the 1916 Proclamation of the Irish Republic."

Ian inspected the proclamation in silence.

Saorla drifted ahead but then turned to face him. "Oh, I almost forgot." Her tone ominous, her eyes darted down to focus on the floor between them. "By a great margin, the most famous possession of this library lies below your feet."

"What is it?"

"Downstairs is where they keep the Book of Kells. More than a half a million people a year descend to the basement level of the Old Library to see the exhibit displaying its volumes, and then ascend here to the main level to walk the Long Room. But make no mistake they come for the Book of Kells."

Ian nodded. "I remember as a teenager seeing the Book of Kells with my grandmother. Can we go down there now?"

"Not after hours. They keep security quite tight."

"I went up to the second floor," Myrna blazed in and interrupted. "Then I headed down an aisle at random, closed my eyes, and picked out a book. I decided that it would be just my luck if the first book I opened ended up being the one we needed."

"So what was the verdict?" Ian asked.

"Guilty of being unlucky in the first degree. The book I chose was on the mating practices of the European porcupine. Obviously not going to help with your artifacts."

Ian rolled his eyes. "I'm not even going to—"

"The answer is yes, I learned something. The female is only available sexually, you know, for ten hours the whole year. Imagine if that applied to humans. It would make most marriages quite dull, no?"

Ian felt his facial muscles wincing. He glanced in Saorla's direction and could have sworn she was blushing, again.

"The male saunters up to the female." Myrna was acting it out, looking more like a penguin waddling. "He then lets out a jet spray of urine from about six feet away that drenches the female. If she's not inspired, she screeches out in disgust and shakes off the urine. But if she's aroused—"

"Okay, I think I've heard enough," Ian pleaded.

Myrna ignored him. "They have to work around the quills of course. She doesn't have any on her belly. So—"

"—Can we get to work?" Ian exclaimed, both amused and embarrassed by Myrna's antics.

"Did you read those ... umm ... 'scientific discoveries' about the porcupine in *Latin*?" Saorla asked.

"Sure did. Late eighteenth-century scientific periodical."

"Your Latin has really grown since last year. Why don't you and Ian start working together? You can go through the same section. Ian can look at the English manuscripts, and if you get one in Latin, Myrna can take a look at that. I'm sure the book I saw was in one of those two languages. If you get a German or French text, we can discard it for now. We need to start on the second floor in the history section."

Ian wasn't sure he would be able to tell Latin from French, Italian from Portuguese. He spoke some Spanish, so he figured he had that covered.

One hour spilled into another. The next time Ian checked on his cell phone, it flashed five-thirty in the morning. They had been at it for over nine hours and had had no luck. Saorla had said that she thought the book they were looking for had the word *Hibernia* in the title. Her follow-up explanation was that *Hibernia* was the Classical Latin name for the island of Ireland.

Still nothing came up.

By the third night, their routine had settled into a distinctive pattern. Each night they arrived at the Old Library after the crowds left and proceeded to hunt for the elusive book that Saorla felt held the clue that would propel them forward. Most nights they quit around 1:30 after six solid hours of pulling one book off the shelf after another. They would get up early the next morning and search until the crowds lined up for the Book of Kells exhibit at 9:30. From there, the three book hunters refueled with an Irish breakfast at one of the local establishments near campus, where Saorla and Myrna drank tea and Ian pounded coffee.

Saorla had been convinced all week that she had been looking in the right area. She'd had Ian and Myrna peruse the card catalogues but to no avail. Optimism remained high on her part, but the morale of her troops waned with each unfruitful hour.

Then, just before midnight on the fourth night of their search, Saorla came to a special section devoted to the Viking influence in the history of Ireland. As she scanned the titles, her eyes alighted upon a tome entitled *Terra Sancti de Hibernia*. Goose bumps formed on her arm. *Hibernia* appeared in the title to be sure, but the familiarity of it struck her at the publication date of 1886 by a Catholic priest named Fr. Frank Conlin.

Turning the pages to the middle of the volume, her eyes zoned onto a print. The campus bell tower rang in the midnight hour, and she felt her heart beating in competition. The print looked exactly like the one she had seen on Professor Greenwald's floor. She rifled through the pages, scanning bits and pieces. Was this text the prize she sought?

At some point, she quit skimming and read the material at a slower and more concentrated pace. The more she read the slower she went.

And then she saw exactly what she was looking for.

A cry, or a heavy gasp at the very least, must have escaped from her mouth because in a few seconds, both Ian and Myrna had climbed the stairs from the first floor and were scrumming around the book she held.

"Don't tell me we're buying *you* dinner," Myrna said, trying to sound disappointed but failing miserably.

Saorla grinned. "Seems that way. Can't believe I didn't look in the Viking section sooner."

Ian looked confused. "What do the Vikings have to do with the symbol etched on the satchel?"

"A lot as it turns out." Saorla turned to the page with the sketch of the same symbol they'd found on the satchel.

Ian's mouth dropped open. "More and more, I'm feeling smarter about hiring you."

Saorla ignored the backhanded compliment. "The book I found is written in English, but the title is Latin and translates 'Holy Land of Ireland.' Father Conlin, who wrote it, says that rumors through the Middle Ages place this same symbol on an Irish treasure chest—filled with gold, silver and untold priceless relics—hidden away somewhere on the island."

"You're kidding?" Ian's face turned pale white, like he saw ghost. His feet began shifting back and forth, like she'd seen with freshly announced graduates just before they threw their caps in the air.

"Ian, she doesn't kid about history. Seriously, you should know that by now."

Drafting on Myrna's words, a silence fell between the three of them, broken only by the loud hoot of an owl in the tree just outside the nearby second floor window.

"Why'd they hide it?" Ian asked.

"Apparently to keep it safe from the waves of Viking raiders that they knew would come." Saorla drew a breath and steadied the heavy tome against the bookshelf. "But that is not even the most important part of what's in that chest, according to Conlin. He says that the chest contains a code or a clue of something even more valuable, but he doesn't mean valuable in the material sense. He means spiritually valuable."

Ian rubbed his temples. He looked worried.

"What's bothering you?"

"I have so many questions. First off, I don't know much about the Vikings."

"The Vikings may seem to be a wee bit tangential to our efforts at first glance. But they may turn out to be the principle cause that led to the concealment of what we're trying to find. I can give you some background if you like?"

Ian gave a quick nod. "I'm all ears."

"Vikings came from what today would be modern-day Norway and began raiding this island in 795 AD. The first raid recorded was off the coast of Antrim on Raithlin Island, where they burned a church. That same year they raided Iona. For the next four decades, the raids increased in numbers and intensity, until they developed some entrenched bases on the island. So much was looted and stolen that it was thought they carried away most of the spoils of the island's economy. Dublin was the chief Viking base. Many people don't know this city was founded by Vikings. Eventually they gradually assimilated into Irish society and became more Christianized. In the tenth century, there was a second wave of raids, and more battles were fought and more treasure carried away. By 1014 AD, however, an Irish leader named Brian rose up, defeated the Vikings of Dublin, and essentially ended the Viking era of power over the island."

"The high king's ancestors hailed from Brian." Myrna flicked back her feathered, silver hair over her ears. "I think Ian should enroll in one of your courses and pay tuition."

Ian chuckled. "I'm done with school. I get why they would have to hide the treasure from the Vikings. But how does that help us? Don't tell me there's a treasure map in that book."

"Very nearly. The book claims that there's a secret code passed down through the centuries dating back all the way to a prophecy given by Saint Patrick in the fifth century. According to Father Conlin, Patrick, by supernatural revelation, had special words of encouragement for the people of *Hibernius* that were to be revealed to them in a time period he called the 'Day of Doom.'"

Myrna's eyes grew wide. "Day of Doom?"

"An apocalyptic term that Saint Patrick used to describe the end-time judgment on the nations just before the return of Christ."

"Are you saying we're living in the Day of Doom?" Myrna asked, her eyes like hubcaps.

Saorla sighed. "All I'm saying is we need the code to go any further in our quest. I'm not a religious scholar."

"What I don't understand is why someone would want to keep such an encouraging prophecy—provided there really is one—under such tight wraps," Ian said.

"There could be a lot of reasons for that," Saorla said. "The first thing that comes to mind is the need to save it for a particular time in history."

"Like the Day of Doom," Myrna said.

"And also, again, to protect it from the Viking raids," Saorla said. "But not only that threat, but all the other threats and ways that documents could be destroyed through history."

"But why wouldn't God simply give the message to a modern-day prophet, pastor, or priest?" Ian asked.

Saorla smiled. "You mean someone like Killian. I shouldn't have to tell you that as impressive as he may be, any impact of a prophecy coming from a mere contemporary man like him would pale in comparison to words that are a millennium and a half old coming from one of mankind's greatest legends."

"Point well taken," Ian said.

"The other thing that I'm just starting to consider is the possibility that God somehow gets pleasure from participating in an endeavor like this with us. I know it sounds strange. But how else to take the repetition of the verse from Proverbs about it being the *glory of God to conceal a matter and the glory of kings to search it out*."

"So let's get the code," Ian said excitedly.

"Not so fast, Cowboy," Saorla said. "There's just one problem."

Ian shrugged his shoulders. "And that would be?"

Saorla pointed to the book she had wedged against the shelf. "It says to get the code, we'd have to take the Book of Kells, hold it up to the light of the full moon, with the forty-fourth leaf of the book facing the sky, and read the code, which it says right here, will then be visible through the translucent calfskin."

"If we do this, we should bark at the moon too, because we would be mad-dog lunatics," Myrna said flatly.

"We've come too far to give up," Ian protested.

"It gets worse," Saorla said. "Conlin writes that no one who has seen the code has ever known what it meant. And he adds that in the hour the code is solved, a great earthquake will hit the island."

CHAPTER TWENTY-FOUR

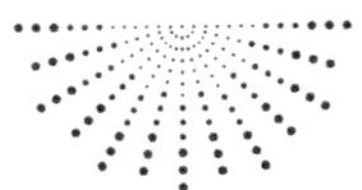

Saorla tossed and turned in her bed most of the night. Sleep refused to come easy. She reached for her cell phone. A few minutes past four in the morning. She would have to get up in a couple of hours, and she hadn't had much sleep all week. The excitement of finding Father Conlin's work acted as a powerful stimulant.

She had to settle her nerves. But how could she? They were on the verge of making some of the most profound historical discoveries in all of the western world.

Or were they?

Perhaps Ian's grandfather George was just a deluded old man, and his dreams were nothing more than indulgent fantasies. Maybe Father Conlin was an imaginative erudite priest that had a hard time separating fact from fairy tale.

Something else gnawed at her, with even more profound ramifications for her personally. She had tried to push it to the recesses of her mind, but in the wee hours of this late October morning, she failed to succeed. She couldn't escape the notion that if the artifacts turned out to be nothing but a cruel hoax, it would for her refute the existence of a supreme being who sought communication with her to direct her life. She would be without purpose. Lost.

On the other hand, if it turned out the God of Patrick was real and that *that* God was *the* God and was trying to communicate with her, it would change everything.

In an instant, she determined to go deeper.

Take the glorious quest.

The words sounded in her head as divine writ straight from the heavens to her soul. Time to jump all in, at least until she found something that would prove her course ill-founded. What she needed was to have a look at the Book of Kells.

But how?

An academic request would take too long, perhaps weeks or months. And what reason could she give anyhow for taking the book outside in the middle of the night that wouldn't get her laughed out of the university.

Her mind traveled back to the nights in the Long Room. She'd noticed that the security guards had left the building every night one-half hour before midnight and returned promptly an hour later. One of the nights, she'd gone outside to an adjacent building to the lounge to buy a bottled water from a vending machine. There, the guards played poker and smoked at a table. What if they took a card break every night? She would have to conduct some reconnaissance to find out. It could well be there was a window when nobody was physically with the book.

The surveillance cameras on campus were the next problem her mind settled on. She would have to find a way to prevent the cameras from recording her presence. Myrna had dated a techie she boasted was so good he could electronically give any college employee he wanted a pay raise and change any student's grade with a stroke of a button. Maybe he could help.

Saorla took turns on the one hand scolding herself for thinking such mischievous thoughts and alternately thinking up more schemes to get access to the Book of Kells. She finally fell into a fitful sleep.

She didn't know how long she'd been out when she awoke to her cell phone ringing in the darkness. Reaching over, she knocked it off the nightstand. Light cast upward from her phone. Amy from the lab in Belfast.

"Are you sitting down?" Amy asked.

"More like lying down. What time is it?"

"Six, but I don't offer any apologies. You're going to want to hear this."

"What is it?"

"The samples you gave both dated to 469 AD."

Saorla launched out of bed and began pacing around, the math rifling through her head. If Patrick was born in 392 AD, one of the accepted dates for his birth, the dating of the satchel would put it within his lifetime. He would have been in his late 70's.

Saorla thanked Amy, asked her to keep the artifacts safe until she could pick them up, and ended the call.

Any lingering skepticism about George's visions was an ice cube melting on a sunbaked sidewalk in the south of France. She would look at the Book of Kells under a full moon even if it killed her.

A FEW SECONDS AFTER NINE ON SATURDAY MORNING, IAN arrived at his office at the legal aid clinic, which Ian utilized to his advantage. He checked the mail and found that his inter-jurisdictional law license had been approved, declaring him legal to practice law in Ireland for the next six months.

Yes!

Hopefully, it wouldn't be necessary for longer than a couple of weeks.

No.

Somehow, the hurry to return to California had diminished.

He checked his office voice mail, and in his first message since his hiring, Sophie Zaworski had called to thank him for his help and explained that more potential clients had desperate need of free legal aid. Monday she would bring in another domestic abuse victim. She also invited Ian to church tomorrow and expressed hope that he could persuade the professor to attend too. Perhaps Ian could sweeten the deal by informing Saorla that the pastor had gone on a ministry trip and had left the church in Killian's care.

Ian spent much of the rest of the morning researching how Irish law handled domestic violence cases. He learned that two kinds of orders of protection existed—a safety order and a barring order. Application for both kinds of orders initiated in the district court and resulted in a hearing before a judge. Safety orders prohibit a non-household member from coming near the home of the victim for up to five years. Barring orders, on the other hand, remove a family member from the home of the victim for up to three years.

The information would be useful for the kinds of cases Sophie planned to bring him. But Ian's thoughts drifted to his own fragmented family. No court had ordered a barring order between him and his father, but the end result felt the same. They hadn't had much, if any, interaction over the past three years.

Ian decided to dial his grandparents. He hadn't had a recent update on Papa George's condition but figured that no news was good news.

Nana's pleasant voice didn't greet him. The gruff tone of his father, Rory, surprised him instead.

"Oh ... hey, I heard you were coming," Ian said.

"It's good to hear your voice, son. You should come back to the farm."

"How is he?"

"Weak. I've never ... ever seen him this way."

Emotion cracked his father's words, something Ian hadn't observed before unless the topic related to soccer.

"Has he been conscious much?"

"Less than an hour today."

Ian decided his grandfather had deteriorated since he had left. "I see."

"Listen, Ian, we need to talk."

"About what? Soccer?" The questions were out before he could reel them back. He didn't care. No matter how much he dreaded the conversation that would surely follow.

"What's wrong with that?" Rory asked, his voice rising.

"Nothing, unless that's all you talk about."

"What's that supposed to mean?"

"You know ... Soccer is all you care about. Ever."

"Listen, I just never understood why you threw it all away. Even now, you're still young. With a year of serious dedication you could probably get yourself up to a professional club level."

"So that's your assessment of how you view my life? You think I've wasted it, thrown it away?"

"Look, I just don't understand you."

"You never tried."

"That's not true. I tried all kinds of ways to keep you motivated."

"That's not understanding. You tried all kinds of ways to *manipulate* me."

"It would be nice if we could spend some time together here. I promise not to talk about soccer." Rory cleared his throat, his voice just above a whisper.

"It would be worth coming just to see if you could keep that promise," Ian said. "Right now I'm helping Papa with a project that's pretty important to him. I'm getting really close to—"

"—He told me some about that," Rory said sharply. "It seems like a fool's errand to me."

"How would—"

Ian's words were interrupted by the sudden voice of his grandmother in the background, calling "Rory."

"Listen, I gotta go. Papa is asking for me. But think about what I said."

CHAPTER TWENTY-FIVE

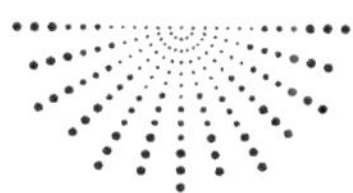

Shards of early afternoon sunshine splayed through the window and greeted Saorla as she entered her office at Trinity College. Many Saturdays she never made it to campus, opting instead to work from home. But Myrna proved to be such a loquacious houseguest that the cloister her office promised would be a welcome reprieve. She closed the door behind her with a satisfying *thud* then settled in at her desk. For the next hour, she delved into Conlin's thick tome, the one she'd taken from the shelf of the second-story of the Long Room.

Nothing new had jumped out at her so far as she read and reread, chewing on the text and then chewing some more. Oh well, she'd found what they'd been looking for. She'd put the book back later this afternoon.

A sudden knock at the door, a tap really, preceded the handle turning it open.

"Working on your CV, love?" Claire asked as she poked her head into the office and then stepped through the doorway."

Saorla shoved the Conlin book into the top drawer of her desk. "And that would be plan B you are asking about?"

"Exactly. You can't be too prepared. Survival of the fittest."

"Suppose not."

"I'm sure of it. You're the gatekeeper of your own destiny."

"What about God?" The words blurted out before she really even thought about the implication of the question. She grappled to offer some context. She and Claire had never before broached the subject of *God*. "I mean, what if there's more than the material ..." her words trailed off—made her feel week and small for some reason.

"You've been under more stress this year than I thought. God is an unrealistic concept. You know better than to believe in myths. I'm not saying there isn't a certain magic about the universe. I've been rethinking many things myself of late. I think there's truth in every religion, but who's to say the old ways weren't best."

"Old ways?"

"The Europe that existed before Christianity."

"You mean paganism?"

"Why not? It offers as good an explanation as any for the mysteries that surround us. And if you're asking me, it's a lot more fun with a lot less hang-ups. No suffocating sexual mores, nor boorish love-your-neighbor bromides. And if there is an after-life, it isn't dependent on who you sleep with or whether you made it to Mass on Sunday."

Saorla sighed. "I just want to know what's true and real. Honestly, I don't know what to think. Can you keep a secret?"

Claire nodded and leaned in. Saorla couldn't quite place the look on her colleague's face. Curiosity, perhaps?

No, something different.

Saorla noted that ninety percent below the surface, Claire concealed a contempt-filled pride. But how could she blame Claire for it? Saorla felt the same way a couple of weeks ago. She owed Claire the gift of honesty, even if it meant that Saorla would be diminished in this woman's eyes because of it.

"Just between you and me, I've seen some things in the past few days to make me wonder if there isn't something more out there. I'm going to investigate. Do you want a report when I'm done?"

Claire laughed as if the whole thing was a silly joke. "If I were you," she said smiling, "I would stay one step ahead of big, bad Dean

Grady. And get that CV ready." She headed toward the door then turned back to Saorla. "What were you really doing in your office today?" The smile had vanished, indicating the gravity of the question.

"Thinking about what to put in that CV," Saorla said, lying. If Dean Grady found out about her plans for the Book of Kells, looking for a new job would be the least of her worries. But the lie confirmed the worst—that she had a long way to go if she was ever going to be a fit candidate to inquire after God.

CHAPTER TWENTY-SIX

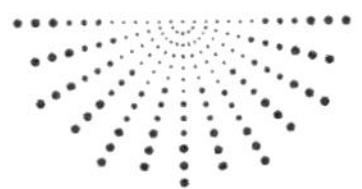

The drizzle started when Saorla reached the bus stop on Merrion Street. She'd walked three blocks from her Georgian to meet Ian. When last they met, they forged the plan to meet and catch a bus to Sophie's church.

Saorla put up her umbrella just as Ian rounded the corner. She started to jog toward him before she caught herself and slowed to a walk. The desire to have a sneak peek at the Book of Kells almost consumed her, and she relished seeing Ian's face light up at the prospect of such an adventure. But she shouldn't be seen running to him like some silly schoolgirl.

Ian's warm smile greeted her, accelerating the beat of her heart. She immediately launched into the details of her scheme. When she came to the part about the guard's nightly poker game, the bus pulled to the curb. They boarded, walked past rows of empty seats, and sat in the back.

"So you see," Saorla said in a whisper, "I confirmed last night that the guards do indeed take a sixty-minute break that starts like clockwork a half hour before midnight."

"It's odd they would leave it alone."

"They're obviously not following the rules. The breaks are

supposed to be taken one at a time. But the two on the night watch fancy a game of chance for an hour in lieu of the routine of protecting the exhibit."

Saorla searched his eyes for some hint of encouragement. Instead, he looked unconvinced and tired.

"What if something goes wrong?" he asked. "What if it rains for Pete's sake?"

"The only thing we really have to worry about besides the guards is the electronic security system. But it's not as advanced as you would think. Last year, an undergrad told Myrna that he got into the museum security network using the password 1234."

Ian shifted in his seat. "I don't know. Myrna hacking into computers?"

"What happened to you? You were ready to go the other night."

Ian shrugged. "I guess my rashness has been replaced by common sense."

"I thought you were always keen for a good adventure."

"I try to avoid *illegal* adventure," he said flatly.

"It's not stealing, more like borrowing. Haven't you ever borrowed anything before?"

He didn't answer, just stared out the window.

This was going to be harder than expected. She had not anticipated the need to persuade Ian toward bold action. Maybe he was right.

They sat in silence for a few minutes as the bus fitfully wound its way through the city traffic. "What about your grandfather?" Saorla finally asked.

"Well, he's still holding on." Ian rubbed his temples as if considering something urgent. "I did promise the old man I would get to the bottom of this. If I knew more about the dating of the lab samples, it might make a difference."

"Oops," Saorla said, "I forgot to tell you. The results came back from the lab in Belfast. You won't believe it. The vellum dated to 469 AD, give or take a few years. At any rate, well within the plausible limits of Patrick's lifetime."

"Wow!"

A frown replaced the initial excitement on his face. "How come you didn't tell me about this?"

"I owed you a surprise after you showed up uninvited on my birthday. Now we're even."

"Ouch, you are a competitor. Maybe *you* should have been the soccer player."

She laughed. "Well, I am competitive. But I also wanted to see your face when I told you, so I waited until we could be together."

"That's sweet." He brightened but then turned to look again out the window. "What if the book gets damaged while we have it out for our little rogue investigation?"

"I have an airtight container we can carry it in. We're only taking out one of the four volumes, briefly at that, and we can do it on a night that is moisture free."

"*Moisture free*," Ian mocked. "It wasn't supposed to rain today. I shouldn't have to tell you there are no moisture-free guarantees in these isles, should I?"

"No need to get hysterical over the possibility of a rain drop. It won't take long to take a peek at one leaf of vellum to see if there is a code encrypted in it. If it's raining, we won't take it out."

"I still don't know. Can't you put a request in to examine it as a scholar?"

"For heaven's sake, Ian, it's just a book! It's not like it's the Magna Carta or the lost Arc of the Covenant. And we're only going to have it for a brief moment. An official request to examine it could take weeks to grant, and you know we don't have that kind of time. Besides, what do you think will happen to my request when I tell them I have to take it outside on the night of a full moon?" Saorla realized she was nearly shouting and hoped her words hadn't wafted over the rumble of the bus to the passengers in the third row and the driver.

The bus halted at the scheduled stop, a block away from the church.

An hour later, they were seated next to Sophie, as Killian preached a message from I Corinthians, chapters one and two. He contrasted the wisdom of the world with the wisdom of God:

"For the word of the cross is foolishness to those who are perishing," he read, "but to those who are being saved it is the power of God."

Somehow the topic of his message irritated her like a bug flying into her eye. Had he chosen this message just to address her?

He continued, "For it is written,

'I WILL DESTROY THE WISDOM OF THE WISE

AND THE CLEVERNESS OF THE CLEVER I WILL SET ASIDE.'

"Where is the wise man? Where is the scribe? Where is the debater of this age? Has not God made foolish the wisdom of the world?"

The longer Killian spoke, the crustier the shell formed around her to fend herself from his words. At one point, Ian tapped her on the shoulder and whispered in her ear. "Isn't this a fantastic sermon?"

"Does he think my book knowledge and wisdom are useless? It seems naive and rude of him to preach that."

"I don't think he means to attack you personally."

"Could have fooled me."

"But you *are* the wise scholar. So if the shoe fits."

"What's that supposed to mean?"

"I mean, much of our lives are so much about our own good ideas and the good ideas of others. But did you ever consider that God has better ideas? Even the best ideas? Have you ever sought true spiritual wisdom?"

Saorla turned away from him and crossed her arms. Why couldn't Killian talk about salient topics—like loving your neighbor and feeding the poor?

Killian continued to challenge her thinking as he spoke of God's preference to use the weak rather than the strong.

"Consider your calling, people, there were not many mighty, not many noble, but God has chosen the foolish things of the world to shame the wise, and God has chosen the weak things of the world to shame the strong ... so that no man may boast before God."

He brought the message to a boil as he outlined how Christianity has as its gateway faith in the "foolishness" of the cross of Christ, which is in reality the power of God and the wisdom of God.

"Christianity is different from all other religions," he said, "because it is ultimately a relationship—the union of the believer with God Himself through the Holy Spirit."

Killian read from John chapters 14 through 16 to show that the Spirit's work is the antithesis of worldly wisdom and is to guide us into all truth and to tell us about things to come. To illustrate his point, he launched into a story about a pastor friend of his from Honduras who saved his entire village from the aftereffects of a Hurricane by listening for the voice of God.

By the time Killian finished his message, Saorla stood up, eager to leave.

Ian took her hand and smiled at her. "Ready for lunch? I'm starving. And wasn't that a great message? I just want God's wisdom."

"Then why don't you just ask *him* to help you with the mysteries of the artifacts? Why come to me?"

"I did ask him, and he sent me you."

Okay, some of the crust over her heart began to melt at those words.

Still, she was as confused as ever. But a silent prayer for guidance sprang from her soul, her first prayer in years. And a thought fluttered to her mind, gentle as dove's wings: *Pray Patrick's words from the "Breastplate."*

MID-MORNING THE NEXT DAY, IAN HUNCHED OVER HIS desk at the legal aid clinic, mulling over his situation. It had been too long since he'd been on a heart-thumping adventure. Yes, since his arrival in Ireland two weeks ago, the drama at Professor Greenwald's coastal home would qualify. But being a near witness to the murder of a good man was not the kind of stress he enjoyed. He needed to forge out onto the sea or hike up into the mountains, but that didn't seem likely in the foreseeable future.

A sneak peek at the Book of Kells under the moonlight would guarantee a rush. The stakes of getting caught red-handed would be high, though likely not warranting prison time. Would it be technically illegal, though, to briefly take one of the four volumes of the book out of its case to have a look for academic purposes? It would entail a minor trespass. Not a serious crime, but it would be embarrassing nonetheless if they were caught. More importantly, his career as an attorney couldn't afford to have another questionable incident.

Ian heard the bell at the front entrance signaling visitors had arrived. Killian and Sophie. They had a woman with them too. Probably the new domestic violence victim Sophie had spoken of in her last phone message.

Ian ushered them back to his office. After hauling in some extra chairs, he had them take a seat, and then he turned to Killian. "Great message you gave yesterday."

"Thanks. I enjoy talking about God."

Ian dipped his head in a knowing nod. "I can tell. Your enthusiasm is contagious. Same goes for Sophie."

Sophie and Killian smiled at each other. They made a great couple. He was as handsome as she was naturally beautiful. Hers was packaged in sincerity and humility. Killian, on the other hand, radiated the calm air of someone who could plug himself in anywhere and lead. He didn't have an accent that Ian could place.

"Where are you from? I'm usually pretty good at telling, but in your case ..."

Killian chuckled. "Not much of a mystery. Typical missionary kid. Born in Bolivia to parents from the UK. Wales actually, but I've never spent much time in Wales. My parents started a ministry called Going the Extra Mile. I did spend a lot of time in South and Central America, the Caribbean, and some time in the States. But for the last ten years Ireland has been home."

"I should have guessed that you were a missionary from your story yesterday. But you look athletic, I would have pegged you for a professional athlete."

Killian laughed. "That's funny cause I did grow up playing a lot of soccer. And my father had me in tennis lessons whenever we were on furlough. When I returned to the UK at nineteen, I got a job teaching youth tennis, which I still do, only now I run my own youth program, but I also dabble in real estate and other small business ventures."

Ian talked with his guests through the morning, fascinated by Killian's story. An artist, musician, writer, on top of running his business ventures, there seemed to be no end to his interests, but it was clear that the overriding concern of his life was to live the message he'd spoken yesterday.

Ian was eventually able hear the story of the domestic violence victim through Sophie's translating. Another sad case of abuse. He promised to set the wheels of justice in motion and do what he could to protect the woman.

As his guests stood to leave, Sophie mentioned that her next stop was to have lunch with Professor Saorla. Killian stared Ian in the eye, unnerving him. Was he about to call out some secret flaw of his?

"I think it is good you're spending time with her."

Ian's stomach twanged with excitement. It was the same sort of half-excited, half-fearful feeling he'd get at Mavs. Killian continued to stare at him, his eyes penetrating and compassionate.

"Can I give you a word of Godly advice?" Killian finally asked.

What if he said something about Saorla being a permanent part of Ian's life? He wasn't ready for that. His stomach turned queasy over what was about to happen next. He found himself saying, "Sure."

Killian's eyes dipped into Ian's soul, searching through him. "You seem to have a lot of courage," he finally said, his tone serious. "An uncommon lack of fear. I believe God wants you to uncover difficult-to-find answers for yourself and others. Be encouraged. He is for you."

Were Killian's words somehow related to Ian's dilemma over the Book of Kells? Or were they just simply an encouragement to keep helping people obtain justice through the use of his legal skills? Ian wasn't sure. And he couldn't very well come right out and directly ask Killian if he thought Ian should steal the Book of Kells.

But what if there was a message contained in the Book of Kells that was meant for him? He had no intent to commit a crime, just an unexplainable feeling he needed to muster the courage to take a look at the book no matter how that decision might impact his legal career.

Saorla had promised that no damage would come to the manuscript by a quick peek. And acting like some wimp who was afraid to take a little risk wasn't likely to engender favorable feelings on her part toward him. The book was regularly taken out of its airtight container to turn it to a different page from time to time. There was no valid concern they would damage it. Was he just rationalizing an excuse for his actions? Or was God calling him to be bold in this instance? This much was clear: God wouldn't speak to him to engage in something contrary to his written word. Stealing would be contrary to Scripture, of course, but he wasn't going to steal the Book of Kells, just look at it.

He now saw that if there was indeed something encoded in that ancient book, it was meant for him. The time was now. And it was the glory of kings to search it out.

There. He had his answer.

As Ian parted with his guests on the sidewalk outside the clinic, he whispered to Sophie, "When you see the professor at lunch today, please tell her that I've had a change of heart. I'm all in with her plan, and I'll meet her tonight at six."

CHAPTER TWENTY-SEVEN

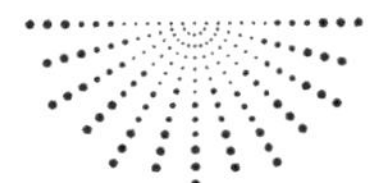

"If there are no hitches it should all go down like this," Saorla whispered to Ian and Myrna over a cup of steaming-hot tea. The three occupied a booth at a no-frills coffee shop located on Anne Street two blocks from Trinity College. "There's always supposed to be a guard standing in front of the bullet proof, climate-controlled display case. Always supposed to be two guards in the building. Except there's not. Thirty minutes before midnight, they take a break, like clockwork, to smoke and play poker. They're usually gone about an hour. The shortest time I clocked them absent from their post was fifty-seven minutes—"

"Great, then we should be in no rush," Ian said.

"Not quite," Saorla said, trying to keep her voice calm. "The problem is that Myrna can only deactivate the system for ten minutes. If it's out longer, it overrides what she's doing and reboots itself, which means that if the book is not there, the alarm activates.

Ian's eyes were like saucers. "Myrna is a computer geek on top of everything else?"

"No. Her friend Jim is."

"Jim from your surprise birthday party?"

"Yeah. He's a computer genius. Told Myrna all she needed to know. But he was busy giving fiddle lessons tonight over at Saint Kevin's Community College. So we're stuck with Myrna."

Ian gave a half-roll of his eyes. "Great, we are being played second fiddle by Jim now."

Saorla chuckled but then punched Ian in the shoulder. "Can we get serious now?"

"ONE MORE QUESTION," IAN SAID. "IF THE DISPLAY CASE IS bullet proof, how are we going to get into it?"

"Before Myrna deactivates the system, she will be able to disengage the locking mechanism. That's how they take it out when they turn the page. She will be stationed at the central computer in another part of the campus. And, thanks to Jim, will be able to get the display case open with a few keystrokes."

"How do we know when to go in?" Ian asked.

"Myrna will shut things down at 11:35, five minutes after the time the guards always leave. It will be enough time for us to make sure they've made it to their poker game. But after that point, the clock is ticking. Remember we just have ten minutes once it goes down."

"Why don't we set another book in its place so that the system thinks all is well while we have the real thing out for a look?" Ian asked.

Myrna who had been sitting back listening patiently up to that point, leaned in to join the conversation. "That won't work. If the network is activated, it's designed to read the current page that's open, if all is not exactly as it should be down to the correct page on display, alarms will sound, and protective safeguards will be deployed. And that of course means trouble. The system is designed to keep thieves inside. If you're anywhere downstairs when it goes off, you'll be trapped on the other side of iron bars until the Gardai arrive to take you to jail."

Ian was losing the color from his face. Saorla didn't want him to back out now. "It shouldn't be a problem," she added. "Ten minutes should be more than enough time to get the book out, take a look at whatever we need to see, and then get it back in the display case."

Ian gulped his coffee then said, "So what you're telling me is there's ten minutes at most from start to finish or else."

"Yep, ten minutes," Myrna said, a smile widening from cheek to cheek, "ten minutes or else it's your Day of Doom."

"That's about right," Saorla admitted wanly.

Ian pursed his lips and gave a single nod. "Okay, how will we know the system is deactivated?"

Saorla took a sip of tea. "The absence of red blinking lights near the display case. In the dark, you can't miss them if the system is live."

"Sounds like you ladies have thought of everything."

Myrna put her hands in the air. "No worries. When this works out, we'll be qualified to work for the G2."

Ian looked puzzled. "G2?"

Saorla tapped at her teacup and smiled. "Irish Intelligence Agency. We can all be spies after this experience."

Ian rubbed his temples in frustration. "People already tell me they think I'm a spy."

"You do look like James Bond," Myrna said.

"Oh brother, here we go again," he said.

Saorla shrugged her shoulders and shared a confused glance with Myrna. "Okay, so you must have hated to play spy games as a kid or something."

Saorla finished casting out the rest of the details of her plan.

"What if it rains?" Ian asked.

Saorla made a goose egg sign with her hand. "Zero percent chance tonight. The forecast for the rest of the week looks progressively worse. A big storm rolls through in a few days. Tonight, however, is perfect for viewing the full moon, a prerequisite to seeing the code according to Father Conlin. And none of us could stand to wait another twenty-nine days or so for the next one."

Ian gave a quick twitch of his head. "And what if something else goes wrong?"

"I knew I was forgetting something," Saorla said. "If there's any trouble, Myrna will bolt to her vehicle parked in the Temple Bar area and pick us up at the corner of College and Pearse Street. We can blend in there."

"Hopefully, we blend with the night," Ian muttered as he cinched down his hood.

Myrna unwrapped a florescent purple scarf from around her neck. "All three of us dressed in black, except for this." She carefully folded the scarf and placed it in her coat pocket. "We're like cat burglars."

Saorla wore a black leather jacket, black boots, black leggings, and a black turtle-neck sweater. She glanced over at Myrna who wore a hooded black coat with some dark-colored jeans and black shoes. Myrna's silver hair would stick out, but she could always cover that with her hood. Ian had on black jeans and a black sweatshirt.

At 11:15, the three conspirators left the coffee shop and huddled outside on the sidewalk for a few final words. When there was nothing more to say, Saorla bowed her head and closed her eyes.

"What are you doing?" Ian asked.

"Praying."

His eyes grew wide. "I thought you weren't a believer."

She enjoyed his befuddlement. "That was last week." The truth was she didn't really know if she was a *believer* or what that even meant for sure. She was just as confused inside as he looked now, but she decided to keep him guessing nonetheless.

His eyes narrowed and trained on her suspiciously. "I've heard of jailhouse conversions, but this seems more like a *pre*-jailhouse conversion."

Myrna stepped away to leave. Her mission in the computer room required her to veer off in a different direction. "Have a whale of time tonight! You two are off to a great first date!"

Saorla shook her head. "You really have no filter, lassie."

"Been told that all my life. I'll pick you up at the designated spot in half an hour if all goes well, and if it doesn't, I'll be there sooner."

"You'll put the heart crossway in me if something goes wrong and you're not there," Saorla said.

"Never fear, Myrna is near." She flipped her hood up, covering her short silver hair, and traipsed off.

FIVE MINUTES OF BRISK WALKING AND THE SIMPLE TURN of the key that Jim had given her brought Myrna to the inside of the room that controlled the campus computer and security network. Her nerves wanted no part of being near the Book of Kells exhibit itself. But she would do whatever she could, within reason, to help the professor that had meant so much to her the past year.

Myrna checked her watch: 11:34. In thirty seconds, if everything went according to plan, she would shut down security without cutting electricity or giving off any signal that something was amiss. This whole episode would make an entertaining yarn next year at Berkley, barring any major snafus. If the planned failed, however, she would have to settle for regaling her fellow inmates with the tale at the Dochas Centre, the female wing of the Mountjoy Prison Complex in north Dublin. Either way it was sure to make a good story.

The timer on Myrna's cell buzzed. Time to flick the switch.

She made two entries into the computer and hit enter. Campus security went into limbo.

SAORLA SET DOWN THE CONTAINER SHE WOULD USE TO transport the book and pulled two pairs of skin-tight black gloves from her coat pocket. One pair for her and one pair for Ian.

They slipped the gloves on. Saorla took keys from her pocket and opened a little-used, unlit door to the Old Library. She picked up her container and shuffled in. Ian followed close.

They'd already checked the adjacent building and had found the two guards, sitting at a table, dealing cards and smoking. So far so good.

They now crept through a deserted walkway of the Long Room toward a corridor of steps leading to the basement level and the Book of Kells exhibition.

Beads of sweat formed on Saorla's forehead, and she felt lightheaded.

She scanned her surroundings. Moonlight shot through windows casting long shadows over the shiny hardwood floor. No sign of movement other than their own. No alarms or sirens. No bars slamming shut on entryways.

She flashed Ian an all-clear sign, and they descended the stairs. Below was the room known as the Treasury, the room where the Book of Kells itself was housed.

Sweat poured profusely over the nape of her neck now as she crept down the stairs like a tight rope walker at a circus, placing her feet ever so softly from one step to the next. Halfway down, her efforts yielded a loud creak.

Stopping, she turned to face Ian on the stairs above her and whispered, "Hold up. I need a tissue."

"How come we're going so slow?"

He was right. They would have to move faster. She yanked a tissue from her coat pocket and wiped the sweat from her forehead. Maybe she could avoid ruining the dark eye shadow she had applied. In a hurry now, she struggled to return the tissue to her pocket. A *rat-tat-tat* echoed below. Had something fallen and tumbled down the stairs? Or was it just her heart rattling outside her chest?

Ian tapped her on the shoulder. "What was that?" he asked in a raspy whisper.

"I don't know. Probably nothing." But it had to be something to make all that racket. No time to think about it now. She'd come back tomorrow, show Ian the exhibit, and look for it then. Whatever *it* was.

It wouldn't matter. As long as there wasn't a guard in the room below, they would get through this. Out and back with the book before anyone knew.

They creeped down the remainder of the steps and entered the Treasury. Saorla removed a small flashlight from her pocket. With the murky tunnel of wee light it projected, she scanned the hardwood floor for any sign of an object.

Nothing.

The only other lighting came from the red glow of an exit sign at the entryway for the stairs leading up to the Long Room. She raised the beam of the flashlight ahead. The calligraphy on the wall read, *Turning Darkness into Light*. Great thought, but they needed to remain *in the dark*. At least for the next ten minutes.

Gingerly, but also a little faster now, she put one foot in front of the other as she made her way across the blackness of the Treasury toward the bullet-proof case that housed the chief paragon of the Irish people.

They were almost there. A few more steps. A noise?

They both halted. Holding themselves unmoving in the near darkness of the Treasury, they listened.

There was only silence.

Saorla checked her watch timer. Well over a minute had passed. Time to kick up the speed.

They moved on to the case. She shone her light into the exhibit. The book rested under a glass counter, its pages open to display the brilliance of its artwork. No blinking red lights near the case. Thank God Myrna had succeeded in deactivating the system. Ian lifted the counter slightly, testing.

No alarms. He easily hoisted the countertop upwards from the center.

Saorla, on cue, lifted out the sacred book and reverently placed it in her container. One leg of their journey was complete.

It was a race against the clock now.

MYRNA SAT AT THE COMPUTER SCREEN AND MARVELED that she had been able to shut down the campus security system without cutting off electricity and without triggering any alarms. Jim was a genius. She'd have to buy him dinner or find some other way to thank him. Honestly though, if she simply let him buy *her* dinner that would probably be enough thanks to satisfy him. As far as she knew, the guy hadn't had a date all year.

Myrna realized, however, that they weren't out of danger yet. Her timer told her that six minutes remained before the system rebooted and the electronic eyes of big brother resumed their all-knowing gaze.

Where were Ian and Saorla now?

Maybe they'd already finished and had returned the book. Or maybe, God forbid, the security guards had turned back early from their poker game.

Again, she was glad that it was not her out there in the night battling against time with the national treasure in her hands. The relative safety of the locked control room comforted her. She knew from her conversations with Jim that no one would suspect that she had tampered with the system. And just as importantly she knew that unlike the Treasury room of the *Turning Darkness into Light* exhibit, there were no full-time guards assigned to the computer room she now sat in.

She checked her watch again. Five minutes and forty seconds left. She looked up at the computer screen.

Something was happening.

But nothing should be happening.

A humming sound growing louder. And why had her screen suddenly come to life?

Her head suddenly felt light as if it were floating away from her body, a swirl of angst swam from her chest to her stomach.

"Rats!" she cried. The system was rebooting itself early.

She punched keys at random, desperate to try and stop it.

It only seemed to be powering up faster.

A shrill alarm screeched in Myrna's ear. She whirled in her seat and fled for the door.

THEY STOOD IN THE OPEN OF THE CAMPUS RUGBY FIELD, lit only by the light of a full moon. Ian worried they'd used too much time extricating themselves from the Old Library building. In his opinion, Saorla had taken too long creeping up the steps and out of the door. Despite the unneeded caution, however, they'd still managed to be nearly on schedule.

Less than seven minutes left and counting down.

He could have sworn that he felt a sprinkle hitting his forehead. A check of the sky revealed a small cloud off in the distance. But the moon was shining in all of its reflected brilliance.

Ian held the ancient volume gingerly and parallel to the ground so that page forty-four hung open and out by itself. Rays of moonlight shone from the sky and penetrated the calf-skin leaf, trickling out the other side. Saorla took off her gloves and put them in her pocket. Placing her reading glasses on, she began to study the page.

"A series of Roman numerals," she said, shaking her head. "And at least three lines of them."

"Numbers?"

"Yes, no words, just numbers."

Ian leaned his head around and glimpsed at the numerals: V, I, VII, VII, IX, VIII ... This was odd.

Saorla had a pen and paper pad in hand now. "I'm going to transcribe the Roman numerals into our familiar Hindu-Arabic system. It'll be faster."

"Huh?"

"Never mind."

She scribbled some numbers onto a pad. "The first line is 51.779833481191585. The second line starts with a negative number."

"What are they supposed to mean?" Ian asked. "They sound like credit card numbers."

"Or temperature readings. Except the Romans didn't use negative numbers or decimal signs."

"This is too crazy."

Saorla shrugged her shoulders. “There is also a third line. It simply reads, *79 m.*”

“Let me take a look at it.” Ian maneuvered the book so he could view the leaf with the backdrop of the moon. The three lines became visible on the translucent calf skin when he turned the page just right.

“It’s bizarre.” Ian studied the leaf another moment. “What is the Scripture verse that the numbers appear over?”

“Oh, that’s right, you can’t read Latin,” Saorla teased. “It’s over Matthew 13:52. *‘Thus, each scribe who’s trained for the kingdom of heaven is like a housemaster, who brings forward out of his treasure both the new and the old.’*”

Ian pondered the words for a moment, especially the reference to the word *treasure* and then looked down at his watch. “Look at the time.” There was less than six minutes left.

“We can sort out the meaning later.”

SAORLA HAD JUST BEGUN TO FOCUS IN ON TRANSCRIBING the second line when the alarms began to wail. Breath left her chest.

Can’t be! They should still have more than five minutes. What had gone wrong?

Saorla looked to Ian. He hesitated a moment, then grabbed the book from her, and sprinted toward the building. “No!” She howled as she chased after him.

He had already begun his descent down the stairs from the long room to the Treasury when she caught him. “Wait, Ian.”

He turned toward her but continued to make his way down the steps. “Let’s get this back before—”

“I didn’t get the second row of numbers down yet,” she cried. “We have to take the book with us. We’ll never get another chance with it.”

The news froze him in his tracks. And then a loud clank of iron bars sealed off the bottom of the stairs.

“Back up,” he shouted, which Saorla barely heard over the wailing of the sirens.

In a panic, she bounded the stairs.

The exit above them was about to seal them down. She strained every muscle in her body to keep ahead of him as they took the stairs two or three leaps at a time.

Two more stairs to go.

A loud clank resounded above her head. Iron bars descended from the door frame, steady and inexorable. The exit at the top of the stairs would be sealed off in another second.

She leapt forward and made it through. A thud sounded behind her, and Ian scrambled past the entry way just as the bars fell behind their heels.

Unscathed on the freedom side, she let out a sigh of relief.

Ian now stood ahead of her, motioning for her to get beside him. From the cover of a Greek column, he squatted and pointed. "Security guards ahead," he whispered soft as a breath.

Saorla saw them as she tucked in behind him. About sixty or seventy meters away at the opposite end of the Long Room, the guards drew their weapons and crouched.

"Is there another way out?" Ian asked, once again breathing the words into her ear.

"Yes … at least I think so."

Saorla trained her eyes on the guards, who now seemed unsure of what to do next. The two men began yelling into their cell phones and then disappeared down a stairwell. She glanced off to her side and saw an old door.

"Come on," she said. "There's a little-used exit over there."

Little used?

She had never seen it used before, but it was a door. Saorla sprinted in its direction and hoped Ian was following. No time to look back.

They came to a ramshackle wooden door that was partially obstructed by a fake potted tree. Saorla slid the pot out of the way and was about to yank on the knob.

"Where does that lead?" Ian asked. "And won't an alarm sound?"

"You're kidding, right? In case you haven't noticed, the sound of alarms is pretty thick already."

"The last question was a joke. You didn't say where this leads, though."

"A wee bit away from here, I hope."

THE DOOR LED DOWN A SERIES OF DILAPIDATED STEPS TO A long dark corridor running underground of campus. Probably hadn't been used in a hundred years. Where would this come out at? How come she didn't even know this passageway existed? She'd have to ask Myrna, the former campus tour guide, about it.

The meager light from their two small flashlights strained to lead the way ahead. The flooring was rotted wood at first, but the longer they travelled through the tunnel-like corridor the worse it got, until finally giving way to gravel beneath their feet.

"I hear rats," Saorla said, her voice rising. "I hate rodents."

"Who doesn't?"

"But I *really* hate them. Not a wee hate, a big hate. Borders on a phobia."

"I betcha they have some big ones down here," Ian said.

"Would you *not* say that please?"

She suddenly held a picture in her mind of a rat climbing up her arm to gnaw at her nose. She sped up her stride to match Ian's gait and tucked her arm under his.

Several minutes passed before it dawned on her that she was clinging to him. She pulled away with a jerk to his arm.

"Sorry. I ... uh ... guess I got scared." She was glad it was dark enough to cover for how red her face must be.

"Don't be sorry. I mean ... It's okay to be scared, and I liked having your arm there."

Saorla wondered what he meant by that. She had to admit that she liked having her arm there too. But why did she still feel a tinge of guilt?

They hurried through the tunnel until they reached a place where it narrowed to such an extent that they could only walk single file. Ian led the way.

"There's a stairway here," he said. "Watch your step."

"This leads somewhere."

"Beats a tunnel to nowhere."

Or a tunnel to jail.

They climbed more rickety steps and reached another old wooden door. Ian turned the handle, but it didn't open. "I think it's locked."

He rammed it with his shoulder several times. On the fourth attempt, it gave way and they found themselves in a dark hallway. Light from her flashlight casted from the floor to the ceiling.

Where were they? It looked familiar, but Saorla couldn't quite place it. Pictures of plants with Latin names lined the walls. The dots connected. They were in the Botany building on the east end of campus behind the rugby field.

Looking out a window, Saorla saw Gardai descending like a plague of locusts. The grass was thick with them. "We need to get out of here, quick." She felt the panic rise in her voice. "The northeast gate is our best chance."

They ran out of an exterior door of the Botany building, sprinted past two buildings, and then saw four Gardai rushing through the east gate and heading south around the O'Reilly building.

"Wait a second," Ian said, pulling Saorla behind a bush with him. "If they spot us, it's all over." The Gardai disappeared around the building.

"Come on," he urged, and they sprinted toward their ticket to freedom, the northeast gate.

"You still got the book?" Saorla rasped.

"You bet."

"Glad you didn't leave it in the tunnel."

"I didn't think of that. Besides, how would we ever get another chance to look at the rest of those numbers."

They made it to the far northeastern gate of the college and slipped out onto the public sidewalk. She filled her lungs with air, willing her breathing to return to normal. On the opposite end of campus now from where they had come in at Parliament Square, Saorla thought for the first time of connecting with Myrna. The city at night was normally filled with a discordant din, but tonight a cacophony of alarm bells and sirens deafened the ears. More Guardia sirens were growing ever closer with each step they took.

Pearse Street came into view, and there, they crossed the sidewalk to the other side of the thoroughfare.

Where was Myrna?

In another moment Pearse Street would be occupied by a dozen Gardai patrol cars that would fill the area with their familiar white, fluorescent yellow and blue colors. The streets would be cordoned off, roadblocks would be set up, traffic and pedestrians would be stopped and searched.

Saorla reeled at the thought that Ian had the Book of Kells tucked tightly under the arm pit of his sweatshirt. The Book of Kells that was now in Saorla's home-brewed container.

Saorla prayed, no, begged actually, that the bulge under Ian's sweatshirt was not obvious to anyone on the street. To whom her desperate plea was directed was unclear, the Cosmos or the God of Killian and Sophie. What was clear was that her desperation struck her as having all the fervor of a wee eight-month-old crying for a diaper change and milk.

Patrol cars were beginning to arrive and dozens of Gardai on foot were flooding into the entrance to the college that Ian and Saorla had just walked out of. The two joined a crowd of onlookers that had gathered on Pearse Street and were heading north toward College Street.

Torn between desperately trying to blend in with the throng and trying to vacate the area as soon as possible, they walked briskly toward College Street.

"I see her blue Corolla," Saorla said.

"It's a sight as sweet as Dawn Patrol at Mavs."

"Huh?"

"Never mind."

The chaotic crowd continued to brew on the sidewalk, as they navigated through it, then jumped into the back of the waiting Corolla.

Gardai swarmed everywhere now. One glanced in the direction of their Corolla and began to raise his hand. Myrna sped off. She made her way up Tara Street and peeled across the bridge over the River Liffey into the north side of Dublin.

Myrna sighed. "You two made it out just in time. I'm so glad—"

"Not exactly," Ian said, pulling the container with the book from under his coat.

Myrna gasped and her face turned ashen. "Don't tell me it's in there."

"Yep."

"Fantastic, so now we're responsible for the illegal possession of the most delicate and valuable artifact in all of Ireland?"

"Afraid so," Ian said.

"The *two* most valuable artifacts in Ireland," Saorla corrected. "Don't forget the copy of the *Breastplate*. If it turns out to be what we think it is, an original penned by the hand of Saint Patrick himself, then we have two of the most valuable artifacts in all of western civilization."

"Why do I seem to be the only one worried about this?" Myrna asked.

"Saorla will be the one under suspicion," Ian said, "so she can't keep the book with her."

"I'll take it," Myrna said, her voice cracking.

"That won't do any good because you live with Saorla," he said. "I'll have to take it and find a safe place for it. Maybe I can open a safe deposit box at a bank and stash it there until we can sort all this out, or maybe I can take it to the farm. I don't know. I'll figure something out."

"Don't forget we still have to find a place to stop so I can take a look at the book again," Saorla said.

"Oh yeah, the second line of numbers," Ian said.

"You mean you're not finished looking at that thing yet?" Myrna squawked.

"Moonlight's burning," Saorla said.

CHAPTER TWENTY-EIGHT

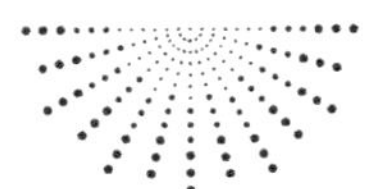

Lorcan arrived at the crime scene at 5:00 a.m., after an aide had awoken him with news of the heist. Oversight of the investigation had been assigned to a veteran detective by the name of Sean Callahan by the Superintendent of the Special Detective Unit, aka SDU, an arm of the Gardai responsible for national security and the most serious matters involving the well-being of the Republic of Ireland.

Lorcan stepped over the yellow police tape stretched around the perimeter of the Old Library and made his way downstairs to the Treasury. He found Callahan conferring with a young Gardai detective with unusually large ears and interrupted their huddle.

"Mr. Duihbur, it is a privilege to see you again," Callahan said.

"Likewise, Sean, I want to offer any help I can with the investigation."

"Of course, your expertise would be more than useful."

"Do you have anything to go on? Any prints, hair follicles, DNA?" Lorcan asked the question even though he already had a rather good idea who had stolen the book. He'd pieced it together after considering the details provided by his informants about the behavior of the professor and the American during their late nights in the Long Room.

All he needed to know now was what the professor had learned in the Long Room that had made her want to heist the Book of Kells. He aimed to figure out why before the day was out.

"There are hundreds of prints on the glass case of the exhibit," Callahan said in his working-class Dublin accent.

"Tell me something I don't know, Detective," Lorcan said. "Have you checked the internet chatter?"

"No, I'm just getting up to speed on the investigation myself," Callahan said. He then pointed to the young detective. "Mr. Duihbur, meet Jumbo, my crack assistant. Jumbo, meet our nation's Minister of Foreign Relations. So tell us, Jumbo, what do we have so far?"

Jumbo plucked a gold ring out of an evidence bag with a metal utensil and displayed it for Callahan's examination. "We found this on the floor by the steps." Jumbo handed Callahan a magnifying glass.

Callahan squinted through the lens. "A wedding ring? There's an inscription on it: *To Saorla My Love*."

Bingo. There was no question who'd taken the book. They had their proof now even if Callahan and Jumbo didn't know it yet.

"We saw the inscription," Jumbo said.

"Make an inquiry to see if that name is connected to anyone at the university," Callahan said to Jumbo. "Obviously, anyone in the world could have taken it, but we have to start somewhere. Also check the credit card transactions from the gift shop and all of the registrars on campus to see if there's been anyone buying something with that name."

Jumbo scratched his enormous ear. "There is one other thing ..."

"Go ahead," Callahan urged.

"We think the perpetrators left through a door that leads underground to the other side of campus. The door is never used, I'm told, but we were able to get a print off it."

"You should run it through the Interpol database," Lorcan said. I'll let the French know we may need their help. It's likely we are dealing with international smugglers. They may try to get the booty out of the country immediately, or they may wait things out a while. But we need to be vigilant at our airports, other ports of exit, etcetera."

Eager to get to his headquarters at the Leinster House, Lorcan began to step away. Was there something he was missing? Yeah. He turned back to face Callahan and Jumbo. "There's one other thing. You should review any footage caught on security camera from the surrounding area and put a watch on all local pawn shops or anywhere you think someone might be likely to show up with the item."

"Good idea," Callahan said, turning to Jumbo now. "And I want to know who tries to open up a new bank account or visits an existing account with an astronomically large sum of money—online or in person—in case they've sold it.

"We are going to need some kind of special search warrant for that," Jumbo said. "I'm not sure—"

"Get it done! We're going to catch these perps. Have the banks report immediately on anyone who shows up in person and even looks like they are thinking of anything suspicious. Have them detain them until we can get someone on site to take them in for questioning."

"I'm on it," Jumbo said.

"Wait a minute," Callahan said. "Scratch the last part about bringing them in for questioning. Better if we simply tail them and monitor their activities. It might lead us to more in the end. If someone turns up suspicious, we'll get a search warrant."

Lorcan nodded and walked away. He would make sure the Book of Kells never made it back to the college. Various fates for the book flashed through his mind, all of them involving ends that would be very pleasing to the Goddess.

After coming out of her bedroom closet with a pair of black boots she chose for their comfort, Saorla made her way to the veranda and peered out to the street below. A patrol car pulled up and parked along the curb.

Her heart skipped a beat, and her breathing quickened.

A short moment later, a second patrol car scooted in behind the first.

This couldn't be happening. Not to her. How had they found her so fast?

Keep a level head.

The Gardai would be at the door in a minute. Sophie was downstairs. Perhaps there was time to get a message to her.

She grabbed a pen and paper and quickly scrawled a note asking Sophie to catch Ian at the bank on Grafton Street before he made his deposit and to tell him to go to plan B.

She raced out of her bedroom—boots and note in hand—and bounded halfway down the stairs.

Too late.

The Gardai were already through the door and into the kitchen, confronting Sophie, who must have let them in. Saorla dropped the note in her tracks on the steps.

"Can I help you?" she asked from her stance on the stairs, trying hard to muster the appropriate level of surprised outrage, despite the sudden pang of nausea in her stomach.

"Police matter," a large Garda with a thick, blonde mustache said from the kitchen while flashing a badge at her.

Remain calm.

She sat on the stairs and stuffed her feet into her boots.

"We need to take someone in for a wee bit of questioning," the Garda added politely. "Might I be having the pleasure of speaking with Professor Saorla O'Rourke?"

"What's this about?" Saorla began to walk down the stairs toward the Garda. She hoped he hadn't noticed the paper she'd dropped behind her.

"I'm afraid there's been a robbery at the college. We need to bring you there to speak with the lead detective."

"Why me?"

"Probably just routine questioning of all the faculty. But I have my orders."

This was anything but routine. She doubted Gardai had sent two patrol cars to bring in each member of the faculty. She met the Garda in the kitchen. "I was going to campus anyway. You'll save me the walk."

As she trudged out to the patrol cars waiting at the curb, she offered a silent prayer that Sophie would find the note on the stairs.

"I'M ASSISTANT SUPERINTENDENT CALLAHAN OF THE SDU. I'm going to have to ask you a few questions. You can call me Detective Callahan if you like."

Saorla's stomach had churned during the ride from her house to the college, but it now reached a maximum roil as she stood face to face with a man that seemed to be looking right through her.

A Garda with large ears handed Detective Callahan an envelope. Callahan reached inside and removed an object. "Do you recognize this?" he asked.

Boy, did she recognize it. The sweat drops formed on her neck and her insides spun faster than an Olympic skater pirouetting out of a triple axel.

The loss of that ring had been the cause of a sleepless night for her. She'd been so focused on the mission of sneaking into the Treasury to get the book, she hadn't realized at the time what she'd dropped. But when she'd arrived back at her Georgian early this morning, it became clear. That's when the worry entered liked an armed bandit.

She took a step closer to Callahan and the ring.

Callahan handed it to her. The familiar inscription was right there on it all right.

"It's my wedding ring." She'd meant to show more surprise with her voice than she did.

Callahan smirked. "It's part of a crime scene investigation now. Do you have any idea how it got here? How it just happened to end up in the Treasury room on the night the Book of Kells was stolen?"

"I hope you don't think I had anything—"

"—Answer the question please."

The right to remain silent was one that all Irish citizens possessed.

But should she assert it? If she clammed up, she would only look guilty. And what good would that do? An inner compulsion gripped her to be as truthful as she could short of giving herself up. Surrender wasn't an option. She wasn't really a lawbreaker. This would be sorted out with time, without her having to suffer the embarrassment of being outed as a common criminal.

"I'm waiting for an answer, Professor."

Her nausea abated, replaced by the feeling that she wouldn't let this man get the best of her.

"I dropped it there yesterday, I guess. I was showing a friend from America the book, you know." This was indeed true, she told herself. She prayed a silent prayer that Callahan didn't ask her what she'd been doing just before midnight.

"Pardon me for asking, but why weren't you wearing the ring on your finger?"

She didn't want to play the grieving widow card. Just stick to the truth. But the truth included the fact that she felt too ashamed to continue wearing the ring after the accident, the accident and death she should have been able to prevent.

"My husband died about two years ago. I keep the ring with me, but I don't wear it on my finger anymore."

"Ah, my deepest condolences."

Saorla detected no empathy in his tone.

"So what were you looking for during those nights you spent in the Long Room last week?"

If he knew about that, what else did he know? The sweat droplets trickled from her neck down her back.

Keep cool.

She shrugged a shoulder at him. "Looking for a book?"

"What kind of book?"

She hoped the color wasn't draining from her face. "A book about the Vikings."

"That's a lot of time spent looking for a book?"

"It was an important and elusive book."

"Care to elaborate?"

"No."

"I didn't think so."

"It was just an old history book that I was having trouble finding but was crucial to some research I was doing."

A Garda appeared behind Callahan and tapped him on the shoulder. He whispered just loud enough for Saorla to hear most of it. Something about several calls from banks about safety deposit boxes that were opened.

Callahan took a few steps away from her and continued to whisper with the Garda. She couldn't make out any words now. The two men became increasingly animated. It had to be a new development in the case.

Please don't let it be Ian.

She decided that if he asked her about anything that could incriminate her, she would demand to see an attorney and assert her right to remain silent guaranteed by the Irish constitution. That course, she knew, would only increase the suspicion mounting against her, but she saw no other choice.

Callahan broke from his conversation with the Garda and marched toward her. He was going to handcuff her and tell her she was under arrest. She just knew it. Instead, he took the ring and held it in front of her face and dropped it back into the envelope.

"We'll keep this as evidence," he said simply. "You are free to go, for now, but you know the drill …"

"Not really."

Don't wander too far beyond the city limits of Dublin. I'm going to have more questions for you."

He walked away, and she just stood there, staring at his back and finally able to let herself blink.

Why hadn't he arrested her? Or continued to question her? The questions floated through her head as she started to slog away.

He's probably just giving you a wee bit more rope to hang yourself.

She would have to walk with her eyes wide open from here on out. That much was for sure.

IAN ARRIVED AT THE BANK ON GRAFTON STREET AROUND 10:15. As far as he could tell, he'd not been followed. He passed through the dark-tinted, revolving door at the entrance and queued in an all-purpose line waiting for the next clerk. Fourth in line was his position, and it stayed that way for a long time.

What was taking so long with the man now at the counter?

After what seemed like an eternity, but was probably no more than five minutes, the man concluded his business and walked off.

Now third in line, Ian's thoughts drifted to the strange numbers he'd seen on the leaf of the Book of Kells under the moonlight. What could they mean? Perhaps they were dates in history, or pages in another book, or some kind of numerological code. The list was endless. He had to admit he didn't have a clue. He could only hope the professor's years of learning would prove sufficient to crack the mystery.

Second in the queue now, he turned to look back. Several others had fallen in behind him to wait. His eyes caught those of the last man in line. Where had he seen him before?

Ian's eyes redirected from the man to movement at the revolving door behind him. A familiar face spun through.

Sophie.

What was she doing here?

The woman made a bee line for him.

"Come with me." There was a quiet urgency in her tone.

An irritated clerk called to him.

"Never mind," Ian said, before bolting in the opposite direction with Sophie.

Passing the man at the end of the line, Ian suddenly realized where he'd seen him. At the National Museum, he'd been one of the men in the security detail.

Once outside, Sophie took Ian by the hand and began walking briskly. She handed him a piece of paper.

"I find this after officials take the professor from her house for questions. Can you tell me what this is about?"

Ian told Sophie about the plan to take a look at the Book of Kells, how it had gone wrong, and how he came to carry in his briefcase what the whole world was now looking for.

"I will help you," Sophie said simply. She seemed unfazed.

"I couldn't let—"

"—You have no choice. I will pray and know what to do."

Ian checked behind him and saw that the man in line from the bank was following about fifty yards off.

They walked north for several blocks, navigating their way around the college and onto O'Connell Street. The man still trailed them.

Ian ducked into the lobby of an old, ten-story hotel with Sophie in tow. A scaffold bridged over the entrance inside, and the place was one big remodeling project.

"Can I help you?" the clerk at the desk asked.

Ian ignored the man and kept walking with Sophie, leading her into an elevator, which they immediately took up.

Sophie removed a thick English book from her backpack and held it up. "I will trade you books, no?"

"What?" Ian asked.

"Yes. I will take your problem. There will be no suspicion with me."

Before he could protest, she'd taken the briefcase from him and had handed him her English book. She opened the briefcase and took the container with the Book of Kells and placed it inside her backpack.

Ian didn't argue. She exuded an air of confident certainty that made challenging her plan seem like folly. After the trade was completed and the elevator door opened, they made their way down a tight hallway to a flight of stairs, which they hastily descended. They escaped out the back of the hotel and onto a side street that intersected O'Connell. After darting across the street, they entered a small souvenir shop, passed through it, and out the back entrance into an alley. From there, they skittered down the alley and ended up on Cathedral Street in front of a pub.

A yellow cab rolled down the street. Sophie hailed it. Ian started to ask her what she was doing but then fell silent.

Sophie tugged on her long blonde ponytail and cinched it tighter. "I will find safe place for it." She tossed herself into the back of the cab while clutching her backpack in both hands like an NFL running back trying hard not to fumble.

In another second, the cab barreled off. Just like that, one huge problem was lifted from his shoulders. Ian scanned his surroundings for any sign of the man who'd been following him.

Nothing.

The best course of action now was to let his trail go cold. Disappear from the streets for a while. He went into the pub in front of him, sat at the bar, and ordered a coke. A rerun of a World Cup Soccer match played on the HD TV that hung on the wall behind the bar. Wales had beat the Republic of Ireland 1-0. He'd read about it in the paper this morning. A couple of older men sat in the bar seats next to him sipping on their whiskeys and watching the game as intently as if it were a live broadcast.

Looking at the older men at the bar, Ian couldn't help but think of his own father who no doubt thought Ian should be out playing on a field like that. Considering where he sat now, he wasn't at all sure he'd made the right choices with his life. His license to practice law dangled over the flames, as did this crazy effort to help his grandfather. The heat was also about to be turned up by the Gardai. And what about those goons who had been following him the past week and a half?

Ian finished his coke and left a tip at the bar. Looking out the front of the pub, he noticed two large men stationed on either side of the doorway. The goons were back.

The main exit was no longer an option. He grabbed his briefcase and walked down the narrow hallway leading to the restrooms. The men's room was a few feet from the back exit. Pictures of soccer stars from yesteryear lined the walls. A few feet from the last photo, he skidded to a halt. His father kicking the winning goal in some championship game from the gloried and storied past. He should have been proud, but instead it only made his stomach crawl. He pushed out the back door in a funk.

Then, wham.

A punch stung the side of his face, followed by another to his nose. His cartilage crunched. Pain seared his head.

A heavy man stomped a knee into his stomach and sent him reeling to the ground. When Ian's eyes cleared, the man held a knife to his neck and had one knee on Ian's chest pinning him to the cobblestone of the alley. A second man stood above him, rifling through Ian's briefcase. He picked out Sophie's English book and threw it to the pavement.

"We want to talk to you," the man standing yelled. "Where's the book?"

"Eat crap." Ian gasped, as he fought through the pain in his head.

The man with the knee on Ian's chest dropped the knife and punched him in the mouth.

"Where's the book?" the man repeated, before shouting an obscenity. Ian tasted the hot blood as it trickled from his lips down his chin. His nose burned like a roasted marshmallow.

The pain caused the adrenaline to surge through his arteries and explode into his veins. Infuriated, he swung his right arm from the ground. It hooked a blast to the side of the man's head. In a nanosecond, the man fell off Ian and moaned on his side.

Ian flipped to his feet to confront the other man, who brandished a club and was pulling it back to swing. Ian spun around and landed a roundhouse kick to the collarbone.

The man tottered but held his balance and swung the club at Ian's head. Ian ducked. His counter-punch connected flush with the man's jaw. Ian kneed him in the groin. The man doubled over, dropping the club. An elbow to the man's back sent him hurtling to the ground.

The heavy man who'd had the knife now rose to his knees, the knife again in hand. One kick from Ian sent him down again.

Both men lay in the alley groaning.

Ian brought a hand to his aching nose and jaw. He was more banged up than all the injuries from his mixed-martial-arts training combined. Satisfied the men on the alley pavement were worse off than he was, even though they'd probably broken his nose, he hesitated between calling the police and fleeing.

But who were these people? Did they have any form of identity on them? Wallets, phones? He needed to know. Were they the same people who tried to kill his grandfather?

While reaching for the nearest man's pocket, movement down the alley arrested his gaze.

Two more goons came running toward him, with guns drawn.

The same two he had spotted positioned in front of the pub. Friends of the guys on the ground no doubt. He wasn't sticking around to find out.

Sharp cracking noises filled the air and whisks of air brushed past his head. Silencers? It took a moment to register, but they had silencers on their guns.

And they were firing them.

A bullet grazed his cheek.

His limbs exploded forward in an adrenaline-fueled blur. Before his mind caught up with what his body was doing, he collided with a garbage dumpster and twirled off balance. He stuck a one-legged landing and blurted out an expletive he hadn't used in years.

He gained some equilibrium, started running.

Box crates were splayed across the alley ahead. He hurled them with a scream.

Voices shouted behind him to stop.

He bolted down the alley toward the main street, running for his life.

CHAPTER TWENTY-NINE

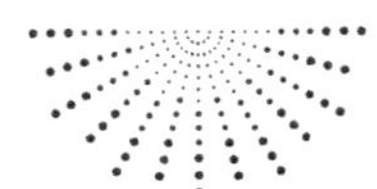

Lorcan waited on hold at his desk phone for Callahan to pick up. Pleased that his offer to assist with the investigation had been gratefully accepted, Lorcan could now keep a close eye on anything the SDU might learn about Shaw, O'Rourke, and their spunky silver-haired assistant.

By the chessboard across the room from Lorcan, Kirby sat holding a chess piece in the air, contemplating his next move. They'd started up another game. And Kirby was again on his way to losing.

"So you say Torna came through for us, ay?" Kirby asked.

"It was in his best interest to make himself useful again."

"I knew he would after that screw up with the professor in Wexford. He's generally reliable."

"He logged a lot of hours and late nights spying on our three little mice over at the Long Room," Lorcan said. "But are you sure you want to talk about screw ups. We've been over this. You and your men couldn't even subdue the American and get the Book of Kells. And the way I understand it, you fired your weapons, which would have been a greater screw-up than the one down in Wexford if you'd have hit him."

"He didn't have the Book of Kells on him. And we fired a few warning shots to try to get him to stop running. Didn't work."

Lorcan tapped his desk with his fingers. "We know they have the Book, though."

"How exactly do we know that?

"The Gardai found the professor's ring at the scene of the crime. We know that. And based on Torna's observations, I made my own inquiry and found what caused them to make the heist. An old dusty book written by an inane priest named Conlin. It talks about the Book of Kells containing a code that would lead to a sacred prophecy from Saint Patrick that would bring tremendous change. It was the same sort of nonsense our men found on the computer of that unfortunate professor in Wexford just before Torna put him to sleep for a trip to the morgue."

"If it's all nonsense, what are you so worried about?"

"Nonsense or not, the discovery of an ancient prophecy purporting to be from Patrick could have the potential to do great harm to our noble cause. You know how much the legend of this man is still revered by the people. If they come to think he has a prophecy for them ... well it could negate our goal of discretely serving the Goddess. That means it would be more difficult to bring about an enlightening and empowering of humanity. And the Goddess would never forgive us if we fail."

A silence filled the room as Lorcan looked off at the wall where a life-size artist rendition of the Goddess Maeve hung from the wall. An unbuttoned red vest barely covered the nipples of her ample bosom. And her fiery red hair flowed past her shoulders down her otherwise naked body to the length of her knee-high red boots. The muscles of her legs were flexed as she partially leaned, partially sat on a throne made of stone. She held a long spear in her right hand like a scepter.

Lorcan stared into her all-searching eyes and whispered, "I will never fail you."

Detective Callahan's voice suddenly chirped in from Lorcan's speakerphone. "Mister Duihbur, good to hear from you. Delighted to have you consulting."

"Thanks, Sean. Wanted to give you an update from my investigation. I went to the Long Room yesterday where I found the volume that your suspects were likely looking at. It was definitely about the Book of Kells."

"That only adds to our suspicions. Good work."

"I just gave the book to your investigators to dust it for prints."

"Thank you. It may end up being a crucial link in the chain of evidence we need."

"I have something else for you—a slip of paper I found near the book," Lorcan said gravely, knowing that a few carefully placed lies interwoven with the basic truths of the black-market underworld would focus even more suspicion on the three mice that were about to be caught in his trap.

"A slip of paper?"

"Yes, indeed. Written on it are the names and phone numbers of two men, operatives of the most notorious black market antiquities operation in the world. A group known as the Art of Death. From my work, I know this network has a world-wide reach. They're connected with Hamas, ISIS, and Boko Haram. Various mafias. They themselves are every bit as bad."

"I'm vaguely familiar with this. But we haven't had occasion to—"

"Understandable," Lorcan said, knowing he would have no trouble leading Callahan to conclude that O'Rourke was connected with the black-market underworld. Lorcan had dealt with these terror groups for several years now and was comfortable in their world. Asim Nassar, who'd been in his office the other day, was one of them.

"Much of the black-market trade flows through Turkey. Lebanon and Jordan are big players too. The terrorist groups operate like a diversified criminal business and buyers all over the world are filling the extremists' coffers. They run their own digs and trades now. But they also buy low, sell high. And, as you might guess, they aren't the Little Sisters of the Poor. If they get screwed with or if those they're in bed with don't produce, they love to spill blood."

Callahan grunted and sighed.

And Lorcan eased back in his chair and relaxed. It was always a pleasure when the spell of your words could cast a web of persuasion over a man's grey matter. When the three mice ended up dead, it wouldn't come as much of a surprise to anyone. The newspapers would very soon be full of phony headlines and stories—with abundant quotes from Detective Callahan himself—about an illegal conspiracy to steal the Book of Kells formed between an Irish professor, her assistant, and an upstart American attorney, all of whom were outwitted and killed by the Art of Death, the group who now likely held the Book.

CHAPTER THIRTY

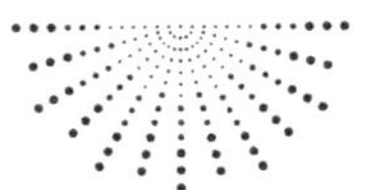

Walking along the north side of the Quay, with the River Liffey and the Temple Bar area to the south, Ian scanned his surroundings for any sign that he was being followed. Nothing caused alarm, but he knew he couldn't be too careful. It was late Thursday evening. Several days had passed since the trio had unwittingly pulled off the heist of the century.

His nose still hurt, and he had a bandage to hide a nasty cut to his lip. But his physical infirmities were the least of his problems.

News chirped in earlier in the week that the California State Bar Court had decided to proceed against him in his absence. They'd found probable cause for a formal prosecution on the charges of behavior unbecoming an attorney in connection with his brush-up in the Castro district. To make matters worse, he was so preoccupied with events unfolding the last couple weeks in Ireland, he'd not had time to retain decent counsel in his defense, other than having Jarvis Reed appear on his behalf to ask for a continuance that would stretch out the proceedings. The request had not only been denied, the matter was expedited.

Another grave concern was the health of his grandfather. He dialed his grandparents' number now as he stopped walking and leaned against a bridge rail overlooking the River Liffey.

Nana answered on the first ring. "Ian, I'm so worried." Her voiced cracked.

"About Papa? Can I speak to him?"

"He hasn't been awake all day. That makes twenty-fours of sleep straight." She began to cry softly.

Ian honestly didn't know what to say, so he just listened to her cry.

She blew her nose and regained her composure. "I'm worried he might continue this way until his death."

"What about my dad?" Ian asked. "Is he still there?"

"Yeah, he says it must be George's medication making him tired. And he says not to give him so much. I've got a call in to the doctor. I'll let you know what he says."

"I'll be praying."

"Me too. I'm still believing for his full recovery."

His grandmother ended the call, and Ian continued walking.

Would he even have a chance to say goodbye to the old man and tell him about the amazing things they had found so far?

The glorious quest.

The phrase seemed obscene as it reverberated in his head. It was hard to see how their pursuit so far had risen to the level of glorious. Angst-filled and pain-filled quest, perhaps, but not glorious.

Ian peered across the river and spotted a place on the Quay called Locutions, a popular 24-hour internet cafe, where he was to meet Saorla and Myrna to plan their strategy. A check of his surroundings indicated that he was not being followed. He'd have to be careful to watch his perimeter after that brush with death in the alley.

He dialed Saorla's new burner phone.

"How's my favorite professor, and how was her day?"

"Professor Marvel from the Wizard of Oz isn't here I'm afraid."

Ian laughed. "I meant you."

"In that case, cheers. I'm as well as can be expected for a suspect whose probably being watched by police as we speak. But I taught my Irish history class today. The usual stuff."

Ian gripped the phone tighter to his ear to hear her over the din of the street. He was crossing a stone bridge with his eyes on the cafe. Through the large windows of Locutions, he could see Saorla with her phone to her ear. The place was mostly empty, so it wasn't hard to spot the attractive brunette.

"I worked at the legal aid clinic," Ian said, almost at the door of the cafe now. "The usual for me too, drafting orders of protection, keeping low-rent landlords honest. Things that none of the barristers in town want to do."

"Serves you right," she said sniggering.

She had her back to the door. Ian walked in and cut off his phone. He stood behind her now and leaned in to whisper in her ear. "Just a couple of normal hard-working people by day, but by night, robbers of museums and plunderers of national treasures."

Saorla turned, chuckling. The smile fled from her lips, though, replaced by a shocked frown when she examined Ian's face. "What happened to you?"

"Looks worse than it is."

She brought her hand to his chin. "Ian, how did this ...?"

The warm touch of her hand startled him, and the magic of her nearness sent him reeling. She dropped her hand, and he regained some of his composure.

"They were only trying to scare me, I think. Because if they had actually wanted to shoot me, I don't think they would've missed."

"They shot at you?" There was no mistaking the concern in her eyes.

"Didn't want to scare you, but I figured you should know."

"I can handle it. You don't have to protect me from the truth. We're in this together."

Ian nodded his head, reassured by her words. He glanced around the cafe. Nobody appeared to be paying them any attention. A couple of people slept, propped in their chairs at their computer screens, and a third man was sprawled out on the floor in front of a computer space.

"Are they homeless?" Ian asked.

"They are sleeping rough," Saorla corrected. "It's cheaper to buy a few hours of time on the internet than it is to get a place at a crowded hostel. And it's better than braving the brisk fall nights out on the mean streets of Dublin."

"Sleeping rough, huh, that's sad."

"Yeah, it's a problem the government has let them down on."

"You think the government should provide everyone with housing?"

"For sure."

Ian was used to this. San Francisco was filled with moonbat idealists like her. "You're a socialist."

"Why do you say that?"

"Where's the personal responsibility? The government should guarantee equality of opportunity, not equality of outcome."

"Giving people with no place to live and nowhere to go a place to stay is hardly *guaranteeing an equal outcome*. Besides, it's better than forcing them to be on the streets and then arresting them for doing it. Where's the fairness in that? But you're American. You should be used to such ideas. It's important to have an imagination that includes room for a better future."

"How do you figure the future will be better with—"

Myrna sprang through the door, snapping her fingers at them.

"I don't have much time. Can we get this going?"

Ian turned to Saorla and shrugged his shoulders.

"She's got a big test tomorrow," Saorla said. "Come on. I reserved some private seats in the back."

They ordered hot drinks at the front counter and made their way to the rear of the cafe to a semi-private area where they could talk and look at computer screens. It was an area reserved for groups and was more expensive to rent, which explained the lack of homeless people using it to bed down for the night.

Once seated at the table, the conversation turned to an attempt to decipher the meaning of the mysterious numbers encoded in the Book of Kells. Saorla slid the numbers across the table toward Ian. They passed them around several times. After fifteen minutes of unfruitful discussion, an obviously exasperated Myrna said, "So, the bottom line is you two haven't got a clue what they mean."

It was quiet except for the snoring of a rough sleeper in the front of the cafe.

Myrna threw her hands up. "If you ask me, it's numerology. Each numeral has a meaning."

Saorla gave a slight shake of her head. "It's possible, but not probable."

What's numerology?" Ian asked.

Saorla had the look of the learned professor he'd come to recognize. Her eyes flashed and her jaw tightened as she began to form her words. "Numerology, broadly speaking, is basically a mystical attempt to draw pseudo-scientific or factual inferences from a pattern of numbers. There are many different kinds of systems and numerical codes."

"I've heard of that," Ian said. "Someone at my church told me that Isaiah 53, a Scripture Christians see as a clear prophecy of the coming of Yeshua as the suffering messiah, has a code in it. The letters at equidistant spacing throughout the chapter spell out the name Yeshua, the Hebrew word for Jesus."

"That's different from numerology, though," Saorla said, "because the equidistance spacing is just an undeniable phenomenon that it is either there or it isn't. It's not occult."

"What if the numbers we got from the Book of Kells are some sort of number pattern?" Myrna asked.

"Numerology is considered an occult practice," Saorla said, seemingly ignoring Myrna's comment. "Scientist don't believe in it. And it was condemned early on in Christian church history by the leadership. Obviously, if this code comes handed down from Saint Patrick himself, the Catholic Apostle to Ireland, it wouldn't be through an occult practice."

Ian scanned the numbers, zoning out on the conversation between the two women. He first skimmed the Roman numeral version and then Saorla's conversion to the Hindu-Arabic system. There was something that seemed strangely routine to him about the figures.

The quantity of numerals, the decimal points, the negative sign before one of the numbers.

"Did the Romans use periods or decimal points?"

"No, I added that period because there was a double space to the next digit, which would indicate a pause between sentences in effect."

"What about the negative sign?"

"I can't explain that. The Romans didn't use negative numbers. But there was an unmistakable dash to begin that second sequence."

Ian continued to study the numbers. They reminded him of GPS coordinates he might see when tracking one of his off-trail, cross-country scrambles through the mountains. It was as likely as anything else they'd come up with to this point.

"I think those numbers might be GPS coordinates," he said. The idea was growing on him now that he'd said it aloud.

Myrna tapped her fingers on the table. "That makes no sense. They didn't have GPS coordinates in the fifth century."

"But maybe we're looking at it the wrong way," Ian said. "These men … men like Patrick … were not led by sight, but by faith and the Spirit. Maybe Patrick received those numbers by revelation."

Myrna grimaced. "You're serious?"

Ian avoided her gaze and turned to Saorla. He spun his computer screen in her direction to show her a map. He'd entered a website that matched GPS coordinates with places on the globe. He typed in the numbers that Saorla had transcribed from page forty-four of the Book of Kells under the moonlight of three nights ago and hit enter.

Myrna now turned to pleading with Saorla. "You're not falling for this too, are you?"

"I don't think it's that far-fetched. Maybe, as Ian says, Patrick received the numbers by revelation—in a dream, a vision, an angelic voice, an audible voice of God, or an impression to his heart. Who knows? But suppose he was confident enough in what he received that he gave careful instructions to quietly pass it down through the centuries. Suppose that it made it, successfully preserved for a few rough centuries until the monks at Iona around 800 AD crafted their book of books. Something they thought would last the test of time.

And suppose they put the clue to Patrick's prophecy encoded into the vellum."

"That's another thing that has me completely puzzled," Myrna said, in an argumentative tone. "How did they get the numbers inscribed into the vellum?"

Saorla took a sip of tea. "I have a theory on that. Given the incredibly exquisite detail it took to do the miniature of the artwork, I have no trouble working on the thesis that the artisans of the Book of Kells crafted the vellum at just the precise thickness they needed to slip one piece inside of two outer pieces—like a sandwich and then attached it seamlessly. All done at the precise thickness needed to view the encoded numbers when held up to the wan light shed by a full moon."

Ian had been following the conversation while multi-tasking on the computer. He hit a button and waited for a result of his search of GPS coordinates. A quick scan of the cafe did not reveal anything suspicious. Nobody had slipped in, and nobody was paying them any undue attention. The fear lessened of his repeating another encounter like the one with the goons at the pub. The kind of encounter he might not be so lucky to survive a second time.

Ian looked down at the computer. A rush flooded his insides on par with catching a monster at Mavs.

"Dudes, this is rad!" he shouted. He caught himself before firing off another line of surfer talk. "Ah, excuse me ... I mean, ladies, take a look at this. Those numbers are GPS coordinates. And of all the places in the world, guess where they pinpoint?"

Myrna looked like she was seeing a ghost. "Ireland?"

Ian nodded his head. "The opposite coast. It looks to be well south of the Cliffs of Moher."

Ian pointed to a map with the southwest coast preeminently displayed. "When Saorla wrote down the numbers, she wasn't sure if this coupling at the end of the first line was a 35 or an 85. If it's 35, it's exactly on the coastline, probably in these cliffs here. That makes sense because I think the third and last sequence, the 79m, is a number that describes altitude. It just happens to be about that many meters to the top of the cliffs in that area."

"What if that last coupling is 85 instead of 35?" Myrna asked. The shock on her face hadn't receded yet.

"Then it would pinpoint this small island here, which is just off the coast, probably a quarter to half a mile away from the first location, but obviously you have to go out to sea a bit to get there."

"Great I'll get my sea kayak and rock-climbing gear ready right after I take my test tomorrow," Myrna said, now as perky as ever.

"She has a kayak and rock-climbing gear?" Ian asked.

"No," Saorla said, chuckling.

"If I did, would you go out with me then, Mr. Bond?" Myrna teased.

"Time to go," Ian said, as he deleted his search and flicked off the computer.

"Oh, come now. You can't just take Professor Saorla on an adventure. I'm a college student. Self-discovery is what I do best."

Ian ignored the teasing and rose from his chair. "I'm going to need a ride home from you ladies. Tomorrow's promising to be a big day."

SAORLA WATCHED AS IAN PLACED €20 NOTE ON THEIR table. "What are you doing?"

"Leaving a tip."

Ah, her newfound friend and client had a generous heart, despite his wingnut political philosophy. But he had nary a clue about the culture here. "We don't leave tips in Ireland. It's a bit of an insult, really."

"Ok, let me get this straight. You want the government to raise taxes so they can buy everyone a home, including people who won't work, but it's considered an insult to give someone extra money for performing a service well?"

Saorla shrugged her shoulders. She picked up the €20 and handed it back to Ian. She decided to try this again. "It is never necessary to tip the host on duty, but if you insist, the polite way to do it is to give her the money and tell her you want her to have a coffee on you."

"Got it," Ian said.

Myrna was already leaving out the door.

A ping of trepidation pelted Saorla hard, the same feeling of impending disaster she'd experienced the other day at the National Museum had returned. The same feeling she had in the Alps and in the cab on the way to Professor Greenwald's house in Wexford.

Was something bad about to happen here and now?

Saorla turned to Ian. "Let's go. Myrna's driving. She's in a hurry. Still has studying to do."

Making her way through the cafe, Saorla stepped over a man with an untrimmed beard who was wearing several layers of clothes. He appeared to be sound asleep. Turning back to Ian, she was about to tell him to watch his step, when she saw him place the twenty in the man's shirt pocket.

Saorla made it out the door with Ian in tow, but the foreboding only increased. She picked up her pace, rounded the corner toward the car, looked for Myrna.

Myrna was twenty paces ahead.

The internal alarm intensified.

"What is your day like tomorrow?" Ian asked. "We need to get to the coast as soon as possible and get a look at that location. Something is there. I know it."

Saorla barely heard him. She was praying, asking, listening.

What is this dread I feel?

In an instant she knew.

"The car!"

Her scream of warning escaped her mouth a split second before it happened.

Myrna activated the unlock button on her key.

The next instant a concussive blast reeled Saorla back on her feet.

Pieces of glass and debris blew out. Fire and smoke engulfed the car.

"No!" Saorla wailed. The force of the blast tossed Myrna into the air like she'd bounded from a trampoline only to land hard on the street's pavement. Fire raged high over the roof of the vehicle. The next thing Saorla knew she was kneeling at Myrna's side with Ian, praying. Blood caked Myrna's skin and clothes, but all her limbs were intact and there was no blood visibly spurting. No telling how badly she was injured.

Please, God, let her be all right.

Minutes passed in a blur. The acrid smell of black smoke burned Saorla's nostrils and made her eyes water.

An ambulance arrived, followed closely by the Gardai. Saorla held Myrna's hand as they carried her away on a stretcher. Myrna's eyes were open, but she was barely conscious.

"Hold on, dear." Saorla cried to her. "It should have been me."

A few seconds later, the paramedics closed the door to the ambulance, and the vehicle pulled out onto the Quay heading east to Thomas Street toward St. James Hospital.

With the wounded attended to and the ambulance's flashing lights growing dimmer in the distance, Gardai circled in on Saorla.

Questions and more questions came rapid fire.

What is your name? The same Saorla O'Rourke under suspicion in the Book of Kells case? Were you with the injured woman? What is her name? How do you know her? How long were you here, and what were you doing?

The vultures were thick in the sky, and she was a piece of roadkill. They carefully took down all her answers, beginning with her name, and proceeded to pick her apart. Calls were made, orders were given. She was taken to the back of a patrol car.

Where was Ian?

She didn't see him anywhere.

In a few minutes, detective Callahan of the SDU arrived. He climbed into the back of the patrol car in the seat next to Saorla.

"A bit active in your social life, are you not, Ms. O'Rourke?"

Saorla didn't look up. A tear crawled down her cheek and dropped into her lap.

"Let's see now, there's been a murder, a bombing, and oh yes, the small matter of the theft of that little book everyone is so upset about. You know what they all have in common?"

Saorla still didn't look up.

"You! That's what they have in common. Do you want to tell me what's going on?"

A part of her wanted to come clean about the whole complex mess that her life had become. But who would believe it? She continued to stare at her knees. There was nothing to say that would make any sense at this point.

"I know just the thing to get you in the talking mood," Callahan bellowed. "Some quality time in our local jail."

It took Ian about fifteen minutes to finish giving his statement to the Gardai about the bombing incident. After dispensing some general information as to his name, place of residence, and purpose in coming to the country, Ian adroitly deflected the Gardai's efforts to get to the nitty-gritty specifics. No, he didn't know who was responsible for this dastardly act, he told them. The trio had met to discuss some personal business, and no, he didn't care to divulge the particulars.

When he finished with the Gardai, he wasn't able to find Saorla. Frantic to see her, he checked back in the cafe. She wasn't there. The man with the crisp, new €20 note in his pocket was still sound asleep on the floor.

Ian asked one of the officers still at the scene what had happened to Professor O'Rourke and learned that she'd been arrested.

Torn between going to jail or the hospital, Ian realized there was no way he could spring Saorla to freedom tonight. Even though she had a right to see a solicitor if she wanted to, he wasn't sure he'd be allowed a visit at this late hour.

He hailed a cab to St. James Hospital instead and discovered that Myrna had been admitted to the intensive care unit. His worst fears were allayed, however, when he learned that she was expected to survive the night. Her admission to the ICU had been necessary because of the amount of blood she'd lost before they were able to get the bleeding under control. All in all, she had some moderate bruising, a broken rib and several cuts that required extensive stitching. They'd given her a transfusion and expected her to recover.

Ian wasn't allowed to see her, however. Visiting hours were from 7 to 8 p.m. and were strictly enforced he was told. Law enforcement had placed a guard on Myrna's wing to keep watch.

Back at his room at 2 a.m., he simmered over what had happened to Myrna. He blamed himself, though, even more than he blamed the evil people responsible. They were doing what came naturally to them in their greed and ignorance. He, on the other hand, should have known better than to endanger the professor and her assistant, especially after all the signs he'd seen, signs that showed he was dealing with determined and violent criminals.

Ian turned out the light and climbed into bed. Sleep would not come easily to him knowing that Saorla was spending the night behind bars. He vowed he would spring her free as soon as the District Court opened in the morning.

CHAPTER THIRTY-ONE

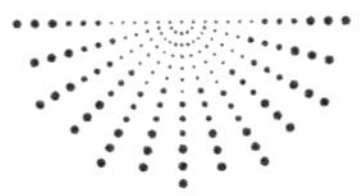

Saorla was fingerprinted and processed at the station. The jailer handed her a set of cheap clothes—jeans, underwear, a white shirt—along with bedclothes, a towel, soap, a toothbrush, and a tiny tube of toothpaste. She was told to change her clothes and place the items she was wearing in a bag provided for her, which she would be able to recover upon her release.

A male jail officer took her by the arm in silence to an eight-by-ten cinderblock cell with two small thin beds attached to the opposing walls. She placed her items on the open bed to her left and heard the clank of the iron-bars locking behind her.

"You better get a good barrister," the jailer said. "Otherwise, you might be here till Saint Peter comes with his keys." He said it while pointing to the ceiling. Or maybe it was heaven he had in mind.

Saorla perched herself on the edge of the bed, her head down, tears welling in her eyes.

I'll call Ian in the morning. He will know what to do, and we'll go from there.

The hope was that by simply telling herself those words it would come true. But it was just a hope, way too fragile to forge a real life.

Nothing was a sure bet in this world. And it hit her full on: God had deserted her.

Again.

First with letting Stuart die and now this.

Such a tough road, heavy load, Darlin' Pretty.

"What's a sweetie like you doing in a place like this?" The question and the voice startled Saorla into an upright jolt. She focused her eyes through cloudy tears in search of the source. Someone was sitting on the bed across from her in the cell. A woman, of course, but not just any woman she saw now as her eyes came into focus.

It was some sort of superwoman.

Panic hit her at the sight, and she blinked her eyes hard to focus.

Muscles bulged from taut arms and shoulders. No fat, all hips and curves, intensely fit, the woman wore jeans and the jail issued white-tank top that pressed back against breasts that stood out like army tanks. A variety of tattoos adorned her arms. But by far her most distinguishing feature was a half-shaved head that showcased a large tattoo that read *Rebel Girl* in black calligraphy. The words bored into the bald half of her head and bordered her otherwise long, raven-black hair. The tattoo on the bald half of her pate was accented by large tomahawk earrings that hung next to several smaller silver piercings in her lobes that matched the silver ones in her nose.

"Hi," Saorla managed to say weakly, her voice cracking. "I guess I was at the wrong place at the wrong time."

"That's usually the case. My name is Tara."

"I'm O'Rourke," Saorla said, not sure why she'd identified herself only by her last name other than it sounded tougher than Saorla, and she was in desperate need of a little toughness.

"What landed you in place like this?" Saorla asked.

Tara clenched her teeth and made a fist. "Had to whip my best friend's arse at the club tonight. She was dancing too close to my man. Know what I mean?"

Irish women could be tough, but this was ridiculous. Saorla nodded her head anyway. "You did what you had to do."

"I'm used to fighting. That's what I do for a living. I'm an MMA trained UFC brawler. I got a fight coming up next week against a woman from Cork. I'm going to kick her arse too. You watch."

Saorla continued to nod her head. How could a woman who looked like that ever lose a fight?

"Last match-up I won in a knockout in the fourth round. You should have seen that girl's face when I got through with her."

"You ever been seriously hurt?" Saorla asked, then added, "In a fight, I mean."

The woman's face turned quizzical to the point where Saorla thought she must think her to be a moron. "I always win. Seventeen straight since I turned pro. But one time I got a concussion ..." Tara had a distant look in her eyes like she was remembering the blow that caused it.

Saorla was about to say that concussions must be one of the hazards of the sport that the athletes have to guard against. "I bet it—"

"—Listen, my agent's going to get me out first thing in the morning, and I have a mega-training session scheduled for ten o'clock. I need to get some rest. Hope you don't mind, but I need the sleep."

With that, the woman fluffed her pillow and flipped onto her back.

Saorla followed Tara's example and fluffed her own pillow and lay on her back.

She thought about Killian's message on how God prefers to use the weak. Despite her initial rejection of it, the message had mesmerized her for the past several days. She'd looked up verses all week on the same theme with the help of an on-line concordance. Those verses now resonated in her head, drowning out the earlier negativity about being abandoned by God yet again. One from Paul— *"When I am weak, then I am strong."* Then one from Jeremiah— *"Let not the wise ... boast in his wisdom, let not the strong ... boast in his strength ... but let him who boasts, boast in this, that he knows and understands me ...."* One from Paul again— *"Finally brethren, be strong in the Lord and the power of his might."*

In the crushing humility of her jail cell, Saorla started to see it all clearly. There could be no doubt her career as a professor at the college was coming to an end even without the layoffs from the budget cuts. Her arrest would surely seal her fate, wouldn't it? And Stuart, the glue that had held everything together for her wasn't coming back.

And perhaps even worse, she might never get out of this cell again.

A glimmer ran down her spine at the thought of just how vulnerable and weak she was at this precise moment. Was she a candidate for God's strength given her pathetic weakness? Her own wisdom and strength were surely not working. That much was certain.

The prayer sprung out in a whisper, straight from her heart to God's. "Jesus, will you exchange my weakness for your strength?"

She waited, afraid to whisper another word into the atmosphere that was all stillness and calmness. A peace blew in and a knowing came, a knowing that it was God who had spoken to her about the danger that lay ahead at the car where Myrna was injured. A knowing that it was God who had been waiting for her to fall into his arms her whole life, was waiting now, arms all warm love. She began to ask for more strength from him to better hear and understand him.

"I choose to trust you," she said with the simplicity of a three-year-old, she knew, but didn't care, knowing that it was right that it was happening this way. "I believe. No matter what, from here on."

She waited, letting those whispered words resonate, holding her breath for some reply. But none came.

It didn't matter. She didn't need a reply.

The thought came to her that she would spend the rest of her life seeking, believing, even if she never heard or saw anything.

The peace intensified, and, in a moment, a resolve and a boldness came over her.

She got out of bed and kneeled on the floor. Tara was snoring softly now. The sudden courage she felt only increased. It was as if she were being transformed into a spiritual UFC fighter with the same toughness in the spiritual realm that Tara possessed in the natural.

No matter what forces she faced in the boxing ring of her life, when she walked out of this jail, she resolved, she would overcome them. Her will, her mind, firmed it up in a promise.

She would *take the glorious quest*.

No matter what it cost her she would go down that unknown road, even if it meant the old Saorla never came back. In fact, she meant for her never to return. If she did come back at all, it would be as a new Saorla, one who no longer had her own good ideas but instead had exchanged them for the better ideas only another realm could offer.

Both quests—her personal one to know God and the mystery of the artifacts—were connected for her now.

She closed her eyes and began praying silently the words of the *Breastplate* that she'd memorized.

A sudden clang on her jail cell lurched her eyes open. It was the jailer who had brought her to her cell. "O'Rourke, you get one phone call. Do you want to make it tonight or wait till morning?"

What did it matter? She was in God's hands now. "You know those keys of Saint Peter you mentioned earlier?" She was smiling up at him still on her knees on the jail cell floor.

He scratched the back of his head. "Uh … oh yeah, that."

The smile on her face couldn't be kept from widening. "Well, I already made a call to someone greater than Saint Peter, and He's already brought the keys."

He eyed her peculiarly. "Is that a yes or no on the call tonight, Ms. O'Rourke."

"I'll make the call in the morning, thank you."

"You're choice," he said woodenly and then walked away.

Tara turned on her side, and the snoring suddenly stopped.

Saorla rose from her knees and climbed into her own bunk. She lay, turned her heart heavenward. And through it all, a peace flowed like a river that never ebbed. A peace that was enough. And she knew —more than she had ever known any historical fact or any intellectual concept or any scientific or political theory—that she never wanted to leave that Peace.

She prayed softly, *Jesus …*

Shield me today
From poison and burning and fire
From floods, from drowning and from wounding
So that I might attain the abundant reward

Christ with me ...
Christ when I sleep... Christ—

Christ WAS THE LAST WORD WHISPERED FROM GRATEFUL lips before consciousness gave way to sleep.

And then the dreams came, dreams of a dark forest where she was required to fend off both fire and flood. Ian was there with her, fighting at her side, two great Fianna warriors kicking up clouds of dust as they ran to a fierce battle of almost certain death.

BIBLIOGRAPHY

O'Loughlin, Thomas *Discovering Saint Patrick*. Mahwah: Paulist Press, 2005

de Paor, Máire B. *Patrick: The Pilgrim Apostle of Ireland*. New York: HarperCollins, 1998

Cahill, Thomas *How the Irish Saved Civilization: The Untold Story of Ireland's Heroic Role From the Fall of Rome to the Rise of Medieval Europe*. New York: Nan A. Talese, Doubleday, 1995

Freeman, Phillip *St. Patrick of Ireland: A Biography*. New York: Simon & Schuster, 2005

Olden, Rev. Thomas *The Confession of St. Patrick: With An Introduction and Notes*. Dublin & London: McGlashan & James Nisbet & Co., 1853

Bieler, Ludwig, *The Life and Legend of St. Patrick: Problems of Modern Scholarship*. Dublin 1949.

Mone, Gregory "Uncorked." *Outside,* February 2008: Adventure ed. 77-83

Sambrook, Kevin "The Irish Apostle." *Charisma,* March 2008: 52-58

Alexander, C.F. "Saint Patrick's 'Breastplate' Prayer." 1889. *The Prayer Foundation,* Accessed July 14, 2021 https://ww.prayerfoundation.org/st_patrick's_breastplate_prayer.htm

"The Legend of Finn McCool" Finn McCool Marketing, Accessed July 15, 2021 https://www.finn-mccool.co.uk/irish-mythology/the-legend-of-finn-mccool/

Yeats, William Butler "The Land of Heart's Desire." (1894) New York: Little Leather Library Corp., 1900 (public domain)

Yeats, William Butler "The Second Coming" 1920 (public domain)

ACKNOWLEDGMENTS

Much thanks to Jenny Dunlap who read an early draft of my manuscript and corrected my mistakes. And special appreciation to Erin Healy who offered her suggestions and guidance and is an editor par excellence. And along the same lines a ton of gratitude goes out to Rowena Kuo and her team of editors at Brimstone—Keith Osmun, Grant Patterson, and Zach Brown.

A huge thank you to my sisters, Lynn Sandberg and Lee Hruby, for taking a trip to Ireland with me for "research," where we navigated the winding roads of the lush Irish hillsides, sometimes at great peril, but also having the time of our lives. The hope is that the landscape we viewed comes across as vivid as any character in the story.

Writing a novel is always a journey in faith that requires lots of encouragement, so I want to thank all those that read my tale while it was still a work in progress and expressed their fierce enthusiasm—Carole Troy, Joy Lang, Donna Friesz, both Patrick McNamaras, Randy Mead, Gunnar Dunlap, and especially Sarah Wagner.

And to Lydia, Liberty, Daniel, Patrick and Dawn, you five are the best and give so much joy. Finally, thanks to my wife Laura who has the gifts of encouragement, prophecy, and discernment to rival that found in the great Saint Patrick himself. Without you I would never have written a single word of this book.

ABOUT THE AUTHOR

As a student at Saint Patrick's Grade School, Michael Penosky developed a love for Saint Patrick and all things Irish. That love led to a dozen trips to the Emerald Isle and the writing of The Patrician Prophecy Series. He holds a Juris Doctorate from Northern Illinois University, and for the past decade, he's been a senior attorney for the Supreme Court of Illinois. When Michael is not writing, he can be found dusting the cobwebs from his basketball jump shot to avoid getting schooled by his teenage boys. He currently lives with his wife Laura, their five children, and his faithful Labrador Retriever, Colter.